Excuses

By

Christopher May

ISBN-13:978-1499723977

Unless otherwise indicated, all scripture quotations or references are taken from the Holy Bible New International Version®. NIV®. Copyright 1973, 1978, 1984 by Biblica Inc.

DEDICATION

To my wife, Mary, the best boss I ever had.

To my sister in law, Dr. Dianne May, thanks for taking on the responsibility of transforming my notebooks of handwritten words into this typed novel.

To my good buddy and fellow baseball fan, Rick McComsey, who always reminds me any winning team has to have a top notch closer. He then presented me with one for mine, his wonderful wife Donna! So glad that her position as my editor is a permanent one!

A special thank you to St. Andrews Presbyterian Church in Charleston, SC for allowing me to feature their beautiful church on the front cover of this book.

Front cover photography courtesy of DianaMo Jones.

CONTENTS

Prologue

Hey, somebody had to take Dr. Graham's place, right?

So why not Rev. Timothy Isaac McDonald?

Tim chuckled to himself and the laugh lines brought out even more his boyish face.

"Yeah, right. First of all, I'm not a doctor. Secondly, I won't be, because seminary isn't in my immediate future. And finally, at age 41, my calling is coming just a little later than Brother Billy's."

And yet, Tim's call into full-time evangelism was most real. Frightening, no doubt, but excitement and a sincere burning of the spirit by miles overrode any doubts or questions.

And Sarah, God bless her. She was in total support of his decision. She had been petrified at first. After all, a bi-vocational pastorate with a nice factory job with full benefits wasn't such a big adjustment – but this?

Sarah, however, did not laugh at God's amazing promise, as her biblical namesake had done. In her heart of hearts she knew the Lord was in this, and it would be okay. They would be okay.

The kids thought it was kind of cool.

"Wow! Will we have our own T.V. show?" asked Gary, their quite precocious fourteen year old, who loved Xbox 360, NBA basketball, Major League Baseball, and girls, not necessarily in that order.

Brooke, their eleven year old Martha Stewart / Rachael Ray wannabe, had gushed, "Oh, I love to travel! We'll see the whole country, and maybe even go overseas! What a background for my career as a gourmet chef and interior designer! Isn't God great?"

Chance, their unexpected blessing appropriately named for his rather late arrival to the family, didn't seem to care one way or the other. At age two, with twin dimples, and a heart melting smile destined to mature into a lady killer grin, he was just happy to be alive.

When Tim, then a nominal, passive believer, had first met his wife-to-be at a frat party at the University of South Carolina, ministry was the last place either one expected to find themselves. Sarah was involved up to her elbows in Alpha Omega Pi sorority. Tim was a BMOC – Vice President of Sigma Chi fraternity and a 3.75 GPA, working, and succeeding quite handily, at carving his path toward an MBA. Their first date was the following evening. Love was instant, and it was consummated long before their spring wedding two years later.

If was five years after this that an invitation to an old fashioned tent revival from one of Sarah's clients in her event planning business in Charleston led both McDonalds into rediscovering the God of their respective childhoods. At first Sarah led the way back, but soon Tim took the reins, as Gary, then later Brooke, entered their family.

1

Sarah got involved with the children's program at Palmetto Baptist Church, and Tim took an interest in the youth. Both also immersed themselves in small group Bible studies. God was working his magic on both of them, and in His always perfect timing, His purposes for their lives began to reveal themselves.

It was during a marriage enrichment retreat in Myrtle Beach that this revealing began. A honeymoon-like feel filled the two as they lavished in their time away from their jobs and the rigors of raising two supercharged preschoolers.

This however, was only the beginning of their weekend experiences.

Tim realized he really did have it all, as far as he could possibly see: a great career – Regional Manager of Sales and Marketing at an innovative die-casting factory; a drop-dead gorgeous wife who adored him and vice versa; and two children worthy of a Currier and Ives – or perhaps a Thomas Kinkade portrait of family bliss.

And yet, as he listened to the message on Christian commitment and finding your place in God's kingdom, an urgent and unrelenting restlessness began to stir. The stirring turned into burning as the topic turned to a shortage of ministers, especially in smaller churches who couldn't support a full-time pastor.

When the call was extended to anyone who felt led to pursue ministerial opportunities in this area as a family, Tim responded without hesitation.

Or consulting Sarah.

He needn't have worried. Sarah's well-manicured, red polished nails and long, slender fingers reached out to clutch and caress his hands.

"What took you so long? I've known this was coming for months!" Sarah spoke with her southern belle drawl that had first melted Tim's heart at the frat party of their initial meeting. As she rubbed the back of his hand with her thumb, he could feel her affirmation – and God's – pouring into him.

It was decided that night. Tim would go to Bible school, seminary, or whatever it took. He would become a bi-vocational minister – trained as a full-time clergyman, and probably working just as hard. He would keep his job at the factory, as well as his benefits, but his vocational focus would definitely take a radical change.

And all went well, through the adventure of Bible College, to his first calling – an impoverished Southern Baptist church in North Charleston, to his current pastorate, a slightly larger congregation in Summerville, a beautiful community on the outskirts of Greater Charleston.

But then, just as everything settled down, and the surprise blessing of Chance dropped out of Heaven into their laps, along came this much more drastic calling.

Full-time evangelism.

Everything about this summons was more dramatic. The restlessness, the burning to serve Jesus, and the peace that came from surrendering to His will.

Sarah's caresses and loving words were even stronger – despite a very real and scary change of lifestyle and leap of faith.

But never, not for one moment, could either of them had guessed what lay in store for them – as this family was swept into the front lines of spiritual warfare.

The battle for lost souls.

~

The transition was no fairy tale.

Tim and Sarah, as well as their three musketeers, hit many jarring bumps, adjustments of their paths, and many dead end roads over the next two years.

For Sarah, it was her one material weakness, jewelry. Back in the day, Tim had invested in diamonds for the diamond in his life, even some pink and yellow "fancy" ones. But now, with and at least for now a greatly reduced budget, even today's specials from HSN and Diamonique® from QVC were a stretch. Tim promised her in due time her patience would be rewarded.

Sarah never complained, at least not much!

For Tim, it was the manly issues. For now, his wife's thriving event and wedding planning business was the lion's share of the McDonald's salary. This pricked his pride, but not his call. He remained steadfast, even if sometimes moody, even down right grumpy and down on himself for not finding a way to make this process more smooth.

Of course, it was really God's timing, and in the end, this is what pushed him onward.

It was a challenge for the children too, of course. No PlayStation®4 for Gary; he had to settle for a couple of Xbox games and some "beastly" clothes from Aeropostle at Christmas that first year (mostly thanks to Sarah's successes). Brook received two new cookbooks and a guide on interior design, which actually suited her just fine. But her clothing allowance had been drastically reduced, which wasn't so fine.

Chance just flowed along, smiling at everyone, and flirting with waitresses on their Friday out to dinner nights.

Then slowly, things began to come together as the master event planner wove his tapestry.

First came the name for the Evangelical organization – TIME Ministries – Timothy Isaac McDonald Evangelical Ministries. "The TIME is now to accept God's free gift of salvation. I tell you, now is the TIME of God's favor. Now is the day of salvation!" II Corinthians 6:2.

Palmetto Baptist Church, where they had first rediscovered God, became the family's local church headquarters. One deacon, one trustee, and the two Sunday School teachers became Tim's Board of Directors, and Pastor

Roger Duncan became Chairman of the Board. The church got behind the effort. So did the Charleston Southern Baptist Association. Soon, revivals and weekend retreats began to dot Tim's ministerial calendar.

Then came two more blessings. Two local musicians with a heart for the Lord stepped forward to become part of the team. Pianist, vocalist and writer, Jamie Ray, and his singing partner, Meghan Amhearst, caught the vision and joined the team. With a variety of musical styles, a heavenly blend, and a desire for full-time music and ministry, they were the perfect fit for the TIME Ministries.

Ironically, the watershed moment was a tent revival.

It occurred in June of 2014 in Folly Beach. Tim's messages were not full of doom and gloom, and yet, their simple clarity and intensity struck a chord in this laid back beach community. Tim spoke from his heart, Jamie and Meghan were in tune with the spirit, and God moved mightily. What was scheduled as a week-long event turned into a month, and several area churches joined the effort. How could a preacher who didn't scream and call down fire from Heaven have such results? It was all about love – and God! Over two thousand souls were saved! TIME Ministries was officially launched.

Now at the beginning of 2015, Tim's calendar had filled up, and talks of a syndicated television show, much to the McDonald children's delight, put Tim on the trail of his hero, Dr. Billy Graham – and even more so, on his truest hero, Jesus Christ. TIME Ministries, no matter how big it might grow, would always first and foremost be about Him.

Sarah's business continued to flourish, but she knew by summer if all went well, she would take a much larger role in the ministry – especially in the television part. For now, though, Tim was on his own as he prepared to embark on his January tour of the Southeast and a late winter and spring Midwestern itinerary. Sarah and the kids would join him in late May, where even more major crusades in New York and Washington, D.C. awaited.

Tim packed his bags right after a postcard perfect Christmas with his family (still no Ps4), and headed to the Charleston Airport to hop a flight to Atlanta (or Hot-Lanta, as Gary, a diehard Braves fan, called it).

"This is it!" Tim sighed as he watched the low clouds give way to sunshine as the Delta jet climbed to 23,000 feet. "God be with me! Fill me up! This is for you!"

Indeed the adventure of a lifetime was beginning, and Tim would need all the help he could get as he stepped onto the front lines of the Battle of the Ages – Spiritual Warfare.

Indeed, TIME Ministries had not gone unnoticed, not even in this realm.

Part One: The First Meeting

Tim was stretched out on the king-sized bed in the Holiday Inn in the heart of "Hot-Lanta," pouring his energy into studying his sermon notes for his largest crusade yet. He had everything down perfectly. He hadn't a clue that before he went to sleep tonight on that very same bed, these notes would be ripped to shreds, never to be used at all.

His cell jolted him out of his papers.

"This is Tim."

"This is Sarah! Hey, darling!"

Tim's dimples sprang forth, along with his smile.

"Hey, baby!" His deep Elvis-like drawl made her giggle, as it always had.

"There's a cold place in my bed that only you can warm."

"You know, it's funny. This Holiday Inn king-size deluxe has the same problem. It's really freezing on one side."

"Back in the day, Gary and/or Brooke would have crawled in with me – but I guess they're too old now!"

"How about Chance?"

"Yeah, he hasn't quite reached puberty yet! He still lets me be a totally mushy mom!"

"You can always be a totally mushy wife to me!"

"Don't worry! I'm saving it up for the weekend after next!"

"I'll be more than waiting!"

They laughed to lighten up the loneliness that only each other could relieve.

"Hey, Boogan can snuggle with you!"

"True! But he snores!"

"Has he torn up anything since I left?"

"Nah, just two pull toys, a pair of my shoes, and one of your belts!"

Boogan was another surprise addition to the McDonald clan – a Jackabee (Beagle and Jack Russell Terrier mix), that the family unanimously voted to save from the animal shelter. This was one good deed paying dividends already, as his deep growl and piercing bark anytime a stranger walked anywhere near the McDonald home, made Sarah and the kids feel safer.

Intruders didn't have to know that Boogan would much more likely roll over for a belly rub than try to attack!

"Hey, darling, I think I have a few of your people here needing to speak to you immediately." The sound of all three children suddenly realizing daddy was on the phone filled Tim's ears. He smiled, wondering who would seize the Galaxy S®5 first!

Chance won the war.

"Hi, Daddy! You bein' a 'vangelis' yet?"

"I start tomorrow night, buddy!"

"I prayin' for ya!"

"Thank you, Chancie, I need prayed for!"

"I wanna go tall baby. Will you please take me?"

"In just a few days, cutie!"

Chance loved to ride on daddy's shoulders which made him a "tall baby." Their favorite stomping ground was Charleston's market place. A wave of home sickness washed over Tim.

"Okay! Love you Daddy!" Chance giggled as Brooke tickled her little bro, snagging the phone in the process.

"Father, are you missing your favorite daughter?"

"You'd better believe it, sweetie pie!"

"You'd better be. I have a new boyfriend and you're not here to ask me questions about him."

This was a ritual between father and daughter ever since Brooke had discovered the opposite sex about two years ago. Tim would ask for more information about each potential suitor of his only female progeny. He figured this would keep the lines of communication open as those always volatile teenage years approached.

"Hey, I can still do that! What's his name?"

"Brett Barrett! Oh, Daddy, he is such a hottie!" Brooke giggled and Tim could feel her blush through the miles.

"Oh yeah, what's so special about him?"

"His eyes. They're big and blue – and soulful! And his hair – blonde – I mean yellow blonde – and curly! And his smile – oh!" More giggles.

"Okay, I get the point. So does he know you like him?"

"Dad, get real! I'm too embarrassed to even speak to him yet – but today, I saw him look at me, I know he did!"

"I see. So when do you plan on talking to him?"

"I don't know, maybe next week. Oh Dad! What should I say to him?"

"Hello might be a good start. Find something you have in common. Become friends first."

"Wow, Dad. You're so cool! Most parents would say you're way too young for boys and dating!"

"Dating? Who said anything about dating? You can date when you're thirty, as we have previously discussed!"

"Oooh! That's so lame! You're ruining my life!" she huffed in disgust, then fell into another fit of giggles.

"Hey, I'm not ready to give up my spot as number one in your life yet, that's all."

Brooke grew silent for a moment, then spoke in a voice that would no doubt reflect her way of talking as a young woman in a few years. "Dad, I seriously miss you! You're the best! I can't talk to anyone like I can to you!"

Tim's own voice choked as he said, "I miss you too, baby, and I love you so much. Hey, I'm going to find you a great cookbook of Georgia recipes."

"Hey, you'd better. God has given you this opportunity to travel, so I expect one from everywhere you go! Oh, I gotta go! *Dancing with the Stars* is coming on. Love ya! I'll be praying!"

Gary was next, as "Dancing" wasn't his thing.

"Yo Dad. Have you found any beastly Braves jerseys yet?"

"Not yet, my man I haven't had a chance to look. But I will. Any player you want in particular?"

"Yeah, I want one with my name on it!"

"Hey, good idea. No one else will have that one!"

"Cool. And, also, a Hawks jersey would be nice, too. Same plan – McDonald, number 77 – God's number!"

"Now, I like that – but where do you think all this money's going to come from?"

"The bank, Dad! Just write a check if you don't have the cash, dude – or swipe that plastic!"

"Oh, it's that easy, eh?"

"Yeah! You're doing God's work! He'll provide. Yo, NBA's coming on ESPN! Gotta go! Love ya!"

Sarah came back on to complete this priceless taste of home. "Hey, sugar! I hope this call has blessed you!"

"Oh, it has, Sarah! It's been perfect – just like you!"

"Oh, you flatterer, you! You are trying to get your way with me or something?"

"Oh, yeah!"

"Well, weekend after next, you got me, big boy!"

"Oh, yeah!"

"Is that all you can say?"

"Oh yeah!"

Laughter broke the tension of separation once again as God strengthened this family for the work ahead.

"Well darlin', I'll let you get back to preparing. I am so, so proud of you. I love you, love you, love you! By the way, I'm wearing your favorite red lipstick and nail polish. Here's a kiss!" She smooched the mouthpiece. "And now, I'm holding your hand!" She then scratched the mouthpiece gently. "Good night! Call me tomorrow!"

Tim glowed and basked in the love of true Christian marriage, then settled back into his notes.

After about a half-hour, a loud knock jolted Tim out of his studies. He hadn't ordered room service, so he wasn't sure who it could be. He jumped off the bed and hurried to answer the door.

Tim opened it to reveal four sharply dressed gentlemen that by their appearance had to be either deacons, pastors, or especially zealous door to door salesmen.

"Brothuh Timothy McDonald?" the eldest, and apparently the leader of the pack inquired.

"That would be me!" Tim smiled pleasantly, despite his confusion.

"Welcome to Atlantuh! I'm Brothuh Wesley L. Williams, Pastuh of Peachtree Baptist Church."

The two shook hands. Brother Wesley's grip was warm and firm.

"Howdy Brother! Lennard Garland, Head Deacon at Peachtree." Again, the handshake was friendly and strong, matching the cowboy-like accent and build of the second man.

"Terry Cantor – Head Trustee – I've heard great things about you brother! Glad to meet you!" No handshake here, Terry was a hugger. So was Tim. A hearty embrace resulted.

"And I'm Don Chambers – Associate Pastor. I'm the quiet one!" The others laughed.

"Now, I'm sure you're wonderin' why we're here, brothuh. Atlantuh's a tough market, so we're here in a spirit of love to prepare you for your ministry," said Brother Wesley.

"Okay!" Tim said, still not sure what to make of all this.

"This city can be quite stubborn, brothuh! The people here like to make excuses. They love to point fingers at the church. Don't get me wrong – there's lots of saved people here, but those that aren't seem quite happy not to be, if you know what I mean."

"It's that way everywhere my friend," replied Tim.

"True. But let me explain what I mean. Here's what I hear a lot of these days, 'you know, I'm doing better than most people. I'm a good person. I was raised in a Christian home. I believe in Jesus. I feel like I'll make it to Heaven. My good outweighs my bad. Besides, God is merciful. And hey I'm kind to people, I give to charity, and I go to church fairly regularly. So I believe I am fine.' Now, how would you respond to that brother?" inquired Lennard.

As Tim's head began spinning up a brainstorm, Lennard jumped in with more than his two cents worth.

"And also, my man, I get a lot of this from people where I work. 'Hey, this getting saved thing sounds nice and all, but not for me. It's too late, and I've done way too much wrong. There's no way I could ever be good enough'. Brother, I've had people tell me they've committed sex crimes, having illicit gay, straight, and sometimes both, kinds of affairs. I've heard embezzlers, gamblers, drug addicts, alcoholics, even one who had committed an unsolved murder, and another who was attracted to children and kiddy porn. Those people are out there brother, believe me."

Tim barely had time to catch his breath, much less think of any kind of reply, before Terry chimed in with his warning.

"I'll tell you what else is killing us – evangelical scandals – Jim Bakker, Jimmy Swaggart, and countless others. Also, stories of children molested by clergymen aren't just exclusive to Catholics. These well-known figures of authority, and in some cases, television and radio stars, are put on pedestals only to fall. There are no good examples or role models anymore. For all I know, maybe even you have skeletons in your closet. No offense, but I hear you're getting your own show soon."

"And," Don, the 'quiet one', decided to make himself heard, "how about all the hypocrites in the church? Just everyday laymen who only live the Christian life on Sunday? The church is not the salt and light anymore. Here in Atlanta, it seems to me to be especially bad."

The others all concurred.

"Brothuh, you'd bettuh lock yourself in your prayuh closet from now till tomorrah night!" said Brother Wesley.

"Hey, and God bless you, brother. We really are just trying to warn you. This is one tough market." Lennard offered a squeeze to Tim's shoulder and a pat to his back. The others then gathered around the totally overwhelmed evangelist and proceeded to lay hands on him. Silent prayers were also offered.

After a few minutes, this group of visitors exchanged nods that it was time to go, as their message had clearly been delivered.

"God bless you, brothuh!" Brother Wesley called and the others echoed as the motel room door closed with their departure.

Tim was rendered speechless and clueless.

After a while, he assumed a kneeling position by his bed and prayed. A strange compulsion filled him. He rose, went to his prepared sermons and notes, and proceeded to rip them to shreds, storing the remains in file thirteen. He then got out his sword – the Holy Word of God, and began to dig for answers.

He was not disappointed.

He stayed up way past midnight, reworking and rewriting his entire crusade. He wasn't sure why those men had come, or who sent them, but maybe now he saw God's reason for it.

He could not wait for tomorrow night to come.

It would have been really interesting to have seen Timothy Isaac McDonald's reaction to all this if he had bothered to do the research.

Peachtree Baptist Church did not exist.

And these men were not pastors, deacons, or trustees with any church.

Not by a long shot.

Excuse #1: Self-Righteousness

Madisyn Wilson was all about business. But to be fair, it was much more than that.

Madisyn was also all about doing right by others. She had worked diligently in her rise through the ranks of SunnyBook, Inc., the phone company's greatest rival in local yellow page advertising for the greater Atlanta area. Madisyn had started out working there during her last two summers at the University of Georgia. It didn't take her long to become their number one producer.

When Madisyn was five, she had made a decision. She loved Disney movies, and decided, like the heroes and heroines of those tales, that she would give her life to helping and being kind to others. Her parents, devout Christians and leaders in their church, Second Street Baptist, couldn't have been more proud of their only daughter.

At age eight, Madisyn found a dog with a broken leg and a couple of fractured ribs from being run over by a careless motorist in her neighborhood. A mix of several breeds, this mangy old mutt became her best childhood friend. He was no Dalmatian, but she dubbed him Pongo, the 101 Dalmatians hero's moniker, anyway.

At age ten, Madisyn took in two stray kittens, and got saved.

Well, sort of.

Second Street had an especially vivacious round of Vacation Bible School that summer. Madisyn had attended all five sessions, and went forward on the final evening. Her parents were both beaming, just as Madisyn hoped, and deep down knew, they would be. She had done it to please them. She felt her desire to be kind rose from her own heart, and her own convictions; thusly she saw no need for all this "born again" stuff. She had seen so many of her friends accept Jesus, but it seemed to have no effect on them, at least not for long. Her "conversion" was within herself. Madisyn, even in this summer of her fifth grade year, was emerging as a leader. She vowed to become a strong woman, one who would inspire others to do the same.

In junior high, she developed an interest in visiting nursing homes and shut-in neighbors. She would read to them, pick them flowers, and sometimes, with her mom's help, would make them homemade cookies. She felt so special, and harbored no doubt that she was getting more out of this than the old folks were. It really was better to give than to receive. Her parents had visions of their budding angel growing up to enter the mission field – perhaps in Africa, India, or some other exotic locale. God had His hand on this child, no question there.

In high school, Madisyn joined a Teens Who Care group that worked with special education children in various Atlanta elementary schools. She felt drawn to the teaching profession – that is, until her junior year when a careers class made her realize something life-changing – the more money she could make, the more people she could help. Teachers were way, way underpaid, and their influence was limited, so Madisyn began to reassess.

Then her senior year, she found her niche when she became a member of FBLA – Future Business Leaders of America. Her leadership skills combined with her compassionate heart, and she found herself in the role of Vice-President by Christmas – despite having only joined in September. She spearheaded the organization's involvement in nursing home visits, environmental projects, and yes, even animal rescue. These activities, along with her other community and church youth group involvement, and stellar grades, won her a scholarship to the University of Georgia. Madisyn Wilson, by her own strength and character, was on her way to being a true world-changer.

~

Ah, college! The parties, the friends pledging the top-rated sorority and being accepted, and the freedom! Madisyn was living high, but still working hard. Yes, she learned how to drink with the best of them, but also knew when to stop. Her sometimes late nights had virtually no effect on her schoolwork. Being an only child, she cherished more than anything the sisterhood of her Tri Sigma sorority friends. She truly believed any one of them would lay down their life for her, and she would no doubt return the favor. She moved out of her dorm room and into the sorority house some well-to-do alumnus had donated for that purpose. Madisyn became a ladies' lady, sticking up for women's rights at school and in the workplace. She did not, however, consider herself a feminist. After all, she had nothing against men, as some of the best looking guys on campus who had taken her out could most definitely attest.

Many of her classes had professors who presented a humanistic world view. Madisyn, having grown up in a Christian home, was shocked, but not totally offended, by their sometimes hostile attitude toward this "out of date" philosophy. After all, she totally believed in the power of self-potential, and it did make perfect sense that right and wrong could change as the culture did likewise. Still, she vowed to be godly about it all, always putting others first, and respecting all points of view. She was told by more than one of her instructors that a fine future as a top tier business executive lay in her path for the taking. Life was so-oo good!

And then came Dalton.

Dalton Dupree, fraternity hero, business school "phenom," and GQ® cover good looks, first asked for Madisyn's help on a marketing project. This led to a late night dinner, a red hot physical encounter, and almost an engagement. For a while, life got even better, until Dalton dumped Madisyn for a less attractive but more connected – as in wealthy family who own a major business – co-ed. Dalton's future was now secure. Madisyn got totally wasted with about ten of her sisters on a Friday night, and by the following Monday, Madisyn was back in control. She was, after all, strong. Strong in herself, and the godly person she herself chose to be. She swore off men, sort of. An occasional physical fling was fun, but commitment had no place, for now at least.

Everyone was scrambling for internships by the end of their junior year. Atlanta had quite a selection, but for Madisyn, SunnyBook, Inc. had the most charm. No, it wasn't a major company, but it was giving a major company a run for its money, despite being locally-owned and starting from scratch. Innovative ideas for their phone book, including business listings by neighborhood, a complete alphabetical listing of all of greater Atlanta's residents, restaurant menus, and virtually any size and color of ad any company could possibly conceive. In addition, their distribution was now wider than the phone companies, and their methods for tracking the ad's results were second to none.

Best of all, their community involvement was impeccable. From school projects to senior citizens' events, to charity work, SunnyBook had all the bases covered. Also, SunnyBook wasn't afraid to go outside the box on hiring minorities. Two African-American, and even a Native American, were all included on the payroll. Also, a Buddhist, a Wiccan, an Atheist, and an Orthodox Jew all worked in comfort side by side. Everyone shared the same goal, sell as many ads as possible, produce the highest quality ads possible, and in the process help as many people and causes as possible.

SunnyBook, Inc. fit Madisyn like a glove. She became the number one sales person that first summer, and upon graduation, became Assistant Manager and Field Trainer.

That fall, Clinton Langston joined the team. His effeminate speech and actions gave him a gay label whether he wanted it or not.

Turns out, he did want it. He became outspoken about his lifestyle, and most people in this diverse atmosphere tolerated him – but not everyone. Bobby Benton, a good old boy hired to win over the construction and general contractor market, couldn't stand him. Clinton knew this, and always went out of his way to be overly friendly.

"Good morning, Bobby, how ya doin'?"

"Don't get in my face, pretty boy!"

"In your dreams."

"You make me sick, faggot. You know, I ought to belt you where it hurts the most and make a man out of you."

Clinton turned the tables by being the victim rather than fighting back. "Hey, that was mean. I am a man, thank you, sir. Just because I choose to be gay doesn't change that."

Just then, Barbie Toom, one of the new administrative assistants who had a secret crush on Clinton but of course had been respectfully turned down by him, sauntered in, a present in hand. "Hi Clinton! Hey, no hard feelings, okay? Here's a gift. No reason why we can't be friends, right?"

Barbie winked at Bobby, but Clinton, curious as to the package's contents, didn't notice. He tore it open to reveal a bright pink dress, along with a note: "Hey girlfriend! Come to my Mary Kay party on Saturday!   Love ya, sis! Barbie."

As Barbie began to giggle and Bobby began to guffaw, Madisyn walked by just in time to see Clinton begin to cry. Right then and there, she suspended Bobby and Barbie, promising their job back only if they would agree to a sensitivity program she would, and did, design immediately. This made her Employee of the Month, won her an award from the Atlanta Chamber of Commerce, got her some media attention, and earned her a promotion to Vice President.

Two years later, she would become CEO.

~

Madisyn became even more known for her acts of kindness than the ever increasing success of her company. She gave 12.5 percent of her check to the United Way and encouraged her employees to do the same. She found work for physically and mentally handicapped people of all ages and creeds. She volunteered one night a week at a soup kitchen, and another night at the nearby Children's Cancer Hospital.

Her generosity extended to her co-workers as well. She did her best to re-create the sorority sister aura of her college days by hosting girls' nights out for her female employees. She offered paid vacations after only six months of service. She had even initiated a small daycare for single moms. Everyone loved Madisyn.

And yet, something was missing.

Madisyn, for the life of her, couldn't figure out what it could possibly be. Yes, she was lonely. There had been no one serious since Dalton. But her life was full of work, fun, and friends. Could it be her biological clock already? Nah, too soon for that, and no time, anyway.

She still attended church with her parents on occasion, but the messages seemed full of words and no action. She was happy in her own strength.

Wasn't she?

All this was passing not for the first time through her mind on that quite raw, drizzly, late January day. Madisyn had more than a bit of a headache, and way more than a bit of a dilemma.

His name was Paul Sanders.

Paul was, well, just a little narrow minded, strong willed, and strong mouthed about his religious convictions. He was the sort that gave being born again a bad name.

Madisyn nervously tapped her immaculately manicured coral-painted nails on her mahogany desktop, and stared at this normally shy but obviously misguided young man. She sought for patience and insight to deal with him correctly.

"Paul, uh, hon, we've got to talk."

"Yes, we do. Did you know I sold my first double quarter column ad this morning? It's a new veterinarian practice downtown."

"Oh, great!" Madisyn's smile was genuine despite her concerns. She patted his hand briefly.

Paul blushed. He was crushing big time, and had been ever since he'd begun his job at SunnyBook back in November. It blinded him to her now stern expression, and her true reason for calling this meeting.

"Oh, did I mention it was in full color?"

"Oh, wow!"

Another hand pat had Paul's heart about ready to jump out of his chest. He gazed at his boss's perfectly permed chestnut hair which flowed to her shoulders, blue eye shadow that matched her eyes yet still brought out their beauty, full lips only slightly glossed because that was all they needed...

"Paul, dear, congratulations! I knew you had it in you!"

"Thanks to you! You're my inspiration!"

Paul looked at her with his Hershey-brown puppy dog eyes, enlarged by his thick glasses. He could have answered, and won, a casting call for the part of "The Nerd." He was dressed in navy plaid pants and a white button-down shirt, complete with matching navy tie. He had his overstuffed briefcase in hand, and his pockets were stuffed with examples of his ink pen collection. She knew he was crushing and felt sorry for him. No, he was not the best looking man in Hot-lanta, but he wasn't the worst either. She sensed he had a sweet spirit that was worth far more than Dalton's outer appearance. She knew, however, that she would only break his heart, especially in light of what had to be talked about next.

"Paul, we do have a problem. I hate to have to bring it up, but..."

"Oh no! I have tried to be on time. I have been, haven't I? My watch broke that one day last week, but since then..."

"No, Paul. It's about your signature."

"What?"

"Whenever you make a sale, you always send out a personal note or email thanking your client, and I love that! Business with a personal touch. That is what SunnyBook is all about!" She flashed Paul her best Crest White Strips grin that kept his focus firmly fixed on her.

"But, hon, that cross symbol has got to go! Lose it, okay? It is not a reflection of this company or its beliefs."

"I know, Madisyn. But it is a reflection of me. Jesus is not just a religion to me. He's my Lord, my Savior, and my best friend. How can I hide Him after all He's done for me?"

"Paul, I know your beliefs mean a lot to you. It's sweet, it really is. And I myself have nothing against Jesus! In fact, I go to church on occasion with my parents. So you see, I'm on your side." She touched the back of his hand lightly to soften the blow of her next statement. "Unfortunately, I am going to have to demand that you refrain from using any religious symbols in your business with us. We have a diversity of beliefs here and all have agreed to make their religion a personal matter. It just works best that way. Can you understand?"

Paul looked crest fallen – totally crest fallen.

"Oh, I hate this, Madisyn. I'll have to pray about whether or not I should continue to work here..." He hung his head obviously torn.

Madisyn found herself gently rubbing the back of his now quite sweaty hand with her finger in a soothing but non-sexual gesture.

"You know I'm right, Paul. It's nothing against you." She pulled away, folding her arms, trying to appear in control.

Suddenly, Paul's face lit up. "Okay, boss lady! I'll make a deal with you!"

"Okay, I'm listening."

"I'll be good and do what you say. I cannot say I'll stop being outspoken. But I will keep within the rules and be professional about it. I've got to be me, but I promise I'll cause you no trouble."

"Okay, so what's the catch?"

"I want you to go out with me tonight."

"Oh, no!" Madisyn's face hardened. She should have seen this coming. She let out a sigh of exasperation.

"Now listen! I want to take you out to eat. Somewhere nice! Just a friendly dinner? Ok? Then, I want you to come with me to the TIME Ministries crusade."

"Oh, Paul, no! I can't!"

"Now, wait! This guy is good! I mean really good! He doesn't scream. He doesn't lecture endlessly about money. He's just good, that's all! I hear the music is great, too! Now, isn't that fair?" Paul favored her with his most earnest, pleading look.

Every fiber in Madisyn's being screamed "no," but for some reason unknown to her, her heart just didn't seem to hear.

"Okay, it's a deal." Her stern expression remained. "But I do demand and deserve the right to bail out early if it's just not my thing. Deal?"

"Deal." They shook on it. Paul smiled. His Lord truly was so good, and so full of surprises. Who would have ever thought that something so good could come from such an awkward situation?

Madisyn sighed heavily once more as Paul whistled his way out of her office. Just what had she gone and done?

~

Madisyn chewed on her oriental chicken salad as she contemplated the situation. Was she leading on this not-so-handsome, but oh-so-sweet man by agreeing to this? She had to give Paul his props – he had some moxie to stand up to her without disrespecting her at all. And his standards were maybe over the top, but he was completely unwavering – even to the point of losing his job he obviously cared a great deal about. Ah, standards. Hers had always been so high, higher than most of the professing Christians she knew. But was there more to it than that? Had her standards kept her from falling in love after Dalton? Had they kept her from finding a deeper truth outside herself as well? A line from an old sixties song by Paul Stookey she'd heard at several weddings came to mind, "If loving is the answer, then who's the giving for? Do you believe in something that you've never seen before? There is love..."

Right now, Madisyn had a confession. She wanted something a lot stronger than the unsweet tea that had accompanied her salad. But, no, the judgment she would no doubt face from Paul...

Ah, Paul. He was different, though. So many people hid behind church, Jesus, and the Bible, maneuvering them around to meet their own needs or make a good appearance. Not Madisyn! Her goodness came as a result of her own inner strength and wise choices. What you see is what you get! She needed no one... But Paul confounded her. His beliefs were truly his way of life. He talked about Jesus like they were best friends. Was Madisyn missing something after all?

She looked warmly at Paul. He had shown such passion, courage, and conviction standing up for himself and his beliefs. That mix of confidence and vulnerability stirred something deep within herself. "Paul?"

"Yes?"

"You really believe this stuff, don't you?"

"Totally. Don't you? You told me you were all for Jesus, and that you attended church on occasion."

"Yes. I do. How could you not believe it?" Indeed. So why was there an empty spot in Madisyn's heart that all her strength and good thoughts and good deeds just could not fill? She reached across the table and gently squeezed Paul's hand as she attempted to regain control. "Thanks for dinner, Paul. It was very sweet. But listen. I honestly do have a very busy day tomorrow. Is there any chance I could take a rain check on the crusade? I will even allow you to walk me to my door."

"Nope. Sorry! A deal's a deal. Business is business. That's what a certain wise woman always tells me!"

"Fine! You're right. Let's just get it over with!"

But as Paul paid the check, and he and Madisyn headed for the exit, the resentment of having to keep her side of the bargain was being overridden by something else, a strange sensation indeed.

It almost felt like relief.

~

"In today's society, it seems like we're all working our way toward something. Maybe it's toward graduation. Maybe it's through college. Maybe it's getting that first job, or that first promotion. Maybe it's toward financial freedom so we can retire early – say age 45? 40? 35?"

The crowd responded with cheers and laughter for Evangelist Timothy Isaac McDonald.

"Working toward achievements and goals is in and of itself not wrong. God wants His children to do well. He wants us to provide for our families and to be great at whatever he has gifted us to do. Whatever your hand finds to do, do it with all your might. That's found in Ecclesiastes, Chapter 9, Verse 10.

"Now, the truth is, I've gone from being a full-time factory worker to a bi-vocational pastor to a full-time evangelist! This has been difficult, frustrating, and scary. But you know, it's always been a fantastic adventure! God has given my dear wife, Sarah, and our three precious children the patience of Job to make it through. Hey, just putting up with me requires the patience of Job!"

Hearty and sincere laughter ensued.

"And whatever you do, whether in word or deed, do it all in the name of the Lord Jesus, giving thanks to God the Father through Him! Colossians 3:17 tells us this. So yes, God wants us to work, and live, and love! All for His glory!"

This time, it was Amens a plenty that broke out.

"But listen dear friends. There is something that cannot be worked for. It cannot be earned. It can only be accepted as the free gift that it is! And yet, nothing we can work for is more valuable than this! I'm talking about Salvation! The free gift of God's grace! Though we do not deserve it, God gave the very life of his son – for us! That is our only way to him. Now listen and listen good. For all have sinned and fallen short of the glory of God! That's Romans 3:23. For the wages of sin is death, but the gift of God is eternal life in Christ Jesus, our Lord! That stop on our Roman Road is Romans 6:23.

"At this time, I want to introduce you to Jamie Ray and Meghan Amhearst, our music evangelists. Jamie wrote a song about what it really means to be strong. Listen carefully."

> But the bitter hurt just wore my heart
> Right down to the bone
> That's when I finally cried out
> "I can't take this alone!"
> I wept in true repentance
> "Dear Lord, I was so wrong"
> That's when he took me in and made me strong!

The power ballad with in the pocket harmonies rained down its blessing on the event, bringing out the message of the night in under four minutes. The applause was almost as long as the song itself.

"In His Sermon on the Mount found in chapters 5-7 of the Gospel of Matthew, Jesus spoke some fairly harsh words against self-righteousness. 'Not everyone who says to me Lord, Lord will enter the kingdom of heaven, but only he who does the will of my Father who is in heaven. Many will say to me in that day, Lord, Lord, did we not prophesy in your name, and in your name drive out demons and perform miracles? Then I will tell them plainly, I never knew

17

you. Away from me, you evildoers!' This very plain passage is found in Matthew 7:21-23.

"Jesus IS our righteousness! Jesus is our ONLY way to heaven. Just doing the things of Jesus, just giving to charity, just going to church, just being a good person – none of these will ever be the answer – they are not enough! It's not about religion, it's about a relationship with Jesus Christ. For everything we do will come from that strength. Jesus said, 'A thief comes only to steal and kill and destroy; I have come that they may have life, and have it to the full!' John 10:10 proclaims this exciting truth.

"Do you want a full life? Do you want to know what it means to live? To love? Then accept Jesus as your Savior tonight. Without Him, nothing else matters. No one can do it for you. You cannot be born into it! It will not sink in by osmosis! You cannot earn it. You have to ask for it by:

A – Admitting you are a sinner;

B – Believing in Jesus as the only way to be saved; and

C – Confessing it to everyone!

Simple right? Yet so many have stumbled. This has to be personal – a matter between you and Jesus! He is knocking at your heart's door. Won't you please let him in?"

~

Paul was so enraptured in the message that at first he didn't notice Madisyn had placed her arm firmly around him. Then he noticed an additional physical warmth to go along with the spiritual warmth his heart was already feeling from hearing the Word preached. He looked unbelievingly at the beautiful hand perched on his shoulder, kneading it tenderly. Was she trying to get his attention to talk him into making an early exit?

But then, he turned and saw her lovely face. Tears were cascading down her cheeks as her body began to wrack with her sobbing.

~

At first, Madisyn had tolerated the preaching and all those Bible verses. At first, she tried to shut it out by concentrating on picking out different people and trying to figure out their true reason for being there.

But then came that song *Strong*. It was as if it had been written just for her. Perhaps it had, because the sermon that followed seemed to be written just for her as well.

That empty spot in her heart was hearing the sweet call of Someone – Someone much more than just a legend or an ideal. The call came from a Person who loved her like no one else could. Was this just a spell being cast in the intensity of the moment? No! He was beckoning her to rise up and be strong – strong enough to swallow her pride and welcome Him.

And she did.

When the invitation came, Madisyn clutched Paul's hand with both of her own and walked – or was it flew? – forward to proudly proclaim her new life!

~

Tim's own eyes brimmed over with tears as he saw hundreds coming forward. Many of these converts appeared professional in nature. Indeed, it would be revealed that many doctors, lawyers, teachers, college professors, and business executives once content in their own success and goodness had now become the recipients of true strength. "What a God I serve!" Tim sighed as he took time to meet as many of these new brothers and sisters as humanly possible. Even as the peace and victory of the night washed over him, he could already sense his work had barely begun.

He was right.

~

Tim McDonald lay in his bed basking in the afterglow of the first night of the Atlanta crusade. He reflected on the many stories of conversion he had heard: Billy Tidwell, the lawyer who did cases pro bono for the downtrodden, but whose own soul had been searching for its own personal, higher connection; Kara Winslett, the special education teacher who was everyone's caregiver, who had finally let herself be handed over to the true caregiver – finding love and peace that had always eluded her; Fred Givens, the church deacon who thought his position and good deeds were earning him a spot in heaven; and Madisyn Wilson, the business executive with a heart, who finally learned she must give her own heart away to become truly strong. And more, so many more, hundreds in fact, and yet...

And yet, Tim knew he needed to preach this same message again tomorrow night, and perhaps, the next night as well.

God wasn't done with Excuse #1 just yet here in Hot-lanta!

Indeed, over twelve hundred new citizens were added to God's kingdom by the time night number four arrived, bringing with it the expository treatment to excuse #2 that Tim had brought to the first. And again, God would be right on time. A very special lost sheep was being prepared to be brought to a place of having open ears.

And an open heart.

Excuse #2: Beyond Forgiveness

Sean Diamond sat sulking in his cell, replaying the horror movie that had been his life up to now. He was coming up on four years in the big house – armed robbery, assault and battery, and grand theft auto rounding out the unholy trinity.

It was the things he had done that he had not been charged for, that few, in fact, even knew about, that were rolling across the silver screen in his mind.

The only person he had ever loved in his life was his momma, and he had lost her at age five in a drive-by shooting reported to be gang related. Sean was uprooted from his home and placed with his grandmomma, whose intentions were good, but she was totally clueless as to what was going on with her grandson and his feelings, and in the real world.

At age eight, ahead of the growth chart by a considerable amount, Sean was given an invitation to join his first gang. Two middle school boys recruited him with a promise of revenge on the rival gang responsible for his mom's death. Sean's initiation was spelled out clearly for him – steal his grandmomma's social security check, get it cashed, then shoplift some clothes and candy from Walmart. As a reward, he would keep fifty percent of the loot, become a full member, and receive his own knife – not a kid's pocket knife, but a deadly weapon. Also, he would be trained to use it, taught how to fight, and personally get to attack the drug dealer who ordered the shooting that had ruined his life forever.

Sean was a natural.

Soon, no motivation was needed, as the thrill of power and wealth intoxicated him to the core. He gained street cred, earning the name "Diamond" for his lust to obtain all the ice he could, from stores, dealers, and rival gang members. He pierced both his ears and displayed diamond studs in each, but his pride and joy was the two carat beauty pierced into his bottom lip.

The legend of Sean Diamond was born, and only grew through his teenage years. Sean could not stand the word "no," taking whomever and whatever he wanted. His thirst for women kicked in at about age thirteen. He would come on to them in an innocent, charming way, but when they turned down his more blatant advances, he forced himself on them, thrilling as their pain snuffed out their protests. "I thought girls liked diamonds," he would snarl as he violated more than a few of Atlanta's young ladies with his burgeoning manhood.

He had yet to commit murder, but Sean Diamond dreamed of it – what power – the ultimate power – life and death at his control. It actually thrilled him more, though, to make his enemies wish they were dead after being inflicted with torturous knife wounds, punches, and pistol whippings.

Sean dropped out of school at fifteen – the streets of Atlanta provided a much more rewarding and fulfilling education. He figured he'd earned a couple of bachelor's degrees and a master's degree in real life. He had the world by the tail, and never once had he faced any charges or been caught committing even the smallest misdemeanor.

Until that wonderful and terrible night that marked Sean Diamond's eighteenth birthday.

"Happy berfday, Gangsta Sean
Diamond's got it goin' on
Here's your present – Manhood heaven
A brand new AK-47!"

Slick Rick, one of Sean's homeboys, rapped out this birthday greeting on this fine specimen of a Tuesday morning in Hot-Lanta. Sean was in a good mood, figuring on celebrating in grand style.

His outlook shot up exponentially when he tore into the package Slick Rick presented to him.

It was exactly what the rapper proclaimed. "Sean Diamond, you are now a man! You have outgrown toys – toys are for boys! Welcome to the big time!"

Sean took out the piece. What a beauty! Brand new, mint condition. Sean could have cried, but he had forgotten how. Instead, he laughed, and then giggled uncontrollably.

"Hey, man, this is righteous! I thinks I'm gonna have to throw a monsta party now!"

"Yeah, we've gotta make your big day unforgettable! I'll call in Krime Dawg! We gonna rock this town tonight!"

Plans were made, masterminded by Sean, and at 3:57 pm, Sean, Slick Rick, and Krime Dawg strolled into the North branch of the Georgia State Bank. Sean's birthday gift was stashed in his bomber jacket, Slick Rick was "packing" a large birthday cake, and Krime Dawg had the drinks covered.

"Yes, can I help you gentlemen?" Sonia Tinsley was the only teller on duty, as the bank was preparing to close. She looked more like a librarian than a banker. Her glasses were thick, her makeup was slight, and her tone was pleasant but quite business-like and no-nonsense.

"Yes, ma'am. My man Sean here is celebrating his birthday today. Won't you join us for a party?" asked Rick.

"Yeah, babe. Rick's got the cake, I got the drinks, and Sean, well, he's basically got the plan, right, homeslice?" asked Krime Dawg.

"You're straight up! How's about a birthday kiss for starters, Sonia?" Sean always made it a point to call people by name when he could. In this case, Sonia's name tag supplied the information.

"You're quite a lovely lady," said Sean.

"We're about to close, boys. What is it you need?"

"I already told you!" Sean grabbed Sonia's hand roughly, bit and kissed it noisily before she could pull it away.

"I'm going to ask you nicely to leave, boys, we're closing in approximately one minute!" Sonia fought to keep her composure.

"Okay, okay. I'll get down to business. I need to withdraw $1,000 from my account. It is my birthday and all. It's under Sean Diamond – like the jewel!" He made a lewd gesture.

Sonia uneasily began to peck at her keyboard, looking for his name, of course, it was nowhere to be found.

"I'm sorry, sir. Apparently you don't have an account here."

"That's funny, because my associate says I do." He whipped out the AK-47. "Now, about that birthday kiss, I mean, a real one!" He reached over, bit her again, then planted a hard, lengthy one right square on her lips, leaving a bruise. Sonia was too scared and shocked to know what to do. As this was occurring, Krime Dawg slipped out to the back parking lot to jack a ride for their hasty exit from this lovely gala.

"Ah, sweet! You're a hottie, Sonia! Now, my associate here says that withdrawal needs to be eighteen large, one for each year! I need it now! You be a good girl, and that kiss will be just the beginning!"

John Sharpton, the bank manager, had been quietly watching the horror movie unfolding. He had the security cameras off, but had quickly turned them back on as he calmly punched in 911.

"Sir, we don't have that much cash up here. I'll have to go to the safe in the back."

"Great! My associate and I will be glad to escort you!" He poked his weapon roughly against Sonia's back as, in total fear, she headed toward John's office. As they passed it, John ducked down, then slid in quietly behind them. Slick Rick had meanwhile slid out the front door to help Krime Dawg prepare the white Hummer H-3 he had chosen for their temporary transportation.

John prayed for his moment. It came when Sean shoved Sonia into the safe she had just opened.

"Count it out right, babe. I might even give you a cut if you'll be my guest of honor at my party!" He slung the gun back carelessly as he was now high on adrenaline and confidence.

John snatched the gun before Sean could react.

"Party's over, gangsta boy!" John trained Sean's present right on his heart. "Don't let the suit fool you. I was a marine for ten years before I came here."

Sean had been in some tough spots before, and he had come out unscathed every time up to this point.

Sean cussed a blue streak. He'd broken one of the gang's basic rules. Never under estimate your opponent.

But he also remembered their most important principle.

Never give up.

Sean slouched in defeat. He hung his head and began to walk away from the safe.

"Okay, man. No harm done, right?" Sean tucked his hands in his pockets and continued to back up.

John's stance was unwavering. His instincts warned him to stay alert. As he was thinking this, a white, blinding pain shot through him. He felt the gun slip from his hand as he fell.

Sonia shrieked.

And so did the sirens.

Sean recovered his weapon, but as he turned to point it at Sonia, he saw with surprise that his masterful movements had not only taken John out, they had also stimulated Sonia into action. She had shot out of the emergency exit in John's office.

What Sean had done was pull out his knife, the same one he had acquired upon his admittance into the gang. He had gripped it, pulled it out, and threw it, all in a fraction of a second; one of the many tricks that had made him a street legend.

Then came trick number two.

As the police burst through the front door, Sean burst out the back, throwing his gun into the open Hummer window. Krime Dawg caught it, and began firing wildly. As the cops focused their attention out back, Sean slipped back inside and jumped into the safe, shut the door, and counted out his eighteen large, as the cops began to pursue the getaway vehicle. Then, he crawled out, regained his knife, and strolled confidently to the front door. Only one cop was guarding it, as everyone thought all the perps were in the car.

Sean repeated his knife trick before the officer could react.

"Cops, marines, it makes no difference to Sean Diamond!"

Before leaving, he whipped out the roll of duct tape he always carried (another principle to live by) and insured that the manager and the cop were trapped securely until the next morning.

They would live. Maybe. At any rate, a move in headquarters was long overdue, anyway. By the time the boys in blue realized the head honcho had flown the coop, it would be too late.

Sean began to whistle as he once again basked in the greatness of the man known as Sean Diamond.

Suddenly, he found himself on the ground. Two officers were towering over him. A third one, balding and red-faced, had tripped him.

"Hello, Mr. Diamond. Nice rocks, especially that one on your lip. It must have been quite interesting to Sonia Tinsley, since you 'favored' her with that birthday kiss. In fact, I know it got her attention, because she described you to a T as the leader. By the way, we got your buddies, too."

Sean's anger boiled as he reached for his knife, but instead of the cold, reassuring steel, he felt a tingle, then a burning as the afternoon faded to blackness.

Never under estimate your opponent.

Or his taser.

~

His friends ratted him out for the price of a lesser sentence. Sean got the word out, and both Slick Rick and Krime Dawg found themselves branded with a large diamond shaped mark, forever reminding them of their betrayal.

His first night in jail, a sex-starved inmate tried to seduce him. Sean did not need a knife to inflict fast and efficient torture. Sean faced no more such difficulties during his stay.

That stay was scheduled for fifteen years. Assaulting an officer did not help his cause. In light of this, Sean Diamond picked up two new habits – smoking and reading; the former to calm his nerves, the latter, he could learn his rights.

He discovered that in less than four years, he could be up for parole – but to accomplish this, Sean Diamond must do something he had never been able to do.

Behave in an exemplary fashion, with no slip-ups, effective immediately.

Okay, fine, but Katy-bar-the-door when he was freed. He would make up for lost time, and so much more – he would make everyone pledge his allegiance to the Diamond, especially his Judas buddies, and that bank teller ho. So, with motivation in place, Sean Diamond, went about becoming a model citizen of Prisonville.

What he didn't bank on was meeting the toughest individual he had ever encountered. At five-two and 125 pounds (all muscle), Ilise Jackson was the most intimidating presence to enter Sean's life.

Since his mom.

~

"You are nothing but a vile earthworm! You are like a pile of filthy, polluted rags that a pack of dogs relieved themselves on! You are a total scumbag, and a waste of everyone's time who knows you."

Sean glared with intense hatred at this middle-aged, quite attractive, and quite well-toned specimen that was his parole officer. His thoughts toward her at that moment lived up precisely to her description of him.

"I can read you like a book! I know every chapter and verse. You want to get revenge on your homeboys who turned their backs on you. I even hear to some extent you already have. I also know you are thinking of tracking down and raping that bank teller, whose description helped bring you down. I also know you are having thoughts of raping me about now."

Sean scowled at her.

"If you do, it won't be the first time."

For the first time, Sean's eyes registered something other than anger – surprise.

24

"Did I catch you off guard finally, Homes? Well, it's true. My first husband abused me horribly. I had to get out, but he found me, and, well..."

"Did you get him back?"

"Not like you're talking about. He was convicted, sent to prison, and then after that, we agreed on a settlement – he owed me nothing if he would just disappear. I could have cleaned him out, so needless to say, he took it."

"So why do you want to help me, if I'm all these terrible things you say I am?"

"That's a good question. Right now, you disgust me – but that's right now. You see, I've learned to see things from a whole new perspective."

"Are you a religious freak or something? And let me guess, I'm the poor, lost cause, right?" Sean's usual persona was returning.

Ilise rose to her feet. "Listen, obviously you're not ready to talk yet. I hope and pray you will be in time. Until then, I'm outta here before I get sick!"

Ilise stormed out. Sean didn't know what to make of this woman who had the nerve to speak to him in such a manner. What a freak! Probably a holy roller. Just who did she think she was? No one defied the Diamond like that.

At least until later that night.

Axe Rottweiler, a member of Sean's rival gang, had recently been brought here for a little involuntary state-paid vacation. Sean had been a thorn in his side years ago, and now, at last, was his chance to make things square by ruining Sean's parole, and at the same time, extolling revenge on a prison guard who had the nerve to bully him.

Axe bided his time, watching for the guard to put down his guard. It happened at 12:24 am. The guard was dozing at his post. Axe paid off the custodian in his cell block to get the key off the sleeping watchman. This was accomplished easily and quietly, as all appeared peaceful, and this guard was usually infallible. Axe stepped out, stabbed the guard several times, rendering him silent and helpless. Axe was wearing a pair of gloves he had hidden under his mattress, so he simply walked over to Sean's cell, put the knife in Sean's hands as he slept, took it back, and laid it across the guard's body as a sign of dominance. The custodian then disposed of the gloves, but not before donning them himself and placing the guard's keys in Sean's hands also before returning them to the guard's pocket.

The next day, Sean Diamond had a rude awakening. He was jerked up out of his bunk and brought before the warden. Sean didn't have to fake ignorance. He had no idea what all this commotion was about. He had literally slept through the entire episode.

Then it hit him.

Axe Rottweiler had just been moved here a few days ago, and he was no doubt laying for Sean!

"No! No! I'm innocent! I'm working to get out of here! It's Axe Rottweiler! He's out to get me! I'll kill him! I swear, I'll kill him!"

But that's as far as Sean's story got. He was thrown into solitary confinement. His hearing would be in a few days – all hope of parole was gone. Especially the next day, when his meager breakfast was slipped through the door. A message came with it that killed any appetite Sean may have had.

Billy Smithson, the guard, had died soon after entering the hospital. Sean Diamond was now looking straight down the barrel of murder charges. His life, if there even had been one in the first place, was over.

But then, Hurricane Ilise exploded on the scene. She, without Sean knowing, burst in, demanding Axe Rottweiler to be questioned. She also interviewed everyone who had been working that night, including a certain custodian whose conscience got the better of him. His confession lost him his job, but gave him peace anyway, as he couldn't stand what he had done any longer.

Sean was fuming in his hell room when a heavenly event occurred. The door burst open, Sean was escorted out, and Axe was ushered in, to the fate he, not Sean, had earned.

Sean, always ready with a rude quip, didn't know what to say. One of his rescuers provided the answer.

"Son, you'd better be thanking God for that parole officer of yours. She moved Heaven and earth for you!"

Now Sean was truly speechless.

~

"But I don't get it! You called me everything in the book. I thought you were a playah hatah!" said Sean.

"I am. That's why Axe is in solitary," said Ilise.

"But how did you know?"

"On my own, I didn't. It's called the spiritual gift of discernment! Sean, I guess I should have made myself clear in our first meeting. Those things I said, I meant, but not about you! It was your sins and your choices! They made you those things! But you, you are a blessing, my dear child! I can see an intelligence in you – a creativity in you – and yes, a good man with limitless potential in you! But I had to shock you into understanding that as of now, you'll never realize all that goodness."

"Listen, Officer Jackson…"

"Child, don't you ever call me that again! My name is Ilise! Now, you were saying?"

"Ilise, I think I like you – you believe in me, that's not something I ever say to anyone – but, if you're talking Jesus nonsense – you're wasting your time with me!"

"And just why is that?"

"Because it's too late for me. My momma used to tell me about this great loving God, but where was He when she was shot? I gave up on that pipe dream at age five – and I think I've done alright. I make my own way."

"Look around you, Sean. Have you really done all right? What if I hadn't intervened?"

Sean sulked and looked down.

"Listen, hon. Jesus loves you right where you are. He's saved souls far worse than yours."

Sean felt a lump in his throat. With horror, he realized he hadn't felt like this since he was five.

It meant he was going to cry. He fought it with all he had to save what little dignity he had left.

"But you don't know all I've done. When I was eight, I stole my grandmomma's social security check. I've beaten up and tortured people, even children, since I was a child myself. I bet I've raped close to fifty women."

"Jesus knows all of that, sweetie, and He loves you anyway. He's waiting at your door. Just open it!"

A few tears leaked from this hardened man. "I'm sorry, I can't take any more today." Sean slumped as he was led back to his cell.

Ilise, however, had seen enough. She knew this mission would not have been in vain.

~

Sean was cooperative as the next few weeks passed, and Ilise was patient, but no progress was being made. She prayed for something that would finish this miracle.

Finally, in January of 2015, it came.

TIME Ministries came to town, and word of a revival unlike since the hayday of Billy Graham was spreading. Ilise had to get Sean Diamond there, somehow.

Then the second piece of the puzzle fell into place, Sean's parole hearing. In light of his model behavior and near tragic injustice Axe had bestowed, the date was moved up two weeks.

Ilise stood by him.

Ilise fought for him.

Ilise won Sean his freedom.

There was one condition, however. Sean, in the company of Ilise, had to attend one service of the TIME Ministries crusade.

Although Sean still knew it was useless, he figured it was a small price to pay. He agreed, then did yet another thing he hadn't done since age five. He gave an affectionate hug to a woman who more and more was reminding him of the last lady he had favored with such a gesture.

His momma.

~

"So, you may ask, who can be saved? Who can claim this free gift, this ticket to abundant life, eternal life, and Heaven? I tell you, EVERYBODY! 'For God so loved the world that He gave his only begotten son, that WHOSOEVER believeth in Him shall not perish, but have everlasting life!'* That's John 3:16, maybe the best known of all the scriptures – but have you really considered what it means? Every single person has a choice, and absolutely ANYONE can be saved. For EVERYONE who calls on the name of the Lord shall be saved! Romans 10:13 makes it clear. Do you realize what this means? Look at David. You don't have to know your Bible to know who David was. You know, the greatest sports upset in history? Teenage shepherd beats 9'6" giant? Yao Ming is a shrimp compared to that guy, yet David defeated him – with a child's weapon – a slingshot!"

The crowd was eating out of Brother Timothy Isaac McDonald's hands, and the pumped up evangelist let them, because this was all about God!

"This man went on to be one of the greatest kings of Israel. We discover political scandal – I mean dirt, ladies and gentlemen. In our time, we've seen a president commit perjury about committing adultery. We've also witnessed the governor of one of our largest states go down for being involved in a prostitution ring – but David? He was worse. He committed adultery, then plotted the murder of her husband, one of his best soldiers, so he could have the woman for himself! There was rape and incest among David's children, Amnon, Tamar, and Absalom. Then Absalom killed Amnon for raping Tamar – then Absalom tried to kill his own father! Talk about dysfunctional families!"

Laughter filtered through the crowd.

"But get this! David repented! He confessed his sin, and repented from it! That means he owned up to it, and turned away from it! And do you know what God did? Called him a man after his own heart! Furthermore, He made an agreement with David that one of his descendants would always sit upon the throne of Israel! My friends, the fulfillment of that deal is Jesus Christ Himself!"

Loud applause and Amens resulted.

"And how about Jesus during His earthly ministry? He was constantly being criticized for hanging out with sinners! Matthew, one of his disciples, was a hated tax collector. He went on to write the book of Matthew! Peter denied Him three times, even spewing some cuss words, but Jesus forgave him, and Peter went on to write two books – I Peter and II Peter! What a Lord!"

The throngs were totally mesmerized.

"Luke 19:9-10 tells us about Zacchaeus. You know, the short guy that climbed up the tree to see Jesus, and got his own song still sung in Sunday Schools across the country today!"

More laughter, and a few strains of Zacchaeus' song could be heard.

"Anyway, Zacchaeus was a hated tax collector. Think of a beady-eyed lawyer who chases ambulances looking for clients to file outrageously large lawsuits. Anyway, he couldn't believe it when Jesus told him it was his house the Lord wanted to visit and stay at that day. Ol' shorty was so grateful he pledged to give half of what he had to the poor, and pay back anyone he had ever cheated four times the amount he owed. How many lawyers or IRS agents
*KJV

do you know who would do that?"

The multitudes rose to their feet in their ovation.

"Now, Luke 19:9-10 says, 'Then Jesus said, Today, salvation has come to this house, because this man, too, is a son of Abraham. For the Son of Man came to seek and to save that which was lost!'

"Then there's Mary Magdalene, a prostitute among prostitutes, and yet she was first to see the risen Lord! She knew she had made a mess of her life, but she knew the one man who could fix it.

"Folks, I don't care if you're a robber, blackmailer, gangsta, rapist, murderer, homosexual, prostitute, or a child molester – God is ready, willing and able to accept you – but you have to confess and repent. Listen to I Corinthians 6:9-11. 'Do you not know that the wicked will not inherit the kingdom of God? Do not be deceived! Neither the sexually immoral nor idolaters nor adulterers nor male prostitutes nor homosexual offenders nor thieves nor the greedy nor drunkards nor slanderers nor swindlers will inherit the kingdom of God!' Now, that's verses 9-10. If I were to stop right there, we'd all be doomed. You know, we may not be gay, or cheaters on our spouse, or a prostitute, or a robber – but how many of us have ever been greedy? This does not eliminate anyone from making it to Heaven, but a change does have to be made. Verse 11 is the key. And that is what some of you were, but, you were WASHED, you were SANCTIFIED, you were JUSTIFIED in the name of the Lord, Jesus Christ, and by the spirit of our God!"

One would have thought the Braves had just won their first World Series in twenty years by the noise that followed.

"Oh, and by the way, Paul wrote those verses. You know, the guy that was blinded on the road to Damascus? You know, he was a Christian killer before that! He was Public Enemy #1 within the church! But he was SAVED – and, speaking of books in the Bible, Paul went on to write about three-fourths of the books in the New Testament!"

~

Sean Diamond's first surprise of the night came as he looked around at the vast number of attendants at this crusade. He saw scantily dressed women, rough looking men, even some gangstas, a couple of which he recognized. So much for the typical uptight goody-goody church crowd.

The second surprise came about ten minutes into the sermon. Ilise reached out a tentative hand, and gently took Sean's into it, tenderly rubbing and patting it. This gesture tugged at the Diamond's heart in a way he thought he'd lost forever during childhood.

Next was the song, *Sinner's Prayer*, sung by Jamie Ray and Meghan Amhearst. No, it wasn't hard core rap, but it wasn't a boring old fuddy-duddy hymn either. It made sense to him, kind of like if he were to try to talk to God himself.

Yes I know I've got to change
My old friends will think I'm strange

It's scary, but I've learned it well
Without you, I'd be headed straight to Hell!
Straight to Hell!

Finally, the sermon itself seemed aimed right at him. He toughened up to it at first, but the words, like fiery arrows, just kept coming, shattering all his excuses and objections. It didn't take long to realize he wanted to lose this battle. A strange feeling entered his heart then. He didn't even recognize it, but he knew he wanted it.

It was hope.

When the invitation came, Ilise's face lit up as she felt herself being led in a death grip down to the front. Sean let his tears finally flow. Ilise embraced him as their tears mingled, and she favored him with a maternal kiss.

Everyone they talked to that night, from fellow new converts to the counselors to Brother Tim himself, all assumed Sean and Ilise were mother and son.

The two saw no need to correct them.

~

Tim was overwhelmed at the response, and the magnificence of the harvest. Georgie Oliver, the convicted child molester, released but feeling the old urges, now knew he did not need to be a slave to sin. The same went for Allen Fogler, a militant homosexual who now had a whole new world view. And how about Roxanne (no last name) who had been a prostitute since age 8? And Sean Diamond, the raging rapist who took whatever he wanted? Tim had a feeling that this young man would wind up in the ministry himself one day.

And that was just a few of the first night's stories.

Tana Peters had left her husband and three kids for another woman who had also left her family. That lady, Cheryl, had also come down, and both had vowed to make things right. Two murderers, neither convicted, a husband and wife embezzler team who had cheated companies they worked for out of millions of dollars, and the head of a child porn ring were added to the roll which would indeed one day be called up yonder.

Again, by the time this series of sermons concluded three nights later, over twelve hundred were saved, proving once again that all things were possible with God. From the most self-righteous to the most purely evil, Jesus saw them all, met them all, loved them all, and saved them all.

What was waiting next?

Tim didn't know, but he could hardly wait to find out!

Excuse #3: Evangelistic Scandals

Danny Driver hated televangelists almost as much as he loved baseball.

Almost.

After all, it was pretty well a given that Danny, at age 20, would make the big league Braves roster this year. After all, he'd hit .357 in A-ball right after high school. He'd followed that up with a .377 average in a season split between double A and triple A last year. He'd also clubbed 25 homers, 45 doubles, 15 triples, and stolen 44 bases. He was ready for the show.

He was thrilled to the core that his two favorite magazines, *Baseball Digest* and *Sports Illustrated*, had already written articles about him, touting him as the hottest rookie prospect in several years, maybe decades. It was projected that he might one day bat .400, hit 40 home runs, 50 doubles, 20 triples, and steal 50 bases. Danny intended to meet, and exceed, these goals.

Even SportsCenter, his favorite television show ever, had run a story, "Will Driver drive the Braves back to glory in '15?" Chris Burman had even dubbed him with one of his patented nicknames: Danny "The Line" Driver.

Life was good, and about to get better.

The road to superstardom, however, had not been a straight interstate by any means. Danny's mom, Julie, had raised him by herself until he was ten. That's when Jerry had come along, and with him, Danny's love for the Grand Old Game.

Before all of this, however, were mom's bedtime stories about great heroes – fearless men and women who gave their lives to God, and in return gained wealth, success, and true abundant life.

Televangelists.

Julie had been an active leader in her church youth group and a model student in school; leading cheers for the sports teams, leading her class in grade point average, and leading souls to Jesus.

Until that one fateful trip to Memphis for a youth retreat her senior year. She had persuaded Chad Hopkins, star quarterback and her pet missions project, to come along in hopes that his bad boy ways just might get washed in the blood of the Lamb. Instead, Chad's smooth talk and charming smile led Julie into what was at first a dream come true – a physical, hot and heavy relationship with the most handsome man in Atlanta, at least in Julie's view. Promises of love, marriage, and a faked Christian conversion swept her into a place she had no business being.

In bed with him.

The results? A broken heart, a ruined reputation, and one bouncing baby boy.

After Chad's predictable vanishing act, Julie gave up her dreams of college and settled into raising her son. She tried in her heart to forgive Chad, but still gave little Danny her own last name, Driver. The only sign of Chad wouldn't emerge until years later – a love and talent for sports.

Julie took on two jobs, waitressing at a local Waffle House, and selling Mary Kay cosmetics out of her home. It was difficult, but the two survived. Perhaps it was the fact that although church lost its appeal to Julie, God didn't, and that's where her heroes, the televangelists, came into play.

There was Jimmy Swaggart, tickling the ivories and wailing away to rival his country cousins, Jerry Lee Lewis and Mickey Gilley. Jimmy's preaching was dynamic and his bold stand on issues and probing the scriptures for answers to tough questions were mesmerizing. His high morals were demanding, but inspiring.

Until he sinned.

With a prostitute, no less.

Then there was Jim Bakker, head of PTL – Praise the Lord – who featured young, beautiful, prosperous Christians on the air constantly. This, in the eyes of Julie, smashed the stiff, no fun churchgoers' image to smithereens. The abundant life was a literal thing – you did not have to be poor and in constant suffering to be a good believer after all.

But then he sinned.

With a church secretary.

He was also accused of using ministry funds to buy an air conditioned dog house – and cheating his followers in schemes of fraud to raise money.

And his wife, Tammy Faye, left him – plus he served jail time.

Still, Julie always found someone new – Benny Hinn, the faith healer. Pat Robertson, who's 700 Club echoed the abundant life of PTL – with politics and end-time predictions mixed in for good measure. Others too – who preached health and wealth, including the guy who had his devotees stuff his pockets with money in the hopes of being blessed many times over for their faith giving.

And how about Jerry Falwell – who built a church and university empire for God on Liberty Mountain in Lynchburg, Virginia? But even he turned his back on Jim Bakker in his time of need, pretending to be his friend. At least these were the stories that leaked to the press. Julie didn't care. She kept searching for a savior to really show her all the possibilities of the benefits of following Jesus. Being a single mom was draining, lonely work, and she had petitioned just about every one of her small screen heroes for a financial miracle and a man to love her and be a father figure to Danny.

As Danny grew older, he began to see the fallacy of all this. Nothing was changing and their money, what little there was of it, was finding its way to all those so-called ministries that could care less about him and his mom.

Everything changed the day Danny decided to try out for his first baseball team in the league for nine and ten year olds.

As it turned out, Danny was a natural, and no one was more impressed than Jerry Farmer, who had dreams of being a major league scout. In Danny, he saw his ticket, a diamond in the rough coming out of nowhere, that no one else had the slightest idea even existed.

Jerry worked with Danny on a daily basis, and Danny felt like a thirsty man in a desert who unexpectedly stumbled onto a Coca Cola plant in the middle of nowhere. All the fatherly attention and affection Danny had never known were now being showered on him, and the young athlete began to blossom.

Home runs are more rare when a player is nine, and hitting and fielding are only just starting to develop.

Not so for Danny. He smacked five homers and hit over .400 his first season. In addition, he showed a knack for fielding and became the starting shortstop for his squad. He even stole ten bases. This, despite only having practiced on his own and from watching major league games on television when his mom was working.

Jerry introduced himself to Julie as he sang her son's praises. He told her the sky was the limit for this young man. He assured her he was a Christian himself, and would also be instilling morals and character into her son as he coached and developed him into a potential star player.

It didn't take long for Julie to become attracted to this charismatic man who seemed to be, at long last, the answer to all her prayers.

Soon they were dating. Within a year the two were engaged. Danny was all for it. Life seemed just about perfect – kind of like PTL or the 700 Club.

Danny's second season was even more impressive, as he smacked eight long balls, batted .450, fielded flawlessly, and stole twenty bases. Jerry and Julie decided to get married at the end of the schedule, then get Danny on the best all-star traveling team possible. The thought of them doing this as a family made Julie cry for sheer joy. God had not forgotten them after all.

That is, until the terrible night just two weeks before their early December wedding date. That's when Mother Nature threw a devastating wrench into all their dreams – and exposing reality in all its horror in the process. The roads were rain slick. It was no one's fault. It was not quite a head-on collision, but close enough. Julie's car was totaled, but her and Danny's injuries were the true tragedies. Julie's legs were badly bent and broken in several places. Her prognosis was a wheelchair ride for the rest of her life. To add insult to injury, a large discoloring and disfiguring scar covered the left side of her face. Danny didn't fare much better. Two broken arms, two broken legs, and several major cuts and bruises would lose him at least a year of baseball.

At least.

The more cruel effect of all was the reaction of Jerry. At first, he feigned support, but little by little he pulled away. Right after Christmas, he called off the engagement. Danny no longer interested him, no time for that.

He would never get a job being a champion of damaged goods. So, just like Danny's biological dad, Jerry vanished.

Mother and son handled all this in totally different ways. For Julie, it was hours spent in front of the TV, hands touching the screen, as she begged for a healing. More offerings, prayer cloths, prayer chains, even letters and phone calls to several ministries pleading her case, brought no acknowledgements, no comfort, and no results. Oh, yes, there were many "God bless you, sister" form letters, but they were totally useless. Julie figured God was punishing her for her fling with Chad so long ago, so she became resigned to her fate as a crippled, scarred woman with no hope.

Danny on the other hand, became more determined than ever. He healed more quickly than anyone could believe, and by summer, although not playing ball yet, he was ready to track down Jerry and show him he'd lost nothing. Jerry had indeed gotten a job with the Braves as a minor league scout, and Danny signed up for one of his camps.

At first, Danny didn't see Jerry at all. He worked with several coaches who could see his potential and were impressed, despite the fact that he was only about 80% of where he had been before the accident. He showed an exemplary work ethic and attitude, however, and was invited back for the next summer.

On the last day, he finally got his chance to confront Jerry. In his heart, still a child's at age eleven, he truly believed he could win Jerry back, both for himself and his mom's sake. As he approached Jerry's office, Danny's spirits soared as he overheard his hero talking about a can't-miss prospect.

"Yeah, he's young, but look at his stats! He could play A-ball right now! And his mom's a fox to boot! I'm so glad I found both of them..."

Danny grinned from ear to ear. Had mom's prayers been answered after all?

"Oh, man, I'm so glad I ditched that other broad. She looks like the front end of a truck smashed her face. Well, actually that's exactly what happened. The sad thing is, her son had some serious potential, but injuries like that will no doubt affect him for years. Oh, well, water under the bridge, right? And with my new ready-made family and meal ticket, I don't even have to play Christian..."

Danny threw his bat, ball, and glove as hard and as far as he could. He almost quit baseball then and there.

Almost.

He never told his mom. She didn't deserve this. He decided instead to throw everything he had into reaching his potential. That way, he could do what all those fake televangelists could not or would not do, take care of his mom. And although Jerry wasn't a televangelist per se, he had still struck the pose of a charismatic man who spoke of a loving God.

A total fraud.

~

Religious matters notwithstanding, better times were ahead for both mother and son. Julie decided to try the scientific, medical approach to healing. She met a kind and gifted physical therapist named Hunter Mason. He believed they could beat the doctor's doomsday forecast.

And they did.

By the time Danny made the starting lineup of his high school team – as a freshman – Julie was there to cheer him on with only crutches to support her. Hunter was also there to support her, for the two had bonded and fallen in love in the process. Her appearance was nothing but beautiful to him, for all he could see was the spirit of the woman within – a true miracle after all.

Danny accepted Hunter because he could sense the love this man felt for and showed his mom was the real deal. Hunter was no athlete, however, and a part of Danny still ached for that mentor relationship he'd found, or thought he'd found, with Jerry Farmer.

Soon, however, Danny had an abundance of mentor prospects who took interest in him. His nearly errorless play, at short and .422 average with twelve homers his first year had the whole school buzzing. This was especially true of Head Coach, Mark Ferguson, who saw in Danny something he had never encountered in his fifteen years of coaching – a true major league prospect.

Over the next three years, Mark oversaw the development of his protégé. Danny's averages were .438 his sophomore year, .457 his junior year, and an off the charts .501 his senior campaign. The power numbers grew, too, from 15 long balls his sophomore year, 18 as a junior, and 22 to round out his high school career. Stolen bases went from the low teens to the upper twenties and his fielding was stellar both at shortstop and centerfield. All these stats had several major league scouts drooling. Jerry was not one of them. He had been fired two years before Danny's graduation and had fallen off the radar screen, just as most of his prospects had.

The icing on the cake was the team's run at the state championship Danny's senior year. The teams breezed through the district and regionals, and were state tournament bound. Danny was voted MVP of the regionals, with 14 hits, 6 homers, and 5 steals in just five games. Danny made a promise to his coach and teammates to bring this title back to their school.

Danny had done a lot of growing since joining the team. Baseball skill was obvious, but it was more than that. Mark had that same religious magnetism as Jerry, but this seemed different. Danny had even attended several church services at Mt. Moriah Baptist Church. The God he heard about there seemed a far cry from the Santa Claus God his mom had always envisioned. Although he wouldn't go as far as to "get saved," his mind did again become more open. Mark's wife, Libby, was like a second mom to him, and their children like the younger brother and sister he'd never had.

Danny developed a yearning to one day have a family of his own. He wanted to be a dad from the get-go for his kids, again something he had never known. He dreamed of all the opportunities a career in major league baseball could give his family.

As far as dating prospects, there was certainly no shortage. He took full advantage of his super jock status and dated them all – at least it felt that way as he lavished in his local celebrity status.

Late in his junior year, however, he met someone special. Karen Wallace was a gorgeous blonde cheerleader that defied the stereotypes of all these facts. She was intelligent – near the top of her class, in fact, and mature beyond her years.

Danny fell in love.

The two dated until the end of the first semester of their senior year. She broke it off, citing her plans to go off to college in Texas to pursue a medical career in cardiology. She thought she should concentrate on that as he focused on his senior season, then his path to the majors.

Danny didn't agree.

He believed, even at seventeen, that love was worth fighting for. He refused to back off completely, but did give her plenty of space, hoping she would come to her senses. They remained on friendly terms as baseball season began, and the storybook trip to the state tournament started to unfold. He did completely concentrate on the task at hand, although the young ladies continued to throw themselves at him. When Karen and Danny were involved, it had been mostly a platonic relationship, despite his intense attraction to her. She said her Christian convictions convinced her to take things slow physically. Hand holding and some light kissing were as far as things had gotten in that aspect.

That had not been the case with his previous conquests, nor was it the case in the propositions he was receiving now. Still, the best friend connection he'd made with Karen was so much deeper, and only made him ache for her more.

But all that was over, at least for now, so baseball became his everything. And now, here his team was, in the deciding game of the state tournament. The score was 10-0 in favor of the favored squad from Augusta. Their pitcher had given Danny's team only two hits, but he was tiring as the top of the ninth rolled in. He surrendered two walks and an infield hit, bringing Danny to the platter. On a three and two pitch, he connected for an opposite field grand slam homer. The sad thing was, not even Danny could make up ten runs with one swing. The score was 10-4, and the next batter grounded weakly to second for the first out.

The boys still had fight, however. The sixth place hitter, a reserve for most of the season but starting due to their third baseman's injury, beat out an infield hit, and the catcher, usually all field – no hit, lined a clean single to left. Following this, the second baseman, a senior demoted to eighth in the order due to a batting slump, drove a ball to right that bounced over the wall for a ground rule double. The score – 10-5, with runners on second and third, and only one out, but still a long way to go.

The pitcher's spot was due up, and Franklin Pierce, an up and comer for a starting spot next year, pinch hit, delivering a single to make it 10-6. A strong throw from center stopped the other runner at third.

The left field playing left-handed leadoff man nearly homered to make it a one run game, but had to settle for a sacrifice fly. Another run scored to make it 10-7, but now they were down to their last out.

The second place in the order was filled by Trevor Stinson, who played a solid right field and could handle the bat well. All he needed to do here was keep the game going. He worked the count to two and two, then connected – a soft liner to first. His heart sank, but Augusta's first base hotshot got a little too fancy and dropped the ball. There was still hope, because now the tying run stepped up to the plate.

Willie Carter was the team's second best player, and a division one college prospect with offers from Georgia, Kentucky, and Mississippi State on the table. He had hit fifteen round-trippers this season, and everyone figured he was dreaming of his own shining moment.

That's why Augusta was totally caught off guard when Willie laid down a picture perfect bunt.

The bases were loaded for Danny.

An out would end it. A hit would make it interesting. A home run would give them the lead.

Augusta's pitcher, the fourth of the inning, bore down, determined to stop this rally, pick up the save, and be the hero. He blew the first pitch past Danny, who was taking. The next pitch just caught the outside corner, putting Danny in an 0-2 hole.

One strike away from defeat.

The next delivery dropped just low of the strike zone, and the following offering drifted just outside to even the count.

Danny then zeroed in to protect the plate, as he just got a piece of two nasty curves and a changeup.

The next pitch dealt was a fastball – a good one.

But Danny was sitting on it.

He deposited it in the third row of the centerfield bleachers, and the biggest comeback in Georgia State tournament history was complete, as Augusta went down one-two-three in the bottom of the ninth.

The choice for MVP was unanimous.

Sadly, however, this would not be the most memorable event for Danny that day. The team got to stay an extra night to celebrate, with a midnight curfew. Most everyone stayed true to the condition of no alcohol and no going outside the motel. A couple of the reserves tried to get into the hotel lounge, but the seniors stepped up and stopped it. After that, the team just hung out together, watching SportsCenter to see if the game made it – it did, and laughing, ordering pizza, and playing MLB-15 on their portable game systems.

Danny joined them, for a while anyway, then decided to head back to his room. Truth was, two grand slams in one inning hadn't been easy. It had only been done once in the majors, by Fernando Tatis of the Cardinals, fifteen years ago.

On the way, he passed Coach Mark's room and thought he heard laughter.

Female laughter.

Libby had not been able to make the trip due to their daughter's illness.

Curiosity got the best of Danny, which turned out to be an awful mistake. Like a moth to a flame, however, he approached his coach's door to see what was unfolding.

"Oh, baby, I got the call today. North Texas State has offered me the position! College ball!"

A flurry of passionate kissing followed, then the voice that pierced Danny's gut spoke.

"That means we can really be together! Does Libby know?"

"Not yet, I'm going to explain to her I have to go first. My signing bonus will allow me to set you up nicely. You know your schooling is taken care of. As soon as I'm settled, I'll break it to Libby. I will leave her. It is God's will for us to be together. Thank you for keeping an eye on my star for me. You befriended him just enough to get his mind off all those other girls. And oh, how he came through – for me – for us!"

"I love you, Mark, so, so much…"

More kissing followed, but Danny wasn't around to hear it.

~

As Danny began his rapid ascent through the minors, baseball wasn't the only reason he was living up to his name. Danny was now driven by his own pet cause – exposing televangelists, faith healers, and other public figures who hid behind religion, and/or used religion to their advantage. So many would-be believers were swindled out of money and given false hope – all for absolutely nothing. It had happened to his mother countless times, yet it was belief in herself that had finally healed her. As for Danny, all those phony would-be mentors so full of God-talk had all proved as genuine as a crisp thirty-dollar bill. Danny had finally learned that he needed none of them, or their God of convenience. Just look at him now! 2015 should finally, at age 20, herald his arrival in the majors, and what a splash he would make! He knew this to be true, because he truly believed in his hero.

Himself.

If people would only see that within themselves lay the power, the love, and the faith, to move mountains – to make their own miracles. Now, with his major league career and corresponding mega-salary impending, Danny could, and would, truly make a difference.

Yet, way back in the deepest part of his heart of hearts, something nagged at him. When Coach Mark, adulterer and manipulator that he was, had Danny out to his church, Danny had felt something - a hope? a warmth? – about the possibility of God being real after all. He had actually gone to see a Christian therapist, Christy Calhoun, about this. Not much progress had resulted – except that the two were now dating!

What a woman! She had just started her practice, and was only five years older than Danny. Karen couldn't hold a candle to her.

But here was this God thing again.

For now, the two had agreed to disagree. However, one event was now occurring that both had an interest in, albeit for very different reasons.

TIME Ministries had come to town, and a revival had broken out! Christy wanted to see and hear this man who was having a hand in a lot of lost souls being won. Danny, on the other hand, wanted to expose another fraud. Despite their opposing motives, they agreed to attend together. There was no mistaking their motives for this, for both were the same.

An incredible chemistry was developing between them.

~

Danny could have had any woman he wanted as his escort to any event he wanted to attend. Publicity about his exploits on the baseball diamond were already winning him a measure of fame.

Danny had no doubt he was exactly where he needed to be, with exactly whom he wanted to be with.

Christy was so kind, yet always honest. She was supportive of whom he was becoming, yet sought to know the man inside. She was always warm and affectionate, but firmly set boundaries for their physical relationship.

He believed he might just be open to loving her. Somehow, he would have to find a way to break these delusions of godly heroes – and this special someone whom they served.

But part of him hoped... no, he had to stay strong. Somehow he sensed a lot was at stake here.

~

Christy knew exactly what she was doing.

Well, almost.

This gorgeous younger man had an intelligence that at least matched his looks. His heart was good and solid, too – the way he loved his mom confirmed this. And his soul? God had given her a vision on that, too. He was searching, and open to the truth, despite all the terrible examples that had tried to block his way to it. She smiled in such a manner as to light up the entire section around them. She draped her arm around his shoulder. Tonight might prove to be a little different than this special man expected.

After all, the Lord she served was full of surprises.

~

Majestic. That was the only word to describe the music and lyrics of the Jamie Ray and Meghan Amhearst duo's special, *You are Lord, You are God, You are King*. The praise filled Christy like a slow flowing river of pure honey, and the chord structure caused an epidemic of goose bumps to break out all over her.

> *You defy all space and time*
> *Yet you're there for us each day*
> *Through you, all is possible*
> *You alone are worthy to be praised!*
> *Let us stand, and let us sing*
> *Through your son, salvation reigns!*
> *You are Lord, you are God, and you are King!*

Even more exciting was the reaction exhibited on the face of the man beside her, a man whom she was praying for with every fiber of her soul. This time, the stakes were personal. His future, and their future together, depended on his eyes being open. To her, it appeared the process might just be underway.

~

Whoa! What a song! Danny could almost believe in a God like this! Christy's face was radiant, even more so than usual. He totally believed that she believed all this. He hoped her heart, unlike his, would never know the pain of a total break.

Yet inside, his soul was stirring.

Well, he'd felt all that before, and every single time, the people who had preached, praised, and promised had let first his mother, then himself, down totally. So how could this God they professed be real? Where was this new creation – this changing, life transforming power? As Brother Timothy Isaac McDonald approached the podium, Danny knew it would all once again sound too good to be true. He looked over at Christy, already rapt in attention, and decided, at least for her sake, he would give this man a fair listen.

But if he caught any flaws, any discrepancies he would not hesitate to expose this man as one more false ray of hope.

~

"Brothers and sisters, it's so great to see everyone. I think this is our biggest gathering yet, and I am humbled beyond any words to see that.

"But, my dear friends, I need to make something totally plain to you – it's not about me! It's about Him!"

The crowd roared its affirmation. Their love for this minister was genuine, because it was rooted in their love for the Lord. Tim felt this wave of affection, and it spurred him head long into his message.

"You know, I'm only human. I didn't even have the sense God gave a peanut till I was out of school for a few years. As for now, that sense hasn't grown much. Just ask my long suffering wife, my tolerating teenage son, and my preteen daughter – who is now knowing close to everything!"

40

Laughter flooded the auditorium.

"In a year and a half, she'll turn thirteen, then she will know everything!"

This time, spontaneous applause was the result along with even louder laughter.

"Anyway, I'll be honest about my mistakes. I drank all through college. I was self-centered. I did not wait until we got married to have relations with my wife – nor, was she the first. I tried, and yes, I inhaled, marijuana a couple of times. I gambled on some sporting events. Even when I got my calling, I ran from it at first – I argued with God – I went into full-blown depression because, for a while, my wife was making more than me, and I resented her for that. Now, there's your evangelical scandal. But at least I'm honest, right?"

The crowd showed by their reception that their love for this man had just grown exponentially.

"Now, let's talk about evangelistic scandals. Yes, Jim Bakker screwed up, big time. He faced the consequences of his sins – jail time, failed marriage, loss of reputability – but in the end, he repented, and I believe he was sincere. Same with Mr. Jimmy Swaggart; his cry of 'I have sinned!' still rings in my memory – but again, I believe he turned away from wrong and back to God. Teddy Haggard, who stood up for family values with his wife and five children; only to have a gay affair. But now he claims repentance!

"There are so many more examples, but I say all that to say this – it's not about the man – it's about the message! Revival has broken out here in the capital city of the South!"

A zealous round of whoops, hollers, and Amens ensued.

"Yes, indeed, revival has broken out, in spite of me, not because of me. All I've done is truly allow the Holy Spirit to move me out of the way and work through me. If I went out tonight and robbed a bank, cheated on my wife, and then ran naked through downtown Atlanta, God would still be God!"

A standing ovation resulted. Among those on their feet was a certain baseball "phenom" who was beginning, despite himself, to be caught up in the magic – true magic.

"Listen folks, my mom used to beg out of going to church anytime her favorite pastor was not preaching. Hero worship is nothing new; but when we put a mere man on a pedestal, there's no way he'll stay balanced on it. Only God is the perfect standard. That's why it took Jesus Christ, His only begotten son, to save this old world. Jesus was tempted at every point we are, but remained sinless. He suffered unimaginable pain and humiliation, and yes, He felt it all, for He was fully God AND fully man!"

Waves of revival ran rampant as the truth rang forth.

"Everyone relates to a different style of teaching at school. I certainly had my favorites. Same with sermons – there are different ways of preaching, and some inspire and move me more than others, and some preachers themselves connect with me better. There is nothing wrong with this. That's

41

why God has given people so many diverse talents and gifts. He wants everyone to be able to relate to His message. But what is true, constant, and unchanging is God Himself. As my brother and sister sang earlier, *All His promises prove true*! God, and only God, can ALWAYS be counted on – in ALL situations! Listen to what Paul says in First Corinthians, Chapter 3, Verses 4 through 7.

"For when one says, I follow Paul and another, I follow Apollos, are you not mere men? What, after all, is Apollos? And what is Paul? Only servants, through whom you came to believe – as the Lord has assigned to each his task – I planted the seed, Apollos watered it, but God made it grow. So neither he who plants nor he who waters is anything, but only God, who makes things grow.

"Yes, we're having a revival, but I ask you, what exactly IS a Tim McDonald? How about Jamie Ray? Or Meghan Amhearst? God gave me the gift of preaching, my praise team the gift of music, and the thousands who now pray for us that gift. The same goes for our financial supporters. Everyone is important, if they allow God to use them. And ultimately, it is God, and not us, who gets the job done!"

The evening was reaching its highest point.

"So, my friends, if you are disillusioned tonight, if the one you idolized fell short, I ask you to come now, and receive the one true Hero, the Star, the Savior. He loves you, and wants you to be on the winning team FOREVER!"

And many did. Lance Burns, who had squandered his retirement fund on a health and wealth shaman; Heather Jones, who had almost lost her life to intestinal complications because a faith healer told her she needed no doctor, just to trust in him instead; and Danny Driver, a soon-to-be Atlanta Braves superstar who has seen his mother's heart broken by false promises, and his own dreams shattered to dust by would-be father figures who hid behind God to hide their own agendas. When all was said and done, over a thousand more found their way to the kingdom over this night and the next.

Tim fell down on the altar and said out loud, long after everyone had left, "I don't have to wait till I get to Heaven to do this..." He reached up and made the motions of removing a heavy head piece.

"I hereby cast my crown of the gifts and fruits of evangelism to you, my only king, and the one True Evangelist!"

~

Tim knew his next excuse would be a touchy one indeed. Hypocrisy within the church! My, oh my. How many souls remained lost by the bad examples set by God's own family? He would no doubt be ruffling some feathers and stepping on some toes, but he knew he could do it.

His Hero had told him so.

Excuse #4: Hypocrisy and Not Getting Along

The thought of ever stepping foot in a church building again made Jo Windsor absolutely sick to her stomach. That's pretty sad when one considers that both her parents are in the ministry; her dad, a youth pastor and her mom, a nursery director and head of children's church and Vacation Bible School.

Oh, but the things Jo had seen.

Josephine Marilyn Windsor had been everyone's darling as she went from toddler to teen in their first church home. "She's so precious!" "What a cutie!" and "What a true angel!" were just a few of the compliments bestowed upon Rob and Samantha Windsor's firstborn, and her heart, full of innocence and childlike faith, believed them all. She believed that church was truly God's house, and the congregation, God's children, from little old ladies dressed to the nines, to the deacons in their crisp three-piece suits, to the too cool for words youth, who showed how fun being godly could be, to Pastor Daniel Bennett, who let her sit on his lap and eat skittles as he explained the plan of salvation.

All that took a drastic turn downward when Josephine turned thirteen. This was the year when she realized "Josephine" was an old-fashioned corny name. "Jo," however, was fresh, so "Jo" she became. Also, this was the year Jo discovered the male species, and found a mutual admirer in Stanley Sturgiss, a fourteen year old dreamboat who just happened to be the son of Matt Sturgiss, Minister of Music – or "Worship Leader" as he preferred to be called, of Pleasant Pointe Baptist Church. The two shared a kiss one night after youth Bible study.

Matt witnessed it, and by doing so seized a long awaited opportunity. Ever since he arrived ten years ago, Rob had been the thorn in Matt's flesh that God refused to remove. When Rob had started, his salary had been identical to Matt's, but subsequently had grown to twelve thousand dollars higher. Good ol' Rob, Mr. Fun and Games – going to video arcades, playing paintball, all-night lock-ins, bowling, miniature golf, even Xbox "LAN parties" – with all clean games, of course. Matt yearned for the days his youth choir and musical mission trips were the core of the youth ministry. Now, only a few graced the choir room, while so many others rejoiced to know that here at Pleasant Pointe, you need not have musical talent to be in the Activity King's Youth Group.

Pastor Daniel offered little encouragement to Matt, other than an occasional pat on the back and a "God bless ya, brothuh!" thrown in now and then for good measure.

Criticism, however, flowed much more freely from the Good Reverend's lips. "Too many old fashioned hymns!" "Not enough upbeat choruses!" "Too few of the old favorites!" "Too much contemporary music!" "The congregation is standing too much, the old folks are complaining!"

"We're not standing enough! We can't be the Frozen Chosen here!" In other words, pleasing this fine flock was totally and completely impossible.

Not so for Mr. Charisma.

Brother Rob was the Golden Boy. Major growth in his department. Innovative ideas to draw in the lost. Perfect wife, perfect children. Cited for excellence and often chosen to speak by the local Baptist Association and invited to host community events.

Matt never got asked to lead any revivals. He was never guest song leader for any associational events. His choir participation had stagnated. People grumbled about practice and about song selections. Matt had had it.

Then came the kiss. How could that Windsor girl be so loose-moraled to lure his boy into kissing her in church like that? Matt went straight to Rob, then to Brother Daniel. A meeting was set up for the following Wednesday night after church.

The meeting was a cordial one. After all, these were three men called of God into full time Christian service. Still, a few sugar-coated barbs were thrown. Matt accused Rob of allowing his daughter's values to fall "just a bit short for a man serving in his position." Rob countered that perhaps Matt might want to take a look in the mirror, since, after all, his boy's hormones were raging, as most fourteen year old boys' hormones will. This led to a couple of comments about Rob's activities-based approach to ministry, and Rob countering with the suggestion that perhaps Matt's musical approach was a bit stale.

Brother Daniel quickly put a halt to this, calling for a quick reconciliation before things got out of hand, but not before agreeing that both men's ministries might need re-examining, as the church had hit a growth slump which not even the youth had escaped. This resulted in both men questioning the sermonizing of their Pastor growing stale, also.

The meeting ended with everyone making nice and a round of forced hugs. "God and the church must come first!" Brother Daniel announced in his booming bass voice that Matt could have used in his choir. Both men nodded at their leader, then left, ending the matter, at least for now.

Except the matter had just begun. For as it turned out, Beverly Long, church secretary / administrative assistant extraordinaire, had eavesdropped. She felt it was her business to know what prompted a meeting between all three full-time ministry staff members. Beverly wasn't evil or anything. In fact, she was an assistant Sunday School teacher. However, she did have a weakness – a love of gossip, and as a result of it, a second flaw had resulted; a taste for drama where drama wasn't needed. It wasn't long before word leaked out that perhaps a sexual situation was developing between the minister of music's son and the youth pastor's daughter. As a result, a feud was no doubt festering between the two men.

Satan saw opportunity knocking, and quickly opened the door, as what should have been nothing, evolved into a full-blown crisis.

Ruth and Martha, two of those "little old ladies dressed to the nines," who used to gush over how cute Jo was, now whispered that perhaps she was a slut in the making, and what a shame that was. Besides, both of them adored Matt, and felt like he was getting the short end of the stick. Cora Smith, a friend of Samantha Windsor, overheard them, reported it to Samantha, and started a rumor about Stanley Sturgiss being a young playboy.

Reba Hoyt, a normally dedicated choir member, had been away for several weeks. She made a return that Sunday following the fateful meeting. She had been dealing with family issues of a sick mother and a rebellious son. Her husband, while supportive to a degree, did not get into the church scene, and had chosen this day to remind Reba this was never going to change, and to just accept that. Reba needed a friend, and Matt had always been a good one. He had seen in her a budding musical talent, and had helped her to become one of the church's favorite presenters of special music. She poured her heart out to her choir director in practice that afternoon. Matt had listened patiently, comforting her, encouraging her, and giving her a warm, brotherly hug.

This was not, however, what Ralph Mitchell, the head deacon who had never cared much for Matt but who fully supported Rob, saw. Instead, he confronted Matt for his "questionable counseling practices," stirring up the other deacons in the process.

One of these men (sharply dressed in his three-piece suit, of course), Calvin Adams, was outraged, but not at Matt. He had been instrumental in Matt's hiring, and saw no wrong in Matt's actions. Instead, he "discovered" a glitch in the youth budget which indicated Rob may have over spent on trips to various game centers and sporting events.

As the controversy which never should have even existed continued to build, the church began to take sides. The musical crowd sided with Matt, while the youth and activity-minded folks leaned toward Rob. The deacons were divided as well, and Brother Daniel began to draw criticism from all sides for "allowing" this to happen.

Then it did happen. Matt got a job offer from a bigger church across town who stressed the music program much more heavily than Pleasant Pointe. Of course, Matt grabbed it, and half of Pleasant Pointe left with him.

So there it was, a true church split, over an innocent adolescent kiss between two ministers' children who had intended no harm whatsoever.

Jo blamed herself. She couldn't believe the horror of all these wonderful children of God showing their true colors when things got nasty. Jo cried and cried. Her parents were so busy trying to pick up the pieces of the church that they weren't in tune with how badly their daughter was hurting.

Enter Calvin Adams.

Calvin was quick to seize the opportunity to give comfort to this budding beauty. Jo, who had always thought of Calvin as a grandfather figure, eagerly accepted it. Evidently, Calvin had bought into the rumors about her.

His kindness soon turned dark and shameful. Calvin warned her not to tell, for no one would take her seriously now. Despite his warnings, she did try to tell – Brother Daniel, her parents, another of the deacons – but no one believed her.

Ironically, the only truly bad act committed was completely ignored, while all the harmless acts of mild disagreements had resulted in the downfall of Pleasant Pointe Baptist Church.

Soon, Rob found a new church of his own, and he, Samantha, Jo, and Eli, their youngest son still far too small to understand all that had happened, headed off to make a fresh start.

Pleasant Pointe never recovered, becoming a mere shell of its former self, and a source of scorn in the community. Brother Daniel eventually left the sinking ship himself, and no one wanted to replace him. Calvin was one of the few who stayed. A sad, tragic tale, no matter how you sliced it.

Jo was glad to erase all this from her mind and heart as she entered the family's new church, Countryside Baptist. The building was breathtakingly beautiful; the people were warm and friendly.

But unfortunately, the secrets of the saints would soon be revealed here, as well.

~

Jo had never gotten saved. Her dad, in all good fatherly and ministerial intentions, had advised her that this most important of decisions must not be made lightly. He knew Jo's love for the church and its congregation would make her conversion almost an act of instinct and nature rather than a true repentant one – a foregone conclusion.

Not so much now.

The Windsors were forced out of Pleasant Pointe as its death throes continued. Rob, with God's guidance, found a new congregation desperate for youth leadership as the blessings of growth had fallen upon Countryside Baptist on Atlanta's south side: a new church, better salary, new beginnings – it had to be right. Right? Rob sure hoped so. He prayed with true urgency for his daughter's soul, for he was now fully aware she had been jaded by all that had occurred at Pleasant Pointe.

So the page turned, and the next chapter of the Windsor saga proceeded to unfold.

~

Jo came to the decision being born again was not for her. All she could see in these so-called converted people was hypocrisy. The talk was pretty, but the actions fell far short. Jo instead, for her parents' sake, decided to be as wholesome of a person as it was for a teenager to be these days. She also committed to be fully involved in her dad's youth group, and help out her mom in the nursery and the children's' programs. Everyone soon simply assumed she had gotten saved somewhere along the line.

Except Rob. He felt led to keep silent, and keep watching. He, unknown to no one, got on his knees daily for this purpose.

In the fall of that year, an angel arrived at Countryside Baptist. Her name was Starla Hastings. She had just accepted a job as a paralegal in one of the neighborhood's leading law firms. She had moved in from Athens, with a glowing recommendation from one of the larger Southern Baptist congregations in that college town which was headquarters to the University of Georgia. She became, much to Rob's delight, the youth Sunday School teacher for the females. Rob took the guys. As a result, they were able to do lots of Sunday School lock-ins and serious examinations of sensitive current issues. Rob's class took on homosexuality, male hormones, how far is too far when dating, and missionary dating – that is, dating a lost person with intent to win their soul. Starla's class looked also at homosexuality, as well as missionary dating. In addition, eating disorders, modest dress, and women's roles in ministry were discussed. Both classes also looked at drug and alcohol abuse, content of music and television shows, and living in sin. This, coupled with Rob's activity driven ministry, caused the youth department to explode in size. Countryside Baptist was a happy ship.

Jo was caught up, despite herself. Starla's biblical breakdowns of why it was wrong to drink alcohol, the dangers of missionary dating leading to unequally yoked marriage, the importance of modest appearance, and self-esteem versus self-centeredness were truly soul stirring. At last, the difference in all areas of life, the real meaning of love, and a personal relationship with Christ, began to gravitate her back toward making a decision to become a Christian. She was almost ready to make the plunge.

Good friends are hard to find; true friends that last a life time, even harder. In Bethany Thomas, Jo believed she just might have accomplished the feat. Bethany became the sister that Jo never had. Bethany confided in Jo about her broken home where her dad had been a drunk and physically abused her and her mother, until he mercifully ran off with a cocktail waitress half his age. Bethany's mom found God, and got her involved in church. Bethany saw what loving families could truly be like. Soon, her mom met a true gentleman who shared her beliefs. Even before they were married, Bethany was already calling him "Dad." Jo, in turn, confessed the story of Pleasant Pointe, not omitting Calvin Adams. They shared lots of hugs, tears, and sleepovers. Rob and Samantha adored her. Rob sensed Bethany could be a key to the answer to his prayers for his daughter's soul.

Jo and Bethany became inseparable. They were at one or the other's house just about every day. They loved hanging out at the mall and just being teens. Boys noticed them both, and many times they would fight over the cutest ones. In the end, however, their friendship always won out.

One night in early November, as a cool breeze, one of the strongest so far, blew in a chill to the usually mild Atlanta climate, Jo and Bethany were having a heart to heart talk about Heaven and Hell.

"So, do you really think everyone who doesn't accept Jesus as Savior is going to Hell?"

"I know it seems harsh, but yeah, I guess I do. He came for that purpose. He'll love you and save you, but He never forces Himself on you."

"What about people who never hear about Him?"

"Well, that's a toughie – I feel like God is merciful. In fact, I know it! But if I knew someone who hadn't heard, or who had heard but who hadn't invited Jesus into their heart, I sure wouldn't want to take a chance."

Jo hung her head. "I haven't."

"What?"

"I said, I haven't. I've never made an official decision."

"Get out! You're the Poster Child for Christianity."

"I know it looks that way. I guess I'm kind of faking it, though. I mean, I love Starla and her teaching. God interests me, I confess. But after the Pleasant Pointe mess – Ugh! Being born again seems like such a joke."

"Hey, how about me? Your B.F.F! I'm for real."

"Whoa! Got me there!" Jo, closer than she had ever been to converting, choked back her tears. "Hey, do you think Starla's still up?"

"Hmm, 11:15 on a Friday. We can try."

Starla was indeed at home. She came over and took her students out for a late night burger at Wendy's. She seemed more animated than usual as she talked their arms off. Sounding like a teen herself as she commented on the hot guy at the drive thru who served them their treats.

"Whoa, babe! When do you get off?"

"Uh, whenever we close, I guess!" the twenty something muttered shyly.

"Maybe I'll swing back by!" Starla winked, giggled, then made the tires squeal as they peeled out of the lot.

Jo and Bethany giggled. What a cool lady!

After wolfing down her midnight snack, Jo was ready to talk about her impending conversation.

"Starla, I have a confession to make."

"Shut up! Not you! You're the purest person in the class, I'd have to guess."

"Well, not totally, I've never accepted Jesus as my Savior."

"Get out! You're kidding, right?"

"Actually, no. But I think I may be ready now. My last church really scarred me and my family."

"Whoa, this sounds heavy. Give me a sec." Starla reached into her purse and pulled out a small flask. She removed the lid and took a long drink, giggling as she quickly closed and returned it to its hiding place. Vodka – colorless and odorless.

"Oops! You didn't see that. My stash is almost gone. Now, sweetie, what were you saying about that stuffy old church you came from?"

Both Jo and Bethany realized with horror what they were seeing. It wasn't hard to put two and two together. It was totally unlike Starla to giggle and talk loudly and constantly. It was also unlike her to flirt so blatantly with a total stranger. Starla had been drinking, even before the drink they had witnessed.

"Hey girlfriends! My job's hard. Even we saints have to unwind sometimes. I'll tell you what! I'll let you both try some of my stash if you promise not to tell. Does that sound like a plan?"

"Starla, could you please just take us home? We won't say anything."

"Oh, c'mon! Loosen up!"

"No, please take us home. Please? We won't tell."

"Pinkie swear?"

Jo and Bethany agreed, just to end this matter as quickly as possible.

Starla proceeded to make an illegal U-turn and sped back to Wendy's. She drove back to the pick-up window.

"Hey, cutie. I'll drop these two children off, then I'll come back. When I do, I'll want something hot and juicy! See ya!"

The worker shrugged and smiled, not knowing whether to be embarrassed or thank his lucky stars.

As they once again made a screeching exit, Jo couldn't help herself. "What about all your teaching? I was really starting to listen to you."

"Yeah, what gives?" asked Bethany.

"Now kids, the Bible never says you can't have fun sometimes. Hey, once a week, that's it. Even God rested on the seventh day, right? Okay, I'll make it up to you! I'll get you home really fast!" Starla pulled out into the intersection despite the light being red.

And despite the bright red SUV coming straight at them.

Jo and Bethany screamed as Starla yelled "chicken!" and pushed down on the gas pedal.

The crash cut out all other sounds, and the darkness cut out all other thoughts.

~

Jo awoke in the hospital, her horrified parents by her side. Their conversation quickly brought back her memory of why she was there.

"I never would have guessed it. She had me totally fooled," said Jo's mother.

"Me, too. She was over twice the limit of legal alcohol consumption. It's a miracle she lived," said Jo's father.

"I'm afraid she's going to wish she hadn't."

So it was true. Jo's new mentor had been just another hypocrite. And she had almost given her life to God. When she had confessed that she was unsaved to Bethany…

Bethany!

"Mom! Dad! Where's Bethany?"

Stony silence met her inquiry which stung and ached far worse than any of her many injuries.

"WHERE IS SHE?"

Screaming hurt more than she could stand, but she scarcely noticed.

"Sweetheart..." said Jo's mother with a tremor in her voice.

"She's gone, honey," Jo's father confirmed.

"NOOOOOOOOOOO!!!"

Jo passed out.

~

Jo attended church one final time at Countryside. It was now early February and she had healed physically faster than the doctors had hoped.

Not so, mentally.

Nor spiritually.

Her parents, knowing her morals and values had been shaken to the core, begged her to get counseling. She had talked to her school therapist a couple of times, but didn't really get that much out of it.

"Listen, honey, Brother Doug is a good man. He has a lot of counseling experience. Please, just give him one chance," pleaded Jo's father.

Rob was frightened, but Satan would not win, not on his watch – not against his family.

It was after church hours, and, praise the Lord, Brother Doug was keeping late hours. He had made it clear that his office was always open, so the Windsors pulled into the church parking lot, and entered unannounced. The middle aged Pastor rose quickly to answer the knock at his door, and invited the family in. Rob and Samantha allowed Jo to go in alone, as they figured their daughter might open up more without their presence.

So surprised was Brother Doug by his youth minister's daughter showing up that he forgot to shut off his computer.

Sadly, the session never occurred, because the computer screen was the first sight that caught Jo's eye.

X-rated internet porn. And she thought the preacher was smiling because she had finally come in to talk to him. That was the last straw. Jo's heart had hardened, and nothing her parents could say or do would ever change her mind.

~

Over the next two years, Jo tried just about everything – drinking, pot, sex, gothic culture, and emo music.

It was all fun, no doubt, but still, it left her empty and alone. So empty and alone, in fact, that the week before Christmas of 2014, she attempted suicide. Rob, who had taken a leave of absence from the church, found her and her bottle of sleeping pills as something had told him to check on her one more time despite her hateful attitude, before he and Samantha went to bed.

Christmas vacation that year was spent in the psychiatric ward of the hospital. At least some progress was finally made. Jo was able to talk about Bethany, and what a true friend she had been. Nothing could or would ever change that. Jo learned to cherish the memories, and to begin living again, because that's exactly what Bethany would have wanted.

By New Year's Eve, the family was back at home, writing out New Year's resolutions.

~

A new year, new outlook. Rob dove back into ministry, kicking his youth into high gear. He wanted to start things off with a bang, so he looked for a major event to get things rolling.

And along came TIME Ministries, and with it, the biggest revival since the hayday of Billy Graham – maybe even bigger! It was a no-brainer to sign up and attend. The kids loved it, and wanted to get involved as the momentum continued to build.

Amazingly, as time for the fourth excuse rolled in, Jo decided, out of love for her parents and little bro (a brand new believer), and in memory of Bethany, she would attend one, but only one, meeting with her family and the youth group. It didn't take long for Rob to realize that God, as always, was exactly on time. If there was still a chance for her to see the light, this was it. He took hold of Ephesians 6:18, and began to pray without ceasing as the service commenced.

~

"My dear brothers and sisters – this fourth excuse, I must confess, held me back in earlier years. I have heard it often, and for a variety of reasons – 'The church is full of hypocrites!' 'Why would I want to be like them?' 'Some of the meanest people I know are church members!'

"Now, people, I'm here to tell you, I've seen these things myself – time after time! Remember, I served as a pastor for two different churches, and have attended countless others! There is more truth in these claims than I want to admit – but hear me out – that's not because of God! It's because of man – and the flesh – and Satan!

"Now, you are the body of Christ, and each one of you is a part of it! First Corinthians 12:25 makes it crystal clear, folks! The Church of Christ should be united! No, we can't agree on every little thing – but we can agree on the two most important things: Loving God with all our mind, heart, soul, and strength, and loving our neighbors as ourselves! Jesus tells us all the law and the prophets are wrapped up in these two commandments! That means this complicated matter of being a good Christian isn't so hard to see, after all! And guess what? As we have already discussed, our only true hero is Christ Himself! We all have sinned! We are all just sinners saved by grace! Listen to Paul's words to the Galatians in chapter 6, versus 1-2 – 'Brothers, if someone is caught in a sin, you who are spiritual should restore him gently. But watch yourself, or you also may be tempted. Carry each other's burdens, and in this way you will fulfill the law of Christ'. Jesus puts it all in a nutshell in John 17:23, 'I in them and you in me. May they be brought to complete unity to let the world know that you sent me and have loved them even as you have loved me'.

We are all in this together, people! We are family! We're all we've got, and yet all we want to do is fight, try to outdo each other, gossip maliciously about each other, and judge each other. Remember, Jesus's biting remarks in Matthew 7:3-5? 'Why do you look at the speck of sawdust in your brother's eye and pay no attention to the plank in your own eye? How can you say to your brother, Let me take the speck out of your eye, when all the time there is a plank in your own eye? You hypocrite! First take the plank out of your own eye, and then you will see clearly to remove the speck from your brother's eye!'

"I know this is a heavy subject, so I convinced Jamie and Meghan to perform a humorous song that still cuts to the heart of this matter – *Sittin' on My Blessed Assurance*. I'll shut up for a few minutes and let them have it all. Besides, my voice is tired. I usually don't holler this much!"

Seems the budget's getting' tight this year
We need more program volunteers
Well, God bless ya, brothuh! I promise I'll
Pray – at least every other – other day!
Call me a pew potato, a benchwarmer, too
But I'm doin' all that I can do
I'm all signed up on heavenly insurance
So I'm sittin' on my Blessed Assurance!

This relieved some of the tension surrounding this tough topic, as laughter returned to the arena – and grew rapidly as Jamie and Meghan's turn at comedy proved most successful indeed!

"Now, just in case you're thinking – Hey, let's just not worry about church at all then – DON'T BE SO FAST! Hebrews 10:25 cuts right to the chase on this issue – 'Let us not give up meeting together as some are in the habit of doing – but let us encourage one another, and all the more as you see the day approaching'.

"Jesus Himself attended synagogue – that's all the proof I need! So, yes, we can make church work – and instead of scaring off the lost, we can make them long for what we have – then we can tell them it's all theirs, too. All they have to do is claim it! Listen to Jesus speaking in John's Gospel, Chapter 13, Verses 34 and 35 – 'A new command I give you! Love one another – as I have loved you, so you must love one another – by this all men will know that you are my disciples, if you love one another!' You know what? I'm through preaching! Instead, we're going to have some church up in here!"

Jamie and Meghan led the audience in some old-fashioned hymns and praise and worship choruses. Soon, large group hugs were breaking out everywhere – along with tears, apologies, prayers, clapping, and even dancing!

Again, the altars overflowed and there weren't enough counselors to go around as once more, over the next three nights, over a thousand new converts were added to the kingdom of God. This time, in addition, whole church bodies came forth for rededication. One had actually had the legendary argument over what color of carpet the church needed. Another had split over whether or not to hire a disabled minister, and yet another had fought over who had power in the church – the pastor, the deacons, or the congregation as a democracy. Tim felt this was the perfect climax to this miracle crusade in Atlanta. Perhaps, as the old Carman classic proclaimed, there truly was a *Revival in the Land*!

~

Jo bent over in laughter, then burst into tears, then did both at the same time as the Blood of the Lamb washed over her at last. Her childhood visions of what church could and should be like became vivid reality around her. She was one of the first to the altar. Her youth group let out the war whoop and Rob actually skipped down front to embrace his precious daughter. God absolutely still works miracles, and still answers prayers.

False Complacency

As the carriage rolled down the Holy City's ancient streets, Tim and Sarah sat cuddled aboard it, listening to the history of their chosen home – a rich tapestry of tales that never grew old. In fact, it was these stories of pirates, ghosts, war heroes, visiting presidents, scandals and affairs of the rich, and survival of so many natural disasters that first drew them here. The southern charm and hospitality finished the job, and their love of "low country cuisine" such as she-crab soup, shrimp and grits, crab cakes, and other locally caught seafood certainly didn't hurt any.

Sarah thrived on the character of the downtown stores, the Charleston Market, and attractions such as Rainbow Row and the majestic southern mansions that could be toured. Her event and wedding planning business had grown out of her genuine love and feel for the culture here. As a result, she was making quite a name for herself.

Gary loved the tours – Fort Sumter, the South Carolina Aquarium, and especially the ghost tours. No, he didn't actually believe in ghosts, but he loved the scary atmosphere, the pure enthusiasm of the tourists from all over the world, and the colorful characters that filled the tour guides' narrations. He was studying to actually be a guide himself. He already had several of them memorized.

Brooke, like her mom, loved the downtown shops, the antiques, the historic homes tours, and the restaurants with their second to none ambiance and cuisine. She knew her talents for design and cooking would fit in perfectly here. She dreamed of one day owning her own restaurant and interior design business, which, of course, would land her both on Home and Garden television AND the Food Network! Who knows, if she were successful enough, she might one day have an address South of Broad, the ultimate mark of success for a true Charlestonian.

Chance loved the hustle and bustle. He wanted action all of the time, and he was right in the middle of everything his family did. He already had a taste for a variety of food. He never seemed to tire of walking downtown through the stores – he only broke something once or twice! As for the tour guides, he was known by name by most of them already.

But nothing could top "tall baby" with daddy through the Charleston Market. He smiled down at everyone and tried to grab a vast variety of brightly colored merchandise. His favorite items by far, however, were the world famous sweetgrass baskets. Due to their cost, he had yet to acquire one of his own, but on this special night, right after the McDonalds shared their private carriage ride, Tim decided the time had finally come. One would have thought the McDonald's youngest had just experienced an extra birthday or Christmas all in one. His face lit up the market place, and the family shared a group hug right there in the middle of it all.

Even Boogan loved it here. Dogs were quite welcome in Charleston, even in several restaurants. He loved to go on walks, go "shopping" in a downtown boutique that specialized in doggie attire and doggie treats, and, of course, to acquire as many belly rubs from the locals and tourists alike as possible. On this same night, he got to partake in all these activities.

After a seafood feast, the family then strolled downtown for a while, just soaking up the scenery. Sarah and Brooke browsed for antiques, while Tim and Gary, along with Chance, took one of the tamer ghost tours that Gary had down pat. The tour guide, a younger blonde with an accent that suggested she came from "away," allowed Gary to assist her, much to everyone's delight.

The night was topped off by a trip to the candy store, where Gary snagged some sour cherries, Brooke snacked on pralines, Tim and Sarah shared dark chocolate and vanilla fudge, and Chance sampled a little of what everyone else was having.

It's hard to beat a vacation, right in your own hometown; and in the middle of winter to boot!

~

After a week of family time interspersed with romantic time for Tim and Sarah, it was time to pray, re-focus, and gear up for the next crusade – Music City, USA. Tim was bursting at the seams. He was fully refreshed and ready to fire up the revival now raging through the South. Still glowing from the hugs, kisses, love, and prayers of his family and Palmetto Baptist Church, Tim boarded the Delta jet and soared off to the next leg of this Heavenly adventure God had for reasons unknown blessed into his life.

~

Nashville was not quite the watershed event Atlanta was, but it was far from a washout. About half as many decisions were made here than were made in Atlanta. Disappointing? A little, but how could one possibly complain about a harvest like this – still way above the norm for an old-fashioned crusade in this day and time.

What made Nashville uniquely memorable were the individual blessings that fell upon the evangelist and music evangelists during their time here. Tim received word that he had a couple of publishers interested in his story, and how this revival had come about. In addition, plans to move up the start date of his television program were pushed up to early June, as a group of promoters wanted something fresh and innovative that would serve as a wakeup call to America. Syndication would triple what Tim had first been told. The group was ready to invest its time and resources fully into this venture. Tim fell prostrate before the Lord and once more cast his crown before his King.

As happy as Tim was for his own blessings, he was even more so for his two musical partners in Christ. Jamie Ray and Meghan Amhearst were happily married, but not to each other! Both their spouses totally backed their partnership, however. Their vocal blend and complimentary talents had to have been woven and brought together by God Himself. Both had been struggling for so long to be able to invest their full working time into their musical and ministry vision. TIME Ministries for them had been the answer to, quite literally, years of prayer.

Now, in one of the country's leading centers of music, another prayer, even more miraculously, was answered. Peter Beck, a record producer and promoter, came to one of the services, and afterward had approached the duo.

"Jamie Ray and Meghan Amhearst, your harmony is second to none. Jamie, your writing isn't the same old ultra-slick commercial thing, and for me, that's a good thing! The way your music fit and even complimented Brother McDonald's message was beyond human calculation. Guys, there are some things that cannot be taught, and being anointed is definitely one of them. Christian music is desperate for some fresh voices, and that doesn't have to mean young voices. Everyone tells me I'm crazy, but that's okay! I follow the Lord, not the latest trends, and you know what? I've done alright. So, what do you say we get you a recording, and distribution deal set up while you're here? Are you guys up for that?"

They were up for it, alright. Neither could sleep as they both called their spouses with the good news. And since in Nashville, events can move quickly, they spent their days recording their first real CD. Both had recorded before, but nothing like this. Featured were the four original songs for the four excuses, along with three traditional hymns and three praise and worship choruses, all arranged with the pair's trademark harmonies and the impeccable skills of musicians who inhabited Music Row.

Now, the crusade was perfectly set. The music could now be purchased and taken home as a keepsake, and Tim's sermons were being recorded, as well. Also, they would soon be televised. After all the hard work and preparation that had gone into this revival, it could and would now virtually run itself, as Tim could begin to gather more material at his own pace and Jamie and Meghan could do the same with their music even as they promoted their CD – *Excuses and Answers*.

Complacency is nice, but it's usually false. This would prove to be no exception.

~

The forces that had sent Wesley L. Williams, Lennard Garland, Terry Canter, and Donald Chambers to Atlanta were now focused on St. Louis, Missouri, the Gateway to the West. The first four had certainly had quite an effect on events and circumstances, but by no means the one they had intended. This praying man had used that age old Sword of Truth much too skillfully for his own good, and as a result, no good was coming from this out of control uprising.

Ah, but now, hope had once again risen. Complacency had reared its ugly, or quite beautiful, depending on one's perspective, head. As a result, the mighty man of God had developed a chink in his armor. Also, things were coming up roses for him, his co-workers, and his family.

All that could change.

So could the tide of this battle.

Even now, the four new representatives were being given their marching orders. This time, the results would be much more personal. After all, this man was mere flesh, and had his own doubts and weaknesses.

These had been made known to this second set of envoys.

Time just might be growing short for TIME Ministries.

~

Between Jamie and Meghan's rush to get their CD done, and some last minute changes in the venue for the St. Louis crusade, Tim didn't get as long with the family this time. Instead of returning home to Charleston, he flew them up to Nashville to observe Jamie and Meghan in the studio, plus a trip to Opry Mills Mall, the Hermitage, and the Grand Ole Opry, and several other tourist attractions that, although certainly worth seeing, still couldn't compare to the ones in their own backyard.

All too soon, it was time to part again. As Sarah, Gary, Brooke and Chance headed back to the mild southern climes of paradise, Tim headed north, only to discover upon his arrival at the St. Louis Airport, that it was a good thing he hadn't delayed his trip.

The area was under a winter storm watch beginning at 6:00 am the next day for a mix of sleet and freezing rain changing to heavy snow.

Talk about being homesick!

The weather arrived right on time that next morning. Tim was able to watch it in the warmth and safety of his Holidome room. He called his family and gave them updates as the storm progressed. To them, this was quite an oddity indeed, as the Low Country very seldom ever saw even a dusting of snow.

Freezing rain first glazed over everything, then sleet gave it all a whiter, grainer coating. By noon, large snowflakes began mixing in, and by dark, just over a half foot of snow served as a very clear reminder of just how far Tim had come from home.

He made the best of it, even venturing out into the storm and catching snowflakes on his tongue, then making and throwing snowballs. The kids would have loved the snow, but the ice made it much too dangerous to venture out far.

Three days later, the weather warmed up and the roads were cleared. This timed out nicely with all the new arrangements for the services. The revival would not even be delayed one day because of this – God's hand was once more at work.

Now, late on this Friday afternoon in late February, Tim glanced over his sermon and program notes. He couldn't help remembering back to that night in Atlanta before all of this started. He thought he was ready to go, but then he was visited by that church leadership group, and his plans were turned upside down, or right side up, as it turned out.

Tim still wasn't sure how he put all of that scripture together so fast, and the sermons to go with them. This time, everything was already laid out perfectly. It was kind of funny how so many people thought he had all the answers to all the excuses for not getting saved. The truth was, he didn't. Deep down, he knew there were reasons he had no answers for.

But for now, God had given him exactly what he could handle, and so many souls were being saved.

That was more than alright with Tim.

His thoughts were interrupted by a loud, persistent knocking on his door.

Part Two: The Second Meeting

"Hey, neighbor! Welcome to the Gateway City! My name's Buddy Belcher! I'm the youth guy from Gateway to Heaven Methodist Church! Pleased to meet cha!"

Tim couldn't help but feel more than a hint of déjà vu! He shook his visitor's hand as he also couldn't help observing, just as before, that exactly three other men were lined up behind the no-doubt honorable Reverend Belcher!

Tyrone Washington, an African American with a throwback name and afro to match, was next to introduce himself. "Bless you, my brother! I'm involved with Habitat for Humanity! It's an honor to meet a true giant of the faith like yourself!"

Despite himself, Tim couldn't help but stare at the contrast between Tyrone's snow white teeth and his Hershey's dark chocolate complexion. His deep vocal timbre only added to his magnetism.

The third man spoke, "I am Samir Muhammed, former Muslim and now head of North American Mission Outreach for the Greater St. Louis Mission Project. It is quite the honor to make your acquaintance, sir." Samir bowed deeply.

Tim didn't know what to make of all this.

Nick Chapman was the final member of the quartet. He was also the most contemporary looking as well as the most handsome. He looked like a young Tom Cruise, and his radiant smile was quite infectious.

"Hello, Reverend McDonald, I'm Nick Chapman. I work with Brother Belcher at Gateway to Heaven Church. I was truly blessed to be asked to come along today. I am only a year out of seminary."

For some reason, Tim was reminded of the overly polite Eddie Haskell on the old classic, *Leave it to Beaver* sitcom. Somehow, Tim got the feeling these guys weren't here just to sing his praises.

Buddy wasted no time in confirming this. "Brother Tim, is it okay if I call you that?"

"Of course, brother!"

"Well, good! Brother, Tim, word of your revival is getting out quickly. The whole city is buzzing. I know your results have been, to say the least, staggering."

"It's all God, my friend."

"Amen, brother, but it's you, too. Not since Billy Graham has there been anything like this. We would love to see that continue in Cardinal Country. Are you a baseball fan?"

"Yes, I am! But I have to confess, the Braves are my team."

"Hey, we all have our faults! No one's perfect, right?"

"Except Jesus Himself!"

"Ay-men! Well, anyway, the Cardinals are known for having some of the best fans in baseball. We have a winning tradition here that has produced more World Series championships in the National League, and second only to the Yankees in all of baseball. We pride ourselves in hard work and dedication."

"I believe that!"

"Missouri, as you know, is called the Show Me State! And now, here you are, with your Excuses crusade! We want to see words become actions. We want to see things proven to us! We want to see victory earned through that blue collar work ethic we mid-westerners take pride in!"

"Hey, I'm ready to minister to you!"

"Actually, you're not. Not at all! That is why we're here."

Tim's face paled as he sank into a nearby desk chair, turning it to face his guests. His heart pounded, sweat began to form on his brow despite the still chilly, late winter day.

"Okay, I'm listening, what do I need to do?" He uttered in a trembling voice, even as he steeled himself deep inside with a wall of prayer.

"Just remember, you did ask. So here goes. I've heard a lot of people, young and old, all say that the Christian religion has way too many do's and don'ts. You can't drink. You can't smoke. You can't get a divorce. You can't buy a Lotto ticket. Some even say, you can't dance, you can't cuss or tell dirty jokes. Some insist even attending the movie theater is wrong, not to mention TV shows and that dreadful invention known as the internet. And music? No rock period, and country has too much drinkin' and cheatin' in it. Supposedly, the truth will set you free. Sounds like prison to me.

"So, what can you do? It seems that list is just as long, but it's not what can you do, it's what MUST you do? You must attend church every time the doors are open. You must be baptized. You must be born again. You must listen only to Gospel music. You must give, give, give, that money. You must put others before yourself. You must deny yourself of pleasure. You must be willing to be a martyr. You must send yourself on an all-expense paid guilt trip at least once a day! Free gift of salvation, my foot! Where's the appeal in that?" inquired Buddy.

Tim looked crestfallen, not only because he had nothing prepared for this excuse, but for another reason Brother Belcher could not have known. These issues had caused Tim quite a bit of confusion over the years. There were so many gray areas, it seemed, and all they seemed to do was stir up trouble. How can life be abundant when you're always second guessing yourself on what you should or shouldn't do? An occasional social drink, popular music preferences, going to the movies, even decorating for Halloween, for crying out loud. Tim always tried to please everyone, especially his Lord, but, no, it wasn't easy. Then, as all of this confusion was permeating through him, Tyrone moved into the batter's box to deliver a blow of his own.

"You know, bro, I'm surprised this one didn't come up in A-Town. After all, the great Ted Turner was quoted as proclaiming it. 'Christianity is for losers!' So many folks I know say this, man! I mean, who wants to turn the other cheek these days? Who wants to get walked all over so someone else can claim that prize, win that victory, or acquire that promotion? And you, dude, how can anyone identify with how the media portrays Christians these days? We are narrow-minded, homophobic, goody-goody two shoes – remember that Adam Ant song from the eighties, dawg? We are seen as an outdated joke! Our hearts are full of hate and judgment! We can't get anywhere in politics because we're offensive to too many special interest groups. Homie, how can we really ever do well on earth if we're supposed to hate money, fame, and possessions? HELLO! I ain't whistlin' Dixie, here! Hah! I bet you never thought you'd hear a black man allude to THAT song, now did you? But seriously, you would not believe what a cancer this school of thought has become. Can you deal with that, my brother?"

And Tim thought the first round had been rough. He himself had wrestled with all this as he had clawed his way to earning his MBA. Of course, back then his beliefs had been nominal, but as he and Sarah had been reawakened, Tim had lost many a night's sleep trying to reconcile the drive to succeed and win versus doing right and putting God and others first as a higher priority. Sharp pain shot through his head and heart as his comfort zone was diminished, once again, to ashes.

Even as this was occurring, Samir, in a quiet but intense tone, voiced the excuse that his former faith itself discredited, sometimes through violence.

"There are so many religions out there. So many cultures. So many who truly believe and devote their lives – so, then, how can one way, and only one way, be right? Just as your Missouri is known as the Show Me State, so the people say 'SHOW ME!' Where is the proof that Jesus is the only way to Heaven? Why couldn't it just as easily be Allah? Or Buddha? Or Confucius? Or even Satan, for that matter? Or, better yet, why not all of them? Truly loving people should be open to this possibility! And how about New Age thoughts like human potential and cosmic energy? Maybe we are all really potentially able to evolve into gods ourselves. It is getting more and more difficult, my friend, for people to accept an absolute one right way. Do you understand this confusion? If you're going to preach here, you must."

Samir bowed deeply to Tim, then stepped back meekly to join the others. There was, however, nothing mild-mannered about the harsh reality of his words.

Tim excused himself for a moment. He needed a drink. In his case, this meant a vanilla Coke. He offered his guests one as well, but they each declined. Tim began to smell the midnight oil he now with one hundred percent certainty knew he would be burning upon his visitors' departure.

At least, the worst had to be over now. Only one more to go, if this pattern from the first meeting held true. Sure enough, Nick Chapman, charismatic grin in tow, was last to voice his mind.

But this excuse may as well have been a hundred more, for this excuse was the one that Tim himself had never been able to reconcile. He had prayed that maybe he would never ever have to deal with it directly.

And this prayer, like so many before, was now being answered, but this time the clear response from God was a resounding "NO, YOU MUST FACE THIS ONE, TOO!" as Nick's radiant glow defied his grim monologue.

"As urgent as all these excuses are, that is, the ones you are currently dealing with, as well as the ones we have brought to your attention today, there is one that trumps them all. Not only does it prevent many multitudes from entering the kingdom, it also sows seeds of doubt even among the most devout of believers. I can tell by the expression on your face that you are already aware of what it is. Perhaps even you have had to deal with its stark reality. Otherwise, you would have exposed it already in Atlanta. So, then, here it is. It must be faced. Why, indeed, does God allow such suffering, even among the best of us? Why do babies and children die? Why must they go through years of physical and/or sexual abuse? Why are they abandoned? How could 911 have ever been allowed to occur? How about Hurricane Katrina? God supposedly is in charge, so why doesn't He do something? How about all the people who get cancer and die slow painful deaths? Even many saints face this; disease and disaster seem both equally impartial to whom they affect. Then there are missionaries, who sacrifice everything to go to the far corners of the world to reach the lost, only to be rewarded with persecution and even martyrdom? Then there's the economy, gas prices, unemployment, foreclosures, bankruptcy, and repossessions – where does it end? Politics have gone to Hell – justice is totally perverted – and religion has no answer – as you yourself have pointed out, evangelistic scandals and hypocrisy and fights within the Body of Christ fill the airwaves daily! Is it any wonder thousands upon thousands are dropping out of ministry? You wouldn't believe how idealistic seminary students start out, only to be totally jaded in just a matter of a few years. Having recently graduated myself, I can tell you how sadly true this is. Brother Tim, this elephant in the room cannot be ignored."

Tim was moved to tears of both bitterness and repentance. How could he call himself an evangelist? Only dealing with what was comfortable for him was a start, yes, but nowhere near enough. Then there was that other issue...

Buddy interrupted this most unwelcome thought.

"As you can see, brother, if we hadn't intervened today, your crusade here would have been an utter disaster. But now you know what you are facing. We'll leave you to go about your business of doing whatever it is you can do to prepare yourself."

Just as before, the four gathered around Tim and laid their hands on him, offering silent prayers. This was followed by a round of hugs and handshakes, then a quick departure.

Did all that Tim had accomplished in Atlanta no longer matter in the future of TIME Ministries?

More shaken than he had ever been since answering God's call, Timothy Isaac McDonald still knew what he must do.

First, he fell to his knees.

Second, he withdrew his trusty sword of truth.

Third, he let the Spirit overtake him as he furiously began to take notes as he attempted to rightly divide the Word.

Before he knew it, midnight had come and gone, and a new day was dawning. But just what would that day bring?

~

"So do you think the fire chief will be pleased?" Nick asked the others.

"Ay-man, brothuh! We are the best squad of firefighters this side of … no, wait, that doesn't make sense! How can we be destined for that place if we FIGHT fires?" exclaimed Buddy.

"We'll just see if that's really where we end up," Samir quietly replied.

"Preach it, bro, preach it!" exclaimed Tyrone.

Tim's "guests," just like the previous four in Atlanta, congratulated themselves on a job well done.

"Our colleagues down South didn't exactly put out any fires," commented Samir.

"True, but we did something they didn't. We hit him where it hurt the most," replied Tyrone.

"Indeed we did. Won't it be shocking when one of the 'greatest' revivals in history suddenly just stops?" questioned Nick.

"Yes, it will. And we'll be there, as always, to lead the sheep back to the broad and crooked path!" exclaimed Buddy.

Raunchy laughter ensued.

~

"Hey handsome. I can't believe such a hottie would be calling this old middle-aged former beauty!"

"There's nothing former about your beauty, Sarah." At this point, Tim choked up and a few tears escaped.

Sarah sensed something wasn't right.

"Baby, what's wrong? The crusade starts tonight. I figured you'd be dancing through the streets."

"It happened again, Sarah."

"What happened, darling?"

Tim told her the story of the meeting, and how creepy it had somehow seemed. He then explained how he had once again completely re-written his itinerary to face these new excuses.

"So what's the problem? God's own genius has struck again. It sounds like divine intervention to me. If I were you, I'd prepare for another watershed!"

"This is different, Sarah. This time I really sensed a personal attack on me. These men seemed to actually enjoy watching me come unglued. Contrary to popular belief, sweetie, I do not have all the answers. Remember how I wrestled with Christianity having too many do's and don'ts and how it really seemed to be for losers?"

"Yes, I do. But look at you now!"

"Yes, just look at me. All those old doubts have re-surfaced. Social drinking, movies, you name it."

"I thought you achieved a peace about all that."

"I did, too. But now, I've been forced to face it all again. And then there's that issue of success, fame, and wealth..."

"And did the Word speak to you?"

Tim sighed. "It did. Of course, it did. The sermons are ready. I had to call in Jamie and Meghan this morning. Their CD is about those other four excuses! They have completely had to redo and re-think everything as well."

"And I have no doubt they rose to the occasion. Am I right? Just like YOU always do."

"How do you always know just what to say?"

"Because I am your wife, the only one for you; and, I just happen to have the spiritual gift of encouragement!"

"That you do, my love."

"So now are you ready?"

Tim grew silent. Suddenly, he began to sniffle. Next came sobbing, followed by all out crying.

Sarah, usually steadfast, suddenly shuddered with dread. She knew Tim was being confronted by his worst stumbling block. The one issue for which no words of encouragement would come. It was something both shared in common, and had helped, ironically, in bringing them together.

Sarah fell on her knees and joined Tim in his tears and pain, praying valiantly as she did so.

The War of the Ages was rapidly intensifying.

God help them both!

Excuse #5: Too Many Do's and Don'ts

There's nothing like meeting your new college roommate, and discovering you have loads of things in common.

Actually, there is something better – finding all of this out over a six-pack of Budweiser, the first taste of alcohol, and freedom from super-strict home lives for these two "brothers" who just happened to be born in different towns to different parents.

And so it was that Brent Bradley and Randy Weatherington became fast friends, best buds over Bud, if you will, on their first night on campus at Saint Louis University.

For starters, both were radio / TV majors. Brent aspired to be a broadcaster who would one day have his own talk show. Randy wanted to be a producer and engineer who would one day be behind the scenes of a major talk show. Randy and Brent vowed that very night they would one day work together professionally, bringing both their dreams to full fruition.

Both had come from ultra-religious upbringings. Brent's parents, and their church, majored in what was forbidden – pop music of any kind, television, movies, celebrating Halloween, dancing, social drinking, to name just a few "vices." In short, pleasure was out – only pure religious thoughts and actions were encouraged. Brent now swore to break free and try everything, beginning with booze, partying, women, R-rated movies, women, sexy internet sites, lewd and crude humor on TV, women… Ah, heaven at last!

Randy's background was more about the do's – attending church every time the doors were open, constant Bible reading, prayer about everything, listening to music – gospel only, giving money – Randy was even forced to tithe from his part-time McDonald's gig, and give additional offerings above and beyond as well – and doing good deed after good deed.

Both Brent and Randy made a pledge that first night to leave their pasts in the past – way in the past! It was time to live!

And live they did. Frat parties, hangovers, and crazy activities like séances, tarot card reading, dabbling in a little weed, and reckless internet surfing mingled with the excitement of classes in their major and the drudgery of required courses.

Even those classes they dreaded, however, sometimes held pleasant surprises of their own. The first such discovery came in General Psychology. Sigmond Freud and all his sexual psychological theories, a section on fetishes, including an article depicting a patient's real struggles with a fixation on boots, and how human potential seemed so much more fulfilling than religious oppression. The college life was fitting these two like a velvet glove.

The next discovery centered around moral relativity versus absolutism. More than one of their professors pointed out that narrow-minded absolutism and fundamentalism were more and more considered the most out dated, hindering, and even dangerous viewpoints. Morals being relevant to culture and circumstances were much more sensible. For example, in the sixties, homosexuality was considered a disease. Today, however, gay people were often admired, and even same-sex marriages were being accepted in more and more places. Randy and Brent felt their minds broadening and opening on an almost daily basis. They decided that the Bible was right about one thing after all. "The truth will set you free!"

So life could be abundant, after all!

And then, life got even more abundant. It happened on September 27, 2014. It was that blessed day they first laid eyes on the Frazier twins!

Intro to Broadcasting had let out a half hour early that Thursday. As a result, Brent and Randy had found themselves in the cafeteria earlier than normal. Neither could later remember what slop was being served that day, because dessert had made its appearance in the lunch line. Not one, but two picture-perfect, co-ed specimens materialized right there in front of them. Brent was the first to speak. He turned on his best hosting voice, which was actually quite dazzling.

"Well, hello, ladies! Welcome to the campus of beautiful Saint Louis University."

Both beauties turned, mouths slightly open at the voice, which truly sounded like a celebrity had invaded.

"The name's Brent. Brent Bradley, future talk show host, and this is Randy, Randy Weatherington, my future producer. Listen, we haven't seen you two around before. Who are you, a couple of Hollywood actresses researching a role or something?"

The sisters gave each other an eye roll, but then smiled politely.

"I'm Stacy Frazier, and this is my sister Tracy!"

Randy, in an attempt at humor, looked back and forth at each of them. "Hey, you guys are twins, aren't you?"

This helped to break the ice, as all four laughed at the wisecrack.

"Well, duh!" Tracy quipped.

More giggles erupted.

"Let me guess, Theater majors, right?"

Brent grinned. "If I were casting, you would definitely get the part."

"Actually, we're both Elementary Education majors."

"Man, none of my teachers were ever that pretty!"

"So, shall we dine together on this fine cuisine?"

"Well, I'm not sure how dineable the cuisine is, but you're welcome to join us!"

The four continued to make light conversation as they passed through the line. Brent and Randy couldn't keep their eyes off these two newly discovered treasures. Both had sparkling blue eyes that danced to the rhythm of life and sang in a variety of nuances that held the boys spellbound. Their smiles were never forced, so at ease with their surroundings. Both guys sensed this would be true no matter what the circumstances.

They were hooked.

Near the end of the meal, if you could call it that, Brent made a proposal to try to get to know these two better.

"Listen guys, we have classes in about twenty minutes. We really hate to leave such splendid company, but our education is important to us, so we have an offer for the two of you."

"Oh, do you now?"

"Indeed, we do. Randy and I have an exclusive invitation to Alpha Tau Omega's kegger tomorrow night! Nothing but good times! Leave your worries at the door. We would be honored to have you as our guests. And believe me, this is no easy party to get on The List for. So, would you honor us with your presence?"

Up till now, the girls had been full of animation. Now, however, both grew quiet and solemn.

"Hey, did we say something wrong? We're sorry, it's just…"

Stacy interrupted. "No, it's not you. Actually, we sort of have other plans already."

"Oh, lucky guys! We just weren't fast enough, were we?"

"No, no! We don't have dates. We just have an activity we're already involved in ourselves. In fact, we were going to invite you to our get-together."

"Oh, okay. We're flexible! What 'cha got in mind? A Sorority bash?"

"No, actually…"

"Actually," Tracy cut in, "every Friday night we have Bible study! We would love it if you guys came! Free Coke and pizza…"

Both Brent and Randy looked like all the helium had burst from their balloons, and now, instead of floating, they were quickly crashing unceremoniously down to earth.

Tracy and Stacy appeared to go through the same transformation.

"Oh, not your scene, huh?"

"Uh, well, you know – been there, done that…"

"Bought the T-shirt, yeah!"

"This is different guys, I'm serious! It's not all religious and stuffy."

"Tell you what, we'll think about it for later. We're already committed to tomorrow night but we'll take a rain check, right Randall?"

"That's correct, Brent, my boy! Ladies, we will be in touch."

"Okay. Maybe later."

The guys took off imaginary hats, bowed nobly and deeply, then headed off to their next classes.

"Oh, well, same old story," sighed Stacy.

"Just like a hose on a wildfire, cools it off every time. The minute they hear the words 'Bible study'…"

"You know what, though?"

"What's that?"

"I have a strange feeling we haven't seen the last of these two."

67

"I have a confession – I was thinking the same thing, and I hope we're right!"

Both ladies blushed, at exactly the same moment.

It's a twin thing!

~

As it turned out, it was a toga party! Brent and Randy were unprepared, but luckily there were plenty of extra sheets available. The spirits flowed, along with an old college tradition, brownies laced with pot. There were plenty of babes for the picking, and the music was a mix of 60's acid rock and modern alternative pop.

Ordinarily the perfect ambiance in the perfect place at the perfect time. Sure, Brent and Randy did some flirting and some making out with more than a few of the uninhibited beauties present. And yes, they both got rather high and forgot about the world outside. And, indeed, they were out till way after midnight.

But something just wasn't the same this time.

Brent and Randy stumbled back into their room at about 1:30 am, lost in the shuffle of all the other party animals. They both fell into their beds, but neither could sleep.

"Some party, huh?" said Brent.

"Oh, yeah, dude."

A few moments passed in silence.

"And we could have been studying THE WORD, brothuh!"

"Ay-men! We could have been rolling in guilt rather than brew!"

"Oh, man! What were we thinking?" Brent slapped his forehead.

"Hey, how about those babes!"

"Totally awesome! There was Vicki, Gina, Juliet..."

"Juliet!? Man! You mean there really are people named that? I've never met a Juliet, or a Romeo, for that matter."

"How about Othello, or Antigone?"

They both giggled like the teenagers they still were.

Just as they calmed down, Brent blurted out, "How about Hamlet?"

The fits of giggling resumed in earnest.

This time, it was Randy who finally spoke in the aftermath. "Tracy and Stacy, those are the two names I care most about," he sighed.

"So, it's not just me, huh?"

The laughter was now replaced by contemplative silence.

"I never thought I'd say this, but I think we could endure it for a night, for their sake."

"So maybe the Alpha Tau Omega's will have to rock on without us next Friday."

"Yeah. So, do we need to like, pray or something?"

"Who to, Othello, maybe?"

More laughter, then silence. Nothing else needed to be said on this night. They were going to do this, for the sake of the most beautiful of God's handiwork – The Frazier twins.

~

Both had dreams that night.

Nightmares, actually.

Nightmares of endless church services. Nightmares of endless hellfire and brimstone preaching. Nightmares of endless pleasure being erased by endless guilt. Still, they woke up the next morning resolved to their course of action.

~

This time, it was Coke products and bottled water that flowed freely instead of booze.

Rather than brownies enhanced with weed, an array of homemade goodies were available, including sugar cookies, chocolate chip cookies, and made-from scratch marble cake. In addition, pizza, ranging from cheese to super supreme, was in bountiful supply.

No togas here, but not suits and ties, either. Instead, some wore jeans, others wore khakis, and several donned T's decked out with religious messages such as "Don't make me come down there! – God," "Driven, not by nails, but by love," and "His life was given, not taken."

Neither was there any psychedelic music to get high by. Instead, a variety of contemporary Christian rock and pop provided a festive, rather than oppressive, atmosphere.

Maybe Brent and Randy could survive this after all, especially when they saw the Fraziers make their entrance, adorned in matching Calvin Kleins and ocean blue tops and just the right amount of makeup.

Ah! Heavenly, indeed!

"Well, hello, gentlemen! You made it!" In perfect synchronicity, Stacy went to Brent and Tracy to Randy, putting an arm around each, and giving them a brief but warm hug.

"Better than the cafeteria, huh?" Stacy smiled.

"Oh, yeah, babe! Five-star dining!" Brent returned it.

"Hey, there's Ricky! I think we're about to start!" Tracy was flush with excitement. Randy wasn't so sure.

Ricky Meeks, decked out in stone-wash jeans and a vertical striped shirt that made Brent and Randy think of Charlie on "Two and a Half Men," did not resemble any preacher either had ever encountered. His mustached, goateed face looked as though life was overflowing from it. He quickly got the crowd's attention!

"Free at last! Free at last! That's right, guys! Freedom is finally yours! Free from parental supervision 24/7, free to try all the pleasures and adult activities you weren't allowed to at home, free to carve out your own future and your own identity..."

Brent and Randy exchanged a grin. They might actually be able to like this guy.

"But, and this is a big but, that wisest of sages we know as Uncle Ben, late Uncle of Peter Parker – that's right, Spidey's uncle…"

The laughter and applause of this young audience would have made Tim McDonald proud. Ricky Meeks had them totally programmed to receive.

"With great power comes great responsibility! So, how many sermons have you ever heard that draw from Spider-Man?"

More applause.

"But guys, the truth is – it's true! When I first came to campus, I hit every frat party I could find. I tried pot, coke, and I don't mean the soft drink, crystal meth – you name it. I had a contest with my roommate to see who could get laid the most times by Christmas…"

Brent felt himself grow red. He noticed Randy was in like mode. The two had virtually the same bet going – until the Fraziers came along, anyhow.

"I now know that is a road reserved for losers! Some nerdy guy in my Organic Chemistry class kept begging me to go to a Bible study quite similar to this one. I finally did it just to shut him up – and you know what? Somehow, Jesus found me!"

A chorus of Amens resounded. Brent and Randy both looked and felt blindsided.

"All drinking does is get you drunk, and as a bonus you get a headache the next day. Getting laid only satisfies lust. It has nothing to do with love – until you are married, of course! Galatians 5:19-21 gives us a list of things we must not do: getting drunk, orgies, debauchery, sexual impurity, witchcraft – that's right, I said witchcraft! That includes tarot card reading, séances, invoking spirits and spell-casting! Also rage, selfish ambition, jealousy, to name a few. And yes, I believe sexual impurity includes homosexuality. I know that makes me unpopular these days…"

Brent's head was filling with a legion of horrible memories from his pre-college days. It was Ricky's next point, however, that would be the last straw.

"Let's talk about selfish ambition a moment. I know a lot about the mindset of many of the professors here. It's all about self-potential and satisfying self above all. I'm telling you, guys, from the heart, Jesus teaches the exact opposite!"

Brent rose, excusing himself as having to use the restroom. He gave Randy a firm eye-signal that he had no plans to return. Not tonight. Not ever.

For the sake of Tracy, Randy decided to brave it out just a little longer.

"So, then, what can we do? What should we do? Galatians 5:22 tells us plainly. The fruits of the spirit, that's what! Love, peace, joy, patience, kindness, goodness, faithfulness, gentleness, and self-control. Do good deeds, expecting nothing in return! Be kind for no good reason! Love people, even your enemies, or your arch-rival, or your strictest professor when he pops a quiz on you..."

Randy felt the deep waters of guilt begin to stir inside him. He began tapping his foot restlessly.

"... and self-control. You know, going to church is hard enough at home, but at school it can become next to impossible. But in truth, we should be in church every time the door is open! It should be a sanctuary, not a prison! And self-control is even about not eating too much, not enjoying anything so much that it takes God's place as number one in your life..."

Randy looked wistfully at Tracy, but knew the guilt would soon drown him, recalling all his past demons. He excused himself as well, following Brent's exact path, as it turned out, a path not to the Alpha Tau House, but directly back to the room they shared. Clearly, an all-night talk session was forthcoming.

~

Like a canvass in the hands of DiVinci, Van Gough, or Picasso, the paper began to transform from bare and white to vibrant and colorful. The nine year old hand of Brent Bradford was waving his Crayola wand with a virtuosity that would have made Harry Potter proud. Materializing were precisely drawn images of glowing orange jack-o-lanterns with shadings Thomas Kinkade would no doubt applaud. A piercing yellow, full moon illuminated the dark landscape which included a scattering of ghosts and goblins, three black cats with lime-green lantern eyes, two black bats with exaggerated wing spans, and a battalion of witches with various colors of hair and a wide range of facial expressions, perched upon majestic broomsticks. The sky was indigo, with a few stars dotting it. The effect was, indeed, magical.

There was, however, nothing supernatural about the time it took to weave this masterpiece. Brent had actually begun laboring right after Labor Day that year, and now, the final product was finally ready.

Right in time for the District-wide Halloween Creative Young Artist's contest and its $250.00 first prize.

Brent had always done well at school, but he'd always seemed to fall just short of receiving any awards.

Not this time.

He had shown it to a couple of his favorite teachers. Ms. Thompson and Mrs. Wilkens. They had both been beside themselves with excitement and amazement. Each had guaranteed him a victory.

The night before the contest was to be held, Brent took out his handiwork one last time to admire it. Ah, yes! His moment of glory was at hand.

Then, his dad had walked in unannounced, which was more than an occasional habit.

"What's that picture, Son, an art project for school…" Ronald Bradford's mouth fell open in horror as he got a better view of the drawing's landscape.

"Get behind me, Satan! Brent, what have you done?"

Brent cowered at the familiar sound of hellfire and brimstone his dad usually reserved for the small congregations he sometimes preached to, not as a pastor or evangelist, but as a layman preacher.

"Dad, listen, this is for a big contest tomorrow. Kids from a lot of different schools are going to be in it…"

"This is the Devil's work! It is demonic! Who put you up to this?"

"No one, Dad. I think I can draw pretty good, and a couple of my teachers think I have a chance to win…"

"There are no winners in Satan's kingdom, young man! Look at this – witches, demon-possessed cats, jack-o-lanterns, ghosts, goblins…"

Ronald seized Brent's pride and joy from his grasp much too quickly for Brent to react to, much less stop.

"But Dad, listen, I've never won anything. This might finally be my chance. First prize is $250.00! Please Dad…"

"1ST Timothy 6:10 says 'for the love of money is a root to all kind of evil!' This proves it!"

"But my teachers were so proud of me. Ms. Thompson, Mrs. Wilkens, they're good people…"

"I knew I should have put you in private school! Well, we'll just put this problem to rest right now!"

Brent's heart was torn into pieces, as Ronald did likewise to his son's treasured work of art. The fragments were heaved into the large great room fireplace.

"Son, we are purified by fire as we are judged by fire. Now, I want you to look up Deuteronomy 18:10-12."

Brent stood frozen in place, tears streaming.

"NOW!"

Brent obeyed.

"I want you to read that passage out loud while this abomination is burned away once and for all!" Ronald lit the fireplace, turning it up to full heat. Brent's once beautiful craftsmanship was obliterated in seconds as the devastated young man read from his Bible given to him by his parents for his ninth birthday.

"Let no one be found among you who sacrifices his son or daughter in the fire, who practices divination and sorcery, interprets omens, engages in witchcraft, or casts spells, or who is a medium or spiritist, or who consults the dead. Anyone who does these things is detestable to the Lord, and because of these detestable practices, the Lord your God will drive out those nations before you…"

"You know, son," Ronald spoke softly now, "I know purging hurts, but it's worth it. I had to take the television out of our room because your mother had gotten hooked on one of those trashy soap operas. She was mad at first, too, but later she thanked me. By the way, you have a nice speaking voice. Maybe you'll be a preacher someday..."

~

Brent cringed as he spun this Halloween horror to Randy.

"Soon afterwards, I faked a born again experience just to appease the old man. I had to do something to get him off my back and out of my face. I did an academy award performance for several years, until, just a year ago, when another contest came my way. This time, I wasn't going to let any self-righteous upbringing get in my way. This time, I figured out a way around it, or so I thought..."

~

The Wind Beneath My Wings. It was perfect! A pop song with a good meaning that Brent could belt. Yes, Brent had a singing talent, a rather strong one, in fact. But the fact that he could duplicate, and perhaps even surpass, Ryan Seacrest, would prove to be his golden ticket.

For the last few years, his school had held its own version of *American Idol*. Always before, "golden tickets to Hollywood" were awarded, but no finals were held. This year, however, Brent's senior year, five finalists would be selected. A second contest would be held, and the winner would receive a pass to skip to the front of the line for the real *American Idol* auditions being held in St. Louis later that year.

Brent's school was blessed with a trio of judges that mirrored the real ones perfectly. Lincoln Abbott, the Choral Director with a rotund frame and cool way of speaking, made a most credible Randy Jackson. Ms. Mary Thompson-Foster, Brent's once and current favorite teacher from his elementary days, newly married and transferred to the high school, did Paula Abdul proud with her hot looks and encouraging words. The finishing touch was Bill Buchanon, the sharp-tongued, no nonsense principal. By putting a British turn on his accent, it was as though Simon Cowell had actually made an appearance in the building.

Brent sailed through the first round, and came out gunning in the finals. At home, nothing had changed since the Halloween Holocaust, but Brent saw in this the one chance to finally go the way he felt led and making his parents proud all in one swoop. Ronald had to work and could not attend, but Shirley Bradford was there with bells on. Brent had no plans to disappoint her.

Competition was stiff, to say the least. Ebony Estes, a true Whitney Houston style diva, brought down the house. Seth Robbins smoldered as a cutting edge rocker. Carol Kennedy did the country genre proud, and Cameron Berkeley soared on the wings of vocal range. Brent played the perfect host for them all, then waited till last to take the stage himself.

"Eat your heart out, Ryan Seacrest!" Brent had the audience already with his hosting chops. Now he proceeded to own them.

"I'd like to dedicate this song to my mom, who is here today. Mom, you and Dad have been tough on me, but look at me now! Mom, you are my power, my strength, the *Wind Beneath My Wings*."

Brent then used elements of rock, country, soaring range, and smooth phrasing to deliver a show-stopping rendition of this so often covered song. A standing ovation ensued, which included all three judges. Not even "Simon" could find anything negative to say. Brent was crowned the winner.

Through the pandemonium, Brent spotted his mom. She was crying. A lump formed in Brent's throat. Maybe at last he had touched her. He reached to embrace her, but surprisingly she ran past him to the microphone, and began to speak.

"Excuse me! Excuse me, everyone! As honored as my son and I are by this, he is going to have to decline this honor. In our family, God comes first. We have no idols, and we feel that this contest puts people on a pedestal and makes them objects of worship! This is wrong, and an insult to God. So thanks, but no thanks."

The entire gym was now hushed as Shirley led her utterly humiliated son out to the hallway.

~

"Now, do you see why I could not stay another minute? All Christianity stands for is 'don't do this, don't do that, but do feel guilty'."

"I'm feeling you, bro. In fact, I'll tell you a couple of tales of my own. Mine, however, will emphasize what we do have to do, and like you, guilt has always been my guiding force."

~

Just who was Randy kidding, anyway? He had never played organized sports of any kind. A little one-on-one basketball with some friends at church, or throwing a few passes with an old worn out football in the Weatherington's backyard with dad hardly qualified him for anything like this.

But, nevertheless, here he was, at tryouts for a twelve year and older traveling baseball team. There were two reasons why he was here. One was Travis Sinclair, the most popular kid in the seventh grade, who unlike him, was not under a religious dictatorship at home and who always seemed so carefree and happy. Travis had already secured a spot on the team, and had dared the shy Randy to do the same. The second reason was linked also to this dare. Mendy Snow, the most beautiful girl in their class, was the love interest of both boys, and just happened to be a huge fan of the Grand Old Game. Her family had held Cardinals season tickets for the last five years.

It was hard, what with all the forced church activity of his family, for Randy to do much else. It was time for that to change.

Except Randy had never been on a baseball team, or even in a game. He just liked it, and on a whim, he decided to give it a shot. What did he have to lose?

Other than the respect of everyone present.

Despite all that, Randy stepped to the plate with confidence and dug in for a series of pitches.

He struck out his first try.

And his second.

Likewise, his third.

He finally hit one grounder and one fly ball, but nothing that turned any heads.

He then tried fielding. He fared somewhat better here, handling most of the ground balls that came to him at first, second, and third.

Then he attempted playing shortstop, and it was here that a subtle change began to occur. It was actually a ball that he misfielded that ushered in that change. He finally picked it up and whipped a throw to first. He whipped it so hard, in fact, that it flew into the dugout. For this, he was immediately thrust into centerfield to try his hand there.

Randy had average speed, so his running down of fly balls was not spectacular, but neither was it disastrous. What got the coaches' attention were his throws to the infield and to home plate. They were quite strong, and fairly accurate to boot. Could Randy have found a way onto this elite team after all?

The coaches called him over to break down his performance.

"Not bad, son. Not bad. Your lack of experience definitely shows, but your arm is a major plus. To tell you the truth, you're right on the bubble. Do you know what that means?"

"I'm not sure." Randy cleared his throat nervously.

"It means you are right on the border of being cut and just making it. Your hitting is not so good. Your fielding is okay. Your throwing arm is definitely worthy of this team's level of play, however."

"Hey, I'll work hard, I promise. You won't be sorry if you give me a chance."

"Let us have a few minutes, son, okay?"

"Yes, sir." Randy faked praying so often at home and at church, but not this time.

Several minutes passed, then one of the coaches came over to Randy, placing a firm hand on his shoulder.

"Son, we're split down the middle, so here's what we're going to do. Let's see if you can pitch. That might just be the difference maker."

Randy breathed a sigh, and headed out to the mound, determined not to disappoint. He threw a few warm-up tosses, then proceeded to give his all. His first few pitches got past the catcher, but Randy bore down, and his offerings grew more accurate, balls that would be called strikes.

Another coach came in and worked with Randy's hand placement, showing him both the two seam and the four seam fastball. Randy continued to show improvement.

"Son, I do believe you've just won yourself a place on our squad. You'll have to work hard, though. You've got some catching up to do, a lot, in fact. We feel like we can mold you into a starting pitcher, and maybe a backup outfielder. Are you willing to put in the work required? We don't like losing on this team."

Randy lit up like a Fourth of July fireworks display.

"You bet I am, sir. I'll make you guys proud, I promise."

Randy received a firm clap on the shoulder from each coach, and, even sweeter, a high five and a grin from Travis. Best of all, though, was the hug and kiss on the cheek bestowed on him by Mendy. Ah, life was good!

Good, that is, until the first practice, when his parents came out to check out the situation. It was revealed that most weekends would be spent out of town, and practices would be just about every night, including Wednesdays. This meant missing church, and missing church was not tolerated. Not for any reason other than severe illness, injury, or emergency. Being on a fancy traveling baseball team did not qualify as any of these.

"Mom, Dad, you cannot do this to me!"

"Yes, son, we can. God has to come first. If you make anything more important than Him, it becomes your idol."

"No! Please! I finally found something I'm good at!"

"Sorry Randy, on this, we have to stand firm."

And so it was that Randy's first practice also became his last. He flung his equipment to the ground and stamped off the field, which would wind up adding to his misery as a grounding from his computer and game systems was tacked on to this most awful of Randy's childhood days.

~

"So in my case, it was the do's instead of the don'ts. To this day, I have bad dreams about that day. But I've got to tell you, it was not the only one, or even the worst one. That one came, as yours did, in my senior year, not long before I finally escaped prison and made it here."

Brent was all ears and hanging on the edge of his bed as Randy began to tell an even more harrowing tale.

~

Randy got over his baseball phase fairly quickly, because his real interest was technology. He did have his own computer, but it was limited to school work only, with no internet access. Whatever online assignments he had must be done at school. Despite all this, Randy became quite a talent in the world of cyberspace. He also worked with recording and production devices programmed into his PC, and became quite the whiz.

Yes, Randy loved video games, but was only allowed ones with an "E" rating, and only a very few with a "T" rating. "M" rated games were taboo, as were any of the fancy game systems. "A waste of money when so many people are in need," his parents had proclaimed, dashing any hopes he may have had of ever owning an Xbox, Xbox 360, Nintendo Wii, or PlayStation®4. All he acquired was an old, much used, Ps3 that only worked right about half the time.

But then came the Golden Arches.

At last, he had a way to get away from the hierarchies of home and church, and appear responsible at the same time. His parents monitored his paychecks carefully, however. He was forced to tithe his ten percent, with another ten percent set aside for charities and special offerings. Fifty percent had to go into his college fund, and what was left over was his to spend. Not a lot, but Randy took it.

His senior year, his hours increased, along with two six-month performance raises. At about the same time, a special from GameStop popped up on his computer. A brand new Ps4 with memory card and two frontline games, all for $499. Randy checked his savings balance via his computer, and discovered he could afford it with room to spare. Unknown to his parents, he had learned to transfer money from his savings to his checking with no receipts sent to their home. Every now and then, he had fudged a little, and treated himself to a couple of pairs of jeans and some overpriced Air Jordans.

This, however, was a much bigger deal. The fear of getting caught was trumped in the end by Randy's desire to finally do something for himself. He had, after all, earned this money himself. Also, it was his senior year, and his grades were quite excellent.

He decided to go for it.

He hid his purchase at his friend Monty's house. Monty came over from time to time already, so he simply began to bring the game system with him, letting Randy "borrow" it more and more frequently. His parents were none the wiser.

For a while.

Randy had all his banking done electronically, but the bank was told to notify Randy's parents if anything unusual ever happened to their son's accounts. They figured that a $500 transfer qualified.

On that fateful day in April, a beautiful, early spring, masterpiece of nature, Randy came home whistling. He had borrowed a cool shooter game from Monty. Before him lay a rare night off – no homework, no McDonald's, and no church, thank God. He hurried to his room, pulled out the game, and prepared to load it.

Except there was nothing to load it into.

The Ps4 was gone, wires and all.

Randy gasped in horror just as he heard footsteps coming down the hall.

His parents, their expressions grim, stood at his door, arms folded.

"Hey, where is it? I'm borrowing that from Monty, you know. If this is a joke, it's not funny!"

"What's the ninth commandment, Randall?" his father asked coolly.

"Pardon me?"

"Your father asked you what is the ninth commandment!" snapped his mother.

"Thou shall not bear false witness," Randy droned.

"And what is a simpler way of saying that?"

"Thou shall not lie." Randy was overwhelmed by a sudden wave of nausea. They knew, but how?

"And yet, you did. You lied to us. You got your friend involved in your sin, and you let God and others down by not being generous with that money. Oh, not to mention the sixth commandment – you stole from your college account that we have been doubling every time you deposit into it with our own account for your future."

Randy hung his head and fought not to vomit.

"Get in the car, Randall. We're going to take a ride of repentance."

Randy had no choice but to obey.

The first stop was the church. The three of them got out, and John, a trustee for ten years now, pulled out his key and let them in. Randy was presented with a copy of the church budget, which was under by over $500 each week. He was then shown minutes from the last business meeting showing forced salary cuts to the bi-vocational pastor, minister of music, secretary, and janitor.

"Son, these people are bi-vocational as it is, but they're being forced to take less money because both attendance and tithing are down. Yes, the economy's bad, but God accepts no excuses for disobedience that is willful.

Randy felt bad. How could he not? He may not buy into this fanatical Christianity, but he was human.

Seeing Randy's genuine grieved expression, his parents were satisfied, and took him to their next stop, but not before his dad put $200 into the offering plate.

The next destination on this trail of tears was the home of Nora Higgins, a newly widowed church member whose husband had left her with nothing due to medical bills.

"Hey, Nora, we're here to bless you tonight. Our son heard about your problems, and wanted to spend a little time with you. Right, Randy?"

"Yes, ma'am." Randy muttered. "Is there anything I can do for you?"

"Oh, what a sweet boy. Yes, hon, there is. Could you read to me? Floyd used to do that for me before he got so sick, and my own children live far away." Nora's face shown like a young girl's as Randy took her hand and sat by her on the couch. He read some *Reader's Digest* articles, some selections from *Guideposts*, and a few scriptures as well. While this was occurring, Randy's parents prepared Nora a nice meal of grilled chicken and mixed vegetables.

Nora continued to glow as the family left her to her feast, the dessert being another envelope containing $200.

"Are you feeling better, son? After all, you had some serious repenting to do; all that money spent on yourself when so many are in need." Marge commented curtly.

"Yes ma'am." Randy whispered as his head hung low.

"We believe you. So now comes your reward, not because you asked for it, but because you truly repented."

Randy didn't say much as houses and streets passed by, giving way to stores and businesses. Randy's heart suddenly leaped as he realized they were heading toward the mall.

Specifically, to GameStop!

The car stopped in front of the mall entrance, but no one made a move to leave the car. The reason soon became all too clear.

"Son, when we learned of what you did, we immediately took back your treasure. We were blessed to get a full refund. You were in line for major punishment, beyond losing your precious game system, but now, all is forgiven. The money you took has been reinvested in the kingdom - $200 to our church, $200 to Nora, and $100 – well, the last $100 is right here. We are going to let you choose where it goes – the church, Nora, another charity – What's on your heart, son? We will trust your judgment."

Bile was rushing into Randy's mouth as he fought back tears. How could they be so cruel as to build his hopes up that he would get back his Ps4 after all?

"Give it to Nora," he choked out as those tears he hoped his parents would mistake for remorse could stay back no more.

~

"That was it. I was done. No more guilt, no more pretending. College could not come fast enough after that. I don't care if I never darken a church door again!"

"Amen, brothuh! You preach it up in here! Let's drink to a revival of freedom and truth!"

They split a six-pack stashed in their fridge for just such an emergency as this.

Even after the beer, and the sleep that finally followed, however, the Frazier twins and the light that flowed from within them refused to leave their minds – like a talisman of things to come and consequences to face that nothing would deny.

~

The novelty of wild parties soon wore off, and was replaced by class assignments and extracurricular activities. Brent got involved with the campus television station as a news and weather broadcast volunteer. Randy got involved too, on the production end, increasing program quality greatly.

Brent's smooth voice was getting increased attention as the semester wound down toward Christmas break.

The theater department also beckoned these two emerging talents to try new things. Brent auditioned for and landed a major role in *Les Miserables*, and Randy signed on for technical support. Both were gaining friends and popularity on a daily basis. Neither wanted the semester to end.

The Frazier twins did not disappear. In fact, a slight shift in scheduling in the education department caused a common lunch time to occur more frequently. The four shared light conversation over continually sub-par dining fare once or twice a week. The twins were excited to hear about the exploits of their two friends, and both promised to come check out the show next semester. The guys always felt so much better after these visits. What was it? Love? Lust? Hope? It was something, and both knew they wanted more. The stumbling block, however, continued to be Friday nights. Not the frat parties, they were so yesterday. But Bible study just wasn't going to happen. But the twins just wouldn't leave their minds.

Or their hearts.

Something would eventually have to give.

~

It was mid-January, and a winter storm was threatening the mid-Mississippi Valley. Not a bad one, just a 2 to 4 inch snowfall with a little sleet mixed in, some wind, and a cold wave to follow. Not a huge deal for this area, but enough to signify that it was indeed winter in the Heartland.

Stacy and Tracy were taking a trip down Memory Lane, which in this case had been their literal address growing up – recalling the good old days when a storm like this would promise at least one snow day.

Not anymore! This was college. It would take a full-scale blizzard to shut down this place.

As the two made their way from Early Childhood Development (not their memories, but the actual class both took) to U.S. History from 1865 to the present, the subject of conversation turned, as it always seemed to sooner or later, to the Bradford/Weatherington duo.

"Oh, those guys! What are we going to do about them?" said Tracy.

"They're kind of cute, but we can't really get involved too deeply – there's that 'unevenly yoked' thing," said Stacy.

"Stupid rule. Who came up with it, anyway?"

"The Apostle Paul. II Corinthians 6:14, I believe."

"Oh, yeah. But still, we both keep feeling led back to them. I think it's a God thing."

"And they are kind of cute."

"And talented, too."

"And smart!"

"And funny!"

"Okay, so Houston, we have a problem! We seriously do need to pray. What is their stumbling block? What is it that freaks them out about Bible study and Christianity?"

"I think it was something to do with how they were raised. Oh, great. Now I'm sounding like a psych major!"

"Heaven forbid!"

They both laughed as they entered history class. It was one of those that students with various majors were required to take. So it was a very large and impersonal classroom setting. The girls settled in and prepared for a long, boring lecture. In this class, it was a recap of the Civil War, including Sherman's march to the sea. Later that night, a story about Atlanta once again being set on fire appeared, not by soldiers, but by revival. This fact would finally prove to be proof that God was at work here after all.

In late February, TIME Ministries would be setting its sights on the Gateway to the West.

~

The mid-February performance of *Les Miserables* was a smashing success. Brent and Randy had their finest hour on campus, and the best part of all was that the Frazier twins were there to see it. They both received warm, lasting embraces from the sisters. Empowered by the magic of the moment, Brent and Randy decided to lay things on the line.

"Look. We think about you guys all the time. We think you are beautiful!" said Randy.

Brent gazed at Stacy and Randy at Tracy as Brent spoke. "And we admire you and what you stand for, even if we can't handle your Friday night scene. But there are reasons for that. Legitimate ones. Anyway, Stacy, would you do me the honor of going out with me, on a real date, I mean?"

"And Tracy, would you do likewise with me?" the much more shy Randy asked.

"All right guys. Here's how it is. You tell us what the God hang up's all about, then we'll talk," said Tracy.

Both guys shared their story, which caused an empathetic enlightenment to fill both sisters.

"Okay then. Now we see. Here's our proposal. TIME Ministries is coming to town in a couple of weeks. Trust me, we've researched it. I believe Brother McDonald can answer your questions and soothe your doubts and fears. He specializes in excuses for not being a Christian," said Stacy.

"But we've heard it all before," said Brent.

"Ah, not necessarily. So here's the deal. You attend one night of the crusade with us, and no matter what happens, as long as you stay for the entire service, we will be honored to go out with you. Is that fair?" inquired Tracy.

Randy and Brent were skeptical, and yet, for some reason, they were willing to try, what could they lose?

But even more important, what could they gain?

~

"Folks, I've got to shoot straight with you tonight. God has given me this ministry of confronting excuses not to accept Jesus as Savior, but the one I'm going to discuss tonight gave yours truly a lot of trouble!"

Right off the bat, Tim's audience was hooked.

"I loved Halloween growing up, trick or treating, all that good candy, dressing up, scary stories, jack-o-lanterns, the whole bit. It wasn't until I was older that I discovered a lot of churches forbid such things! Now, I'll be honest, today, my two older kids have almost outgrown trick or treating, but not quite. What we did was come up with some compromises. No demonic costumes. Our pumpkins have happy expressions. In fact, dressing as Biblical characters is a great alternative. Also, parties with bobbing for apples, haunted houses with a Heaven versus Hell theme, and best dressed contests are, in my opinion, viable choices.

"Ah! Opinions – that, my friends, is the key here. There are many things that are neither right nor wrong. The internet, for example, or television, are just things. We can make them right or wrong by how we use them. Same with movies. There are both good and bad movies. And music, no one style of music is all bad – or all good. It depends on the individual song. I listen to all styles of music, not just Gospel. Jamie and Meghan, my worship team, have taught me that music can be written and sung about all subjects, then applying a Christian viewpoint to it. For example, a romantic love song is a great thing, but a song about cheating, or longing for a forbidden love, is not."

The audience was rapt.

"So, when do we refrain from questionable practices? How do we keep Christianity from becoming the great religion of DON'T! DON'T! DON'T? Listen to what Paul says about this. 'Be careful, however, that the exercise of your freedom does not become a stumbling block to the weak.' I Corinthians 8:9-15 is saying to us that we are wrapped up in a practice, and a weaker Christian is offended by it, that person should become more important than your freedom. In other words, Halloween, playing cards, dancing, buying a Lotto ticket, going to the movies, etc. – may be fine for you and your conscience, but not for all. If it becomes an issue – it's not worth making a brother or sister stumble. In other words, use these things for good, don't be controlled by them. Where is the freedom in that?"

Several people were nodding vigorously.

"I Corinthians 9:19 makes even more clear. 'Though I am free and belong to no man, I make myself a slave to everyone, to win as many as possible.' But listen to the other side of the coin. Verse 22 in that same chapter says this: 'I have become all things to all men so that by all possible means I might save some.' You see, it's not about don't, don't, don't! Instead it's about freedom! Freedom to do things not in contrast to God's word, but also freedom from letting some activity control you to the point of making it an idol. Do you see it?

"I Timothy 4:4 says plainly 'For everything God has created is good, and nothing is to be rejected if it is received with thanksgiving.'

"In those days, people were trying to say it was wrong for Christians to get married and they had to abstain from certain foods. Some of these people even beat their bodies in order to control fleshly desires. Listen also to James 1:17, 'Every good and perfect gift is from above, coming down from the Father of the heavenly lights, who does not change like shifting shadows.'

"Now, as for the real don'ts – adultery just tears up marriages and breaks hearts. Drunkenness leads to acting stupid and even worse, to sometimes deadly accidents. Lying hurts both the liar and the deceived; stealing and murder are obvious, and the same with jealousy or greed. God is not a cosmic policeman. He is a loving guardian, leading us away from what will only harm us. Does this help? I pray it does. To have Christ is to have freedom, not imprisonment!"

The crowd stood as one, including Brent, who felt happier than he had in his entire life. Holding onto him was a most radiant Stacy!

"Now, I know a lot of people say Christianity is just a bunch of compulsive activities we must do: church attendance, constant prayer, keeping your nose stuck in your Bible, and giving every penny to church and to charity. Ladies and gentlemen, I beg to differ! But before we get into that, Jamie and Meghan have a song for you just right for this occasion. Listen carefully to *Ordinary Man*."

I know that I'm not perfect
But I'll do all I can
Have mercy on me, Lord, sweet Lord,
I'm just an ordinary man!

The song indeed hit just the right chord with the crowd, whose hearts and eyes continued to open to the truth.

"In Luke's Gospel, in the eighteenth chapter, starting with verse nine, we find the parable of the Pharisee and the Tax Collector. The Pharisee's prayer is self-centered, as he reminds God of all the religious things he does, and thanks God he is not like the sinners, especially the tax collector.

"Picture if you will a beady-eyed IRS agent who loves to audit the middle class and small businesses, and you will begin to appreciate how hated these people were. When this man prayed, he did it humbly, from far off. All he said was 'have mercy on me, a sinner!' It was this prayer, not the holier than thou Pharisee's, that God heard!

"Check out Romans 1:17, 'for the Gospel a righteousness from God is revealed, a righteousness that is by faith by first to last just as it is written', 'the righteous shall live by faith.' Then get a hold of Ephesians 2:8-10, 'For it is by grace you have been saved through faith – and this is not of yourselves – it is the gift of God – not by works, so that no man can boast. For we are God's workmanship, created in Christ Jesus to do good works which God prepared in advance for us to do'.

"It is nothing we do! It is what He does! We are saved by grace, through faith, because of His mercy and love! Yes, we should attend church; Hebrews 10:25 tells us this. We should pray; Ephesians 6:18 says to do so continually. We should give as we are blessed, and we should rightly divide God's word – but – none of these things should be done compulsively. Instead, they should be a natural result of what God has done for us. The Pharisees became obsessed with piling on more and more rules to try to make themselves holy. It is not how many services you attend per week. It's about what's in your heart as you do these things that do need doing.

"The fruits of the spirit listed in Galatians chapter 5, verses 22 and 23 are the key. Love, joy, peace, patience, kindness, goodness, faithfulness, gentleness, and self-control should become our do's. If they do, all else will follow. Once again, it's all about freedom! So what's stopping you from declaring your freedom tonight? Jesus is your emancipator!"

Randy, flanked by Tracy, now joined Brent and Stacy in the massive flow to the altar. Like his buddy, Randy had never known such happiness and peace in his entire life. Yes, these two were cool college kids with bright futures, but tonight they didn't care one bit who saw their tears of joy flow unchecked!

~

Ah, just like Atlanta all over again! This time, close to 1,400 souls were saved over a three night period, including Mary Jenkins, a private Catholic School graduate with a diploma in Guilt Trip Administration! And yes, it included being hit with a ruler by a nun on the knuckles and told never to think of "nasty boys." Also, Gene Riggins, whose dad had to resign as Deacon of his church because he was caught red handed purchasing a Lotto ticket, came to understand and trust a merciful, loving God, not a prison warden. Then there was Camile Smith, whose parents were publicly humiliated by not being allowed to vote for a prospective new Pastor because they had missed two Sunday night and two Wednesday night services over the preceding month. Ironically, she now planned on attending church as much as possible herself, albeit a different one than her parents attended.

Then there was Brent Bradford and Randy Weatherington, one a victim of "Do's", the other of "Don'ts", and those angelic twin sisters in Christ who had somehow persuaded the two to come out to the crusade. Tim had a feeling he may one day meet up with these four again. He couldn't say how he knew, or what the circumstances would be, but he was pretty sure he would prove to be right.

~

Tim phoned Sarah and the kids and had a wonderful chat with them. As always, waves of homesickness washed over him, but as always, love and peace kept them under control. The weather was warming up back home, and so was his family's feelings. They would be hooking up in a few weeks at home, then go to Kansas City together as Gary and Brooke would be on Spring Break.

The conversation ended on a pleasant note, so Tim was surprised when his cell rang again almost as soon as he had disconnected.

"Hey, sweetie! Need a little more of me, eh?" asked Tim.

"Gee, I'm flattered, but, no, not really!" said Herb.

Tim flushed as he recognized the voice of Herb Paulson, representative of the Calvary Channel, home of Tim's soon-to-be syndicated show. "Oh, sorry, Herb! I had just gotten off the phone with my wife."

"Oh, okay. That's why I couldn't get through."

A pause. "Listen man, I hear you're tearing up St. Louis. Congratulations!"

"It's a God thing, Bro! It ain't me!"

"Amen." Another pause. "Listen, my brother, I'm afraid I have a bit of unpleasant news."

"What's wrong?" Tim's embarrassment instantly converted to concern.

"Believe me, brother, I fought against this tooth and nail, but there's this new evangelist, Phillip Goodman – he's young, Hollywood handsome, and name it claim it, healthy-wealthy gospel through and through! His crusades are blazing like wildfire – and the powers-that-be have decided that he is just the shot in the arm the Calvary Channel needs. We were getting a reputation as a little too old school, so that's the direction they've elected to take. I'm sure God is in this. We still love you, brother, and we know you'll find a place of your own, too..."

Tim was overcome with disappointment. How could he not be? This was supposed to be a done deal. Worst of all, the next excuse was set to begin tomorrow night – "Christianity is for Losers." And now, because he refused to go with the trends, instead, standing firm on the ministry God had given him, he might just be living proof of the validity of this excuse.

Sometimes, however, the help you need is right in front of you, as Tim would soon learn.

Excuse #6: Christianity Is For Losers

Music, despite its beauty, can be cruel. The road to being a full-time musician can also be cruel, but at the same time so addicting it is impossible to leave.

And so it was, on this unavoidable course leading to either disaster or destiny, that the paths of two idealistic and aspiring artists crossed.

As a result, each would become first jaded, then later, redeemed.

It all began at a hair salon.

Jamie Ray chuckled as Sandra Miller ran her long nails through his too-long hair, desperately in need of a shape-up and a good trim.

"Why are all the good ones taken?"

"Now, Sandra, I'm just a part-time musician. I have no money. I have no prospects right now. And besides, I'm not exactly a stud muffin! Look at me!"

"Ewww! No income or looks! What was I thinking?" Sandra pulled her hand away quickly.

They both cracked up.

Sandra resumed her stroking of Jamie's scraggly locks. "Your wife thinks you're hot, and you have a great future!"

"Stephanie's the best! I don't deserve her!"

Sandra slapped his shoulder playfully. "Oh, yes you do! And she deserves you. She is the kindest hearted lady I know, and you're the sweetest man I know! Are you sure you don't have a brother?"

Jamie smiled. "They're both married, too."

"It figures."

Sandra now went about the task of saving Jamie from another bad hair week. As she did, the subject turned, as it usually always did, to music, ministry, and how to coordinate the two.

"Hey, you sounded great over at Harbor Place Saturday!"

"Thanks for coming, Sandra. Unfortunately, you were one of the few!"

"When word gets out, the crowd will pick up. You are one great writer!"

"Thank you!"

"And keyboardist!"

"Thanks!"

"And vocalist!"

"Hey, I promise I'll tip you, even though I'm broke! By the way, how would you like to be my agent?"

"If I knew how, I'd love it!"

A few moments of silence passed.

"So how's your church going?"

"It's okay. You know, same old arguments about hymns versus choruses, and how often the congregation needs to stand."

"Hey, sweetie, it's that way at my church, too. Don't feel bad."

Jamie smiled. Sandra had not always been in church. But thanks to Stephanie, who had witnessed with her life rather than a well-rehearsed presentation, Sandra had accepted Jesus and was now quite active in her congregation.

"You know, it's so sad they call me a bi-vocational minister of music, but with the wages I get, it should be tri-vocational!"

Sandra snorted and patted his shoulder.

"But the worst part is that they won't support the fact that my other job is playing music. How dare I play anywhere except in a church?"

"I bet your witness is at least as strong when you're playing at restaurants!"

"It's not like I'm a Jekyll and Hyde or something. I don't go out to wild bars and sing about drinkin' and cheatin'. I try to perform a mix of old favorites and songs I've written about love and life. No, not everything I write is gospel per se, but it's all from a Christian viewpoint."

"I love those songs I've heard that are for Stephanie! They are absolutely beautiful!"

"Thank you – again! You're worth every penny of the $200 you charge!"

Again, both bent over laughing.

"But I never want to leave God out. I want Him to receive the glory, but it's like if you're a Christian, you can't be successful. I read all those scriptures about not getting hung up on possessions, and how a rich man getting saved is tougher than a camel going through the eye of a needle. But isn't it also true that a man who can't support his family is worse than an infidel? I hate to say this, but I guess I can kind of see how Christians are so often portrayed as losers."

Sandra stopped in mid snip, placed a firm hand on Jamie's shoulder, and gave him a cutting look – sharper than her clippers.

"Jamie Ray, I don't want to hear you say that again. You and Stephanie are my two biggest inspirations. You are a winner! You are going to go far! Trust me! Is that clear?"

"Yes, ma'am."

"Good. Now, we're almost done. Then I'll shampoo it out and make it look great! Stephanie will want a date with you tonight!"

Jamie smiled. Sandra's gift of encouragement was manifesting itself once more. She was a true friend, not always an easy find these days.

"Now don't enjoy this too much, or I'll tell your boss lady on you!" Sandra began to once again massage his hair gently as she started working in the lather of the shampoo. Just as Jamie was relaxing in the warmth of the washing, however, Sandra's hands suddenly went still.

"Hey, that was feeling good!"

Jamie figured he would get a laugh out of Sandra, but she remained still and silent. Finally, she resumed with renewed vigor, and began to talk excitedly, so fast that Jamie had to strain to listen.

"I can't believe it! I can't believe I never thought of this. There's a lady at my church. Her name is Meghan Trenton. She's a great Christian with a voice that gives me, and everyone else, goose bumps. She's all frustrated about what to do with her talent, too. She's a single mom, and her life's not an easy one. You two need to meet!"

"Hey, I'm open to anything right now. The Harbor Place will probably end in a couple of weeks, and I don't even feel secure at my church. Maybe meeting another like-minded person will give me some new ideas!"

"Oh, good! I'll give her your number. Stephanie won't mind, will she?"

"No, we're so in love, and two reasons why are trust and honesty."

"I know that! Great! I'll set it up! Don't be surprised if you hear from her in a day or so."

~

Just as he had been now for so long, albeit for different reasons these days, Troy Trenton filled her dreams. This time, their whole history unfolded before her as Meghan alternated between fitful sleep and fretful awakenings.

It all started in high school. It wasn't the hot shot quarterback or the home run king that stole Meghan's heart. Instead, it was the guitar star with the velvet voice that captured the shy, choir girl's fancy. Every talent show that the school had, Troy won it. Every community-wide talent show he entered, Troy won it. By his senior year, he had put a band together, had his own fan club, and had a couple of pro bono offers from local recording studios.

Troy could have had any girl he wanted. But there was only one girl for him. The girl who refused to surrender her virginity, despite being totally in love with this musical heartthrob. Troy did everything to win her, including making her his backup singer. As it turned out, besides being quite beautiful, the girl could sing!

Meghan stood firm on her Christian values, however. So Troy did the only thing he could to win her intimacy.

Right after graduation, he married her.

He won over Meghan's parents by convincing them he would help her musical dreams come true, also. They invested in the two and helped them move to Nashville.

Troy's career began to take off, first as a session guitarist and vocalist, then as an entertainer in his own right. A Music Row record label caught his act, and took an interest. Meghan couldn't have been happier for her man.

As Troy was surrounded by the town's best musicians, vocalists, and makeover team, Meghan became, unknown to her, a joke among Troy's new friends.

"Lose the choir girl, peckerwood! Your small town churchy days are over!"

Troy had no problem going with the flow. He was embracing his outlaw, playboy image, and talks of platinum CD's, nationwide tours, and major crossover airplay and television appearances had dollar signs dancing in his eyes.

Soon, something else danced into his life – his new backup singer Trish Sturgiss – better known as Trish the Dish. Soon, neither could keep their hands off the other.

Meghan was completely oblivious, much to everyone's amusement. Troy's cohorts helped him concoct a scheme to break the news to his poor, naïve wife.

Troy convinced Meghan to give him a tape of her voice to take to his producer. She did, hardly believing what was happening when she was summoned to the record company's office.

Archie Wayne, the head honcho, called Meghan into his lair.

"Meghan, it's a pleasure to meet you. You have a lovely voice."

"Thank you!" Meghan gasped, trying to catch her breath.

"You have a talent, but it's not what we're looking for here. Get on the church circuit, or maybe even try a little opera. That's more your style."

"Hey, I've thought about that, but really, I'm just happy singing with Troy."

"Well, sweetheart, that's the problem. That's why you're here today, in fact. Troy just can't bear to break your heart, but I'm afraid your stint as his backup has to end. He's going to be a star. You're a good Christian girl. You have no place in this scene. We're talking rowdy, outlaw drankin' music, and Troy is a master at it!"

"Oh." Meghan's face fell.

Troy walked in, Trish the Dish wrapped around him like a grapevine.

"Listen, babe. I have a new backup singer – and a new partner. I didn't know how else to tell you. I'm sorry. But you'll thank me in the long run. Tell her, Arch."

"I'll do better than that. Meghan, Troy has made arrangements to take the best care of you. In this envelope, you'll find an incredibly generous check. All we ask in return is a quiet uncontested divorce, no media involved. Oh, and I have you a list of Christian producers who might just give you a fair listen, especially with my recommendation..."

Meghan woke up crying, tears gushing out of her eyes just as they did on that day of this most strange and cruel end to her marriage. She recalled firing the envelope at Troy and Trish, and ripping up the list of producers, flinging those at Archie in the process. She hurried out of town with what little dignity she had left, and with the one real gift Troy had given her.

Their five year old son, Garth.

~

Troy did help with support, at first, that is, until his flash-in-the-pan career fizzled. He tried to win her back, but it was far too late. She knew the only reason was Trish the Dish had dumped him for the Next Big Thing.

Garth became the center of her life, and she returned to the church of her childhood and began to carve out a life of their own. Was it easy? No. But at least it was real.

But the music never left. In fact, it began to grow inside her as her voice began to improve thanks to some vocal coaching, her only indulgence, and hours of late night practice after all her responsibilities with work and motherhood had been met.

She looked into singing more at churches but soon discovered most of the other women who did this had husbands to support them financially – and emotionally.

She tried out for a band or two – and found she was up to belting out some Celine Dion and Whitney Houston, but her squeaky-clean personality never seemed to mesh with the other members.

Still, the ache continued to grow. There had to be an answer.

Friends were supportive of Meghan upon her return, including some from high school who couldn't believe what a jerk Troy had turned out to be. Garth was a very well-behaved child, so finding a sitter was never a problem. Several men in the church gave him some time and attention, but nothing could replace the permanent father figure he longed for.

One friend in particular, however, stood out. Sandra Miller began doing Meghan's hair soon after her return. At first, the relationship was casual, but, about the time Garth turned ten, their relationship solidified as they took a girls only trip to Savannah for some shopping and fine dining. Garth got to stay with one of his buddy's families, so he was fine. Sandra, a new Christian herself, just had a feeling that Meghan could use a break.

It was during this trip that Meghan was able to share her heartbreak as well as her unresolved dreams of music. Sandra was such an encouragement, and Meghan returned renewed and refreshed. Sandra still longed to somehow be more of a help. She prayed for an answer.

That answer finally came, the day that Jamie received the royal treatment from his favorite hairdresser. As usual, God went beyond the prayer request, and Sandra was able to help not one, but two, of her dear Christian friends.

~

As it turned out, Sandra was not the only one who caught Jamie's gig at Harbor Place.

Also in attendance was Bart Burrows, Head Deacon of Jamie's church, Antioch Baptist.

"Son, the deacons and I have gotten together with the personnel committee, and we all are in agreement. We feel it is a conflict of interest you playing at that restaurant. We realize it is not a bar per se, but they do serve alcohol. Also, although your musical selections were fairly tasteful, they certainly weren't church songs. If you plan on continuing to pursue this line of work as your second vocation, we will have to ask you to step down."

"Sir, with all due respect, I can't. Music is my job. I feel like I can carry my witness a lot of places, and honestly, I feel God wants me to do this. He has given me this talent..."

"So you won't co-operate, then."

"Sir, I..."

"Then I'm afraid we must dismiss you."

Jamie tried so hard to always be nice and respectful, even when he didn't agree. This time, however, something snapped.

"Fine. Maybe God will be able to replace that exorbitant salary of $5,200 a year you're paying me. God bless you, sir."

Jamie arrived home crushed, confused, and already sorry for what he'd said.

He was greeted by the insistent, bright red light blinking on the answering machine. It seemed more harsh than usual somehow.

It was.

"Jamie, this is Kate at Harbor Place. Listen, hon, let's hold off for a couple of weeks. Business is a little slow. I'll give you a call next month if things pick up..."

Jamie buried his head in his hands.

"Maybe Christianity is for losers, after all. So much for trying to do what I feel led to ..."

In his raving, he almost didn't hear the second message.

But the timid yet beautifully timbered alto voice was hard to miss.

"Hi, Jamie. My name is Meghan Trenton. I hear you love music and are serious about making a career of it. Sandra Miller highly recommended you to me. If you would like, give me a call..."

Jamie's day had been a total shipwreck so far. Yet, now, he felt an unexplainable sense of a major shift about to occur in his life.

"Whatever you do, follow through with this," a voice seemed to say from inside him.

He obeyed it.

~

"Are you sure you're up to this, Jamie?"

"Yes, absolutely! I can't wait to hear you sing!" Jamie was struck by the unbridled kindness and sympathy in Meghan's voice. Already, he imagined it set to music.

"Do you know *I Will Always Love You*?"

"I sure do. What key?"

"Try B flat!"

Jamie went into a quite credible version of the song which had become a classic signature song for both Dolly Parton and Whitney Houston. Meghan began to deliver her rendition.

Jamie was spellbound. He almost lost his place several times. To keep focused, he added harmony.

Now it was Meghan who almost lost her train of thought.

"That was beautiful!" The two both said, this time in almost exact unison.

~

Meghan was glowing as she left Jamie's house about an hour and an half later. She would have stayed longer, but Garth needed her, and Stephanie and their young daughter, Isabelle, needed their man.

How refreshing!

This man was obviously in love with his wife and daughter. So many of the other male musicians she had tried to work with always seemed to have an ulterior motive. She found Jamie to be so easy to talk to. She had no trouble telling him her life story – and he actually listened! He had shared his latest disappointments, as well as several of his original songs. These seemed to have parts written in them just for her. She could not wait till next Thursday night. They had agreed to start out making that their standing practice night each week. She hoped that soon they would have to have lots more practice time, as lots of work poured in. It was so nice to hope again.

~

Over the next few weeks, Jamie taught Meghan several of his songs. In addition, they worked out about two hours' worth of standards that would target restaurants. They already both knew a bunch of hymns and choruses for use at churches. Their sound was breathtaking. Stephanie, Isabelle, and Garth all approved.

So now what? It was time to give this dream legs. The first stop was Sandra's salon. Both knew she would be objective without being cruel.

"Oh, my day has been made! Two of my favorite people, right at once! So, can I hear the magic for myself?" asked Sandra.

"You'd better believe it!" said Meghan.

They proceeded to give her an a cappella medley of *Amazing Grace*, *Change My Heart Oh God*, and *How Majestic is Your Name*. They then rendered, *We've Only Just Begun*, *I Will Always Love You*, and *Let It Be Me*. Finally, they put the icing on the cake with parts of two of Jamie's love songs and two of his gospel numbers.

The results? Lots of goose bumps, at least five squeals of delight, and two fierce hugs, one for each performer.

"Okay, I'm good, but I didn't know I was this good! You guys are a perfect musical match!"

"Thank you, Sandra," Meghan said sincerely.

"Thank you, thank you very much! Come on down to Memphis with me baby!" Jamie drawled, causing everyone to crack up. "So, then, what do we do? Find a really nice restaurant? Get on the church circuit? The hotel circuit? Form a band? Hit the studio?"

"Yes!" Sandra replied with a smile that filled her whole face. "All of that!"

"It's been so frustrating. Restaurants are great, but they don't usually last long. Churches can be more political and tougher to crack than the secular market. All bands want to do is practice, have some fun, play some bars, then split up."

"I know. And gospel quartets want to practice constantly. Then, even if they're good and get booked every weekend, they still have to work full time jobs. And hotels? It's so hard to get the managers to see you…"

"And we need to record, but it takes money to do that right, and if you're not working…"

Sandra put an arm around each of them as a gleam ignited in her eyes.

"Let me work on this, guys! God has brought you two together for a reason! I will figure this out! Somehow, I will help you, mark my words!"

~

Before Jamie got out of Meghan's car, he turned to her. "I think we might be good!"

"I think you might be right!"

"We've got to do this! There's got to be a way! I'll think about different ideas we can try! If we can just get some exposure…"

"You're right, Jamie. This is too good to let waste. I'll tell everyone I know about us! I've wasted too much time already!"

"Meghan, you're a genuinely nice person! You're great to work with! You make it fun!"

"You too, Jamie. I know you're a real friend. Where ever this leads, I'm so glad we've met! Thank you for everything!"

They shared a warm hug, full of comfort and encouragement.

Maybe Christianity wasn't only for losers after all.

~

The following Thursday night, Meghan did not come to practice alone, and she was earlier than usual.

Garth was in tow, and quite eager to play with Isabelle.

"I hope Stephanie doesn't get mad, because tonight we have to whip up a demo tape. Sandra assures us we won't be sorry!"

Meghan's enthusiasm was contagious. "Hey, if Stephanie gets some quiet time, she'll love it!"

Recording at home on cheap equipment is tough, but the two had a blast doing it anyway, and in about two and a half hours, they had produced a good sampling of their repertoire. The kids got along great, and Stephanie exhibited the patience that only a long suffering musician's wife can. Jamie made himself a copy of the tape, and gave Meghan the original to give to Sandra.

Before the weekend had passed, Sandra had made their efforts more than worthwhile!

~

Sunday, after church, the Rays had gone out to a nice family meal. Stephanie felt like this happened far too seldom. Between the odd jobs Jamie found to Stephanie's own busy schedule with her executive assistant position, coupled with raising a vibrant, bright daughter, family time was a rare commodity. Yes, it was tough giving away another week night, namely Thursdays, to this Meghan – the singer girl, but Stephanie gritted her teeth and did it anyway. Today, however, was the Lord's day, with family time in between church services.

That's why she got just a bit angry when she saw Meghan's red Camry parked at their house.

"Um, is it Thursday and I just don't know it?"

"No. I wasn't expecting Meghan today."

"Sure you weren't. One day just isn't enough anymore, is it?"

"Honey..."

"Don't 'honey' me! This is our day. I think I've been more than fair about this! Go see what she needs."

Jamie did. She noticed both of them growing more and more animated as the conversation progressed. Then, they ran into each other's arms and shared what seemed like an awfully long embrace. Next they ran over to Stephanie's car window, grinning like opossums.

"Hey, honey. I've got some good news and some bad news."

"Okay," sighed Stephanie, "what's the bad news?"

"You're not going to like this, but Meghan and I have to practice every night this week, that is, up to Thursday."

"Why?" Stephanie did not have a clue where all of this was heading.

"Well, that's the good news! Meghan and I have a gig, a really good paying one, starting Thursday night at Southern Charm Steak and Seafood Emporium!"

Stephanie smiled, jumped out, and hugged them both. So that was what all of this had been about; the tape, the surprise visit today! It had to be the work of Sandra Miller!

"Okay, but you're going to owe Izzie and me lots of presents!"

"Gotcha covered, babe!"

~

The food was delectable (free meals for performers and families were included), the atmosphere was awe-inspiring, and the customers and staff lived up to the name of this earthly taste of Heaven.

Southern charm, indeed.

Tips and compliments flowed freely. It was the highest paying job either Jamie or Meghan had ever held. Stephanie was so proud, and felt so bad for ever resenting those many hours of practice.

Jamie was told he needed to get his songs to the publishers in Nashville. Meghan was told she should head to New York and try out for Broadway shows. Both were told their harmony was impeccable, and they should get themselves into the studio and make a CD – ASAP!

Sandra was a frequent guest, and did her best to promote the two even more. Soon, some wedding gigs and a few private parties began to make Jamie and Meghan even busier.

And yet, something was missing.

No churches.

Jamie and Meghan were not allowed to play anything gospel at Southern Charm. Oh, yes, they slipped a few things in with subtle Christian messages. After all, just about everything Jamie wrote contained them. Still, they felt like they were selling God short.

That's why they were so thrilled when they were approached one Friday evening by a preacher and his family.

"You guys are fabulous! I got chills all through my delicious meal!" The blonde headed wife decked out in red lipstick and matching nail polish exclaimed.

"Amen!" confirmed the evangelist. "Let me ask you, do you all sing any gospel?"

"Absolutely! We love it!"

"We're just not allowed to sing it here."

"Perhaps I can help you with that, and in the process, maybe you can help me!" beamed Brother Timothy Isaac McDonald.

~

As Tim wove the vision of TIME Ministries for them, Jamie and Meghan realized what had been lacking. While their thirst for performing standards remained, the desire to serve God more on the front lines, and to actually win souls, began to boil within them.

"For now, it will be mostly weekends, but this will become full time. God has been preparing me for this for quite a while. I love the music you do here, too. I've always said there should be a place for clean music with positive messages, especially love songs. I encourage you to keep on playing it! We'll even figure out a place for it as we go. The bottom line is, I would be honored to have you two in my ministry. Would you pray about it?"

"We will, but I believe we already have our answer!"

"Yes, we do!" Meghan grinned. "I think this was the real reason we were brought together in the first place."

And so it was that Jamie Ray and Meghan Trenton became an integral part of TIME Ministries.

~

At first, TIME Ministries didn't take up a lot of their time, but the events that did occur thrilled the duo to the soul. There was not much money in it at this point, but God provided by keeping Southern Charm going.

Meghan had to go to Columbia for a couple of weeks in March to help her brother and his family with some personal problems they were having at work that required help watching their children. Jamie agreed to hold down the Southern Charm fort in her absence. Jamie was only human, and had long dreamed of playing a gig like this solo, surviving on the strength of his own music. As it turned out, things went okay. The tips and kind words still ruled.

And yet, it just wasn't the same. Meghan made it so much more fun. He thought about how strong Meghan had to be to do all she did – raising Garth single-handedly while balancing her music and household chores as well. He wished he could find a way to bless her somehow soon. All these thoughts turned into a song, *Too Lovely to be Lonely*. He couldn't wait until her return to surprise her with it.

~

"And now, I want to pay tribute to my most talented singing partner – a great friend and terrific mother! Meghan Trenton, this one truly is for you!" Jamie poured himself into this most special performance.

> *She's too lovely to be lonely*
> *Too strong to be held down*
> *An undiscovered treasure*
> *Just waiting to be found!*
> *In our Lord's perfect timing*
> *Someone shall surely see*
> *She's just too lovely to be lonely!*

Meghan began to cry, then, at the end, she threw both her arms around him and favored him with a kiss on the cheek.

"Just so you know, Jamie's wife, Stephanie, is in the audience tonight. Stephanie, just so you know, you have nothing to fear. I love your husband, but as a friend and musical partner. The truth is, this may be Jamie's best song yet, because it WORKED! While I was gone, I met up with an old friend of mine and my brother's! We have begun dating, and he is planning to move here! His name is Andy Amhearst!"

The crowd roared its approval. The song became one of their most requested, and several people commissioned Jamie to write them a situation-changing tune of their own!

God is good! All the time!

~

But then came the day of reckoning. The school year had just ended for Garth and Isabelle. Meghan and Andy were now engaged, and TIME Ministries was preparing for by far its biggest event yet, a weeklong crusade at Folly Beach. On one hand, Meghan and Jamie were primed and pumped, but on the other, they were frightened. In order to participate, they would have to ask off from Southern Charm. They knew that there were others who wanted their job, and yet, they knew that they could not say no. The owner reluctantly agreed to give them a week off, letting a jazz duo take their place.

That's when God decided to turn everything upside down, as revival exploded on the shores of South Carolina! A week became two, and two weeks became a month. Jamie and Meghan couldn't leave as souls were being saved left and right. Even in the midst of all the joy, however, a blow was dealt to the duo, as the jazz combo took their job. A case could once again be made that Christianity is for losers. Yet, even though TIME was yet to go full-time, Jamie and Meghan felt like they had just won the South Carolina Powerball drawing.

Soon, and very soon, their new job would be full time, and then some.

~

No, things were not nearly as lucrative as they were in the days of Southern Charm. God, however, did provide. TIME Ministries had services, crusades, and events pretty well every weekend now. Even more exciting, though, was the outlook for 2015. Full-time crusade work was slated to begin in January, and talk of a syndicated television show was beginning to become more of a realistic eventuality. Meanwhile, some restaurant work and some weddings kept Jamie and Meghan striving, rather than starving artists. Sarah McDonald's event planning business had more than a little something to do with this.

In December, a wedding of a more personal nature took place, as Meghan Trenton became Meghan Amhearst. Jamie wrote a song for the special day entitled, *Together We Are Beautiful*.

As always, Meghan found the perfect part for herself, and it was definitely a moment no one would ever forget. Jamie had Stephanie come up by him, and Meghan sang to Andy in a declaration of love and togetherness that was beautiful, indeed. They had a gut feeling that one day they would make a CD of love songs, and this one might just be their first release off of it.

Together we are beautiful
Forever we are love
The right words for the right song
Perfect combination
Once empty, our hearts are now full
Together we are beautiful!

And then came January, and the Atlanta crusade. Jamie and Meghan had plenty of hymns and choruses at the ready, and a special song chosen and perfected for each of Tim's messages.

But then, Tim's strange meeting had taken place, and the duo had to rethink everything. Surprisingly, Jamie had a song just right for each excuse. Everything literally fell together overnight, because there was no choice. Because of their willingness to fit into God's plans, history was indeed made in

Hot-lanta, as a Billy Graham size harvest occurred. Never again would Jamie or Meghan ever for a moment think that Christianity is for losers.

But God wasn't done, not even close, in fact, to being done.

Jamie and Meghan would never forget that night in Nashville when the well-dressed but unpretentious man with blue eyes and brown hair streaked with gray had approached them after the service.

"Meghan Amhearst and Jamie Ray. It is a true pleasure to meet you. I love you guys. Your sound is straight from your heart and soul. It's kind of old-fashioned, yet fresh at the same time. Your harmony is quite honestly some of the best I've ever heard!"

"Thank you, sir! You really blessed us saying that!"

"No, thank you! My name is Peter Beck, and I'm a Christian record producer here in town. I can't believe you guys don't have a CD available."

"Well, we're saving up for that. We want to do it right."

Peter chuckled. "I love it! Most people would be groveling at my feet begging me for a contract."

"Well, we'd love a contract one day, when God's timing is right. We're just blessed to be serving Him doing what we love best."

"Guys, I have a news flash. The Head Man just gave me a word for you. The time is now! I would love to sign you two!"

Meghan and Jamie were rendered totally speechless.

"Here's my card. Come to my office at 9:00 am tomorrow. Maybe we can even lay down some tracks."

Jamie and Meghan glanced at the card and their mouths flew open. This man was for real! The label was a major player in the Christian music industry. What had they done to deserve such favor from their Lord? Both knew the answer to that. Absolutely nothing! God did it simply because He is God!

Andy, Garth, Stephanie, and Isabelle all came into town to watch the recording begin. Since this was a quick project, something the two could have for now until the summer when the serious work would begin, it was decided to make it simple, emphasizing the pair's harmony and Jamie's keyboard prowess. The four excuse songs were recorded, along with three hymns and three choruses – a little something for everyone.

Peter talked with Jamie and Meghan about some visions and plans for the future. Talks of extra concerts, the television show, the love songs CD and doing other kinds of music from a Christian perspective, and using all these methods to cross over to a larger audience while never compromising the Christian message. So inspired by these talks was Jamie that he wrote a new song, *As High As It Can Go*, about breaking new ground for God and in love through music and ministry. Peter liked it so much that it was decided it would be the title track of their first national release, slated for July.

Next came St. Louis and the second eerie meeting, followed by the second round of overnight changes. Once again, God provided, including *As High As It Can Go*, finding a place in their plans much sooner than expected.

"And tonight is the night!" Jamie now proclaimed to the Show Me State crowd. "We will now present it to you, then say just a few more words before Brother Tim comes up here. Oh, and by the way, although he allowed us to speak at length for the first time tonight, he promises that he will not be singing for you tonight, or any night in the future, for that matter!"

Peals of laughter filled the building as the two presented their brand new selection, divinely just right for the occasion.

> *I want to go where no one has ever gone*
> *I want to do what they say can't be done*
> *He'll break the barriers down, and*
> *Turn this world around*
> *He'll take my strength as high as it can go*

What followed was the best, loudest, strongest ovation either had ever received in any venue. The audience had been riveted by the life story of these two, and now the songs they delivered were that much more special.

"Just last night, Brother Tim found out his T.V. show set to start this summer had been scratched. It seems a more trendy, but less doctrinally sound program took his place. Now, tonight, he has to come out here and preach to you about Excuse #6 – Christianity is for Losers! Can you imagine how he must be feeling? Even so, he is ready! We hope our story has been a good start in understanding that this simply is not true!"

The crowd roared its affirmation.

"Now, this man of God will come forth, armed with the Sword of the Spirit, God's Holy Word, and totally rip this excuse to shreds!"

A standing ovation greeted Tim's arrival to the front. He smiled, waved, then delivered his opening lines.

"I look at the number of souls saved since this Excuses Crusade began in Atlanta, then I look out at this lovely crowd tonight, and you know what I see? This excuse has already been annihilated!"

The response was thunderous.

"Television shows come and go, but soul winning doesn't! Love lasts forever! God's work is eternal! Now, for anyone who still doesn't believe that, I'll let the sword do the talking for me! We'll look at how this has gotten misconceived, then we'll look at the way it truly is! Are you ready?"

"Yesssss!" they shouted in one voice.

"Matthew 19:24 says this: 'Again, I tell you, it is easier for a camel to go through the eye of a needle than for a rich man to enter the kingdom of God!' If that doesn't point a dismal outlook for earthly success, check this out. Matthew 10:37-39 very loudly proclaims 'Anyone who loves his father or mother more than me is not worthy of me; anyone who loves his son or daughter more than me is not worthy of me. Whoever finds his life will lose it, and whoever loses his life for my sake will find it.' Are you depressed yet? I'll be the first to tell you, I was!! Sometimes, even now, I still wonder – So if you're rich, you are going to have one nasty time of it ever getting into Heaven, and if you love your family too much, you are not worthy of Jesus! And, if you love living, forget you! You should have a death wish and deny yourselves of all pleasures, then you will live! Halleluiah, brothers and sisters! Raise your hand if you'd like to get saaavvvved!"

Some laughter and some musing flowed through the crowd. This really, after all, could get very confusing.

"But wait! What about the fifth commandment, which tells us we are to love your father and mother all the days of your life? How about Ephesians 5:22-25, where Paul puts marriage in the sacred place God intended, 'Wives, submit to your husbands as to the Lord. For the husband is the head of the wife as Christ is the head of the church, His body, of which he is the Savior. Now, as the church submits to Christ, so also wives should submit to their husbands in everything. Husbands, love your wives, just as Christ loved the church and gave himself up for her.'

"Ephesians 6:1-4 extends the love of and for children. 'Children, obey your parents in the Lord, for this is right. Honor your father and mother, for this is the first commandment with a promise – that it may go well for you and that you may enjoy long life upon earth.' 'Fathers, do not exasperate your children, instead, bring them up in the training and instruction of the Lord.'

"Finally on love in general, we turn to 1 John 4: 7,8 – 'Dear friends, let us love one another, for love comes from God. Everyone who loves has been born of God, and knows God. Whoever does not love does not know God, for God is love.' And John 13:34-35 backs this up, removing all doubt. 'A new command I give you: Love one another as I have loved you, so you must love one another. By this all men will know that you are my disciples, if you love one another.'

"So, let's talk about being a winner at love. When Jesus talked about not loving your family more than him – in fact, in Luke 14:26-27, He goes so far as to tell us to hate our wives and families and even our lives – He doesn't mean to have negative feelings for them. He doesn't even mean not to love them with all we have – as the verses I mentioned before make clear. What He means is – nothing can become more important than Him. This isn't an emotional contest, it's a matter of priorities – What if, for example, your son or daughter feels called into foreign missions – perhaps to a place that's dangerous, maybe even life-threatening – and you say 'No!' – First of all, you want your child close by. Secondly, you certainly don't want your baby to be in any danger. Now, if you forbid them from doing the Will of God, you are loving the child more than God. Same with a child who rebels against God, and to make peace and keep your relationship, you allow it. This is loving the child more than God. But wait, is it really love? If you love God first, your love for your spouse, child, parents, friends, and even yourself, is MORE! You heard me, more! If we love our wives like Christ loved the church, what is better than that? Nothing!

"Personally, I can't wait till Jamie and Meghan release a love songs CD! Oh, and remember, Christians even love their enemies! So, when it comes to love, because Christ first loved us, we are Winners!"

The crowd, quiet and attentive at first, was now ecstatic!

"Now, about riches and living. It is the love of money, not money itself, that is the root of all evil. I Timothy 6:10 backs this up. James 1:17 says everything that is great and good comes from up above! Jesus says in John 10:10 that He did not come to destroy but to give us life to the full! Abundant life does not begin in Heaven – it is fully realized there, but it begins now, upon your salvation. No, it does not mean all your problems are solved, but it does mean He is with you every step of the way – and along with those rough times will come many blessings!

"Does that mean material blessings, too? It must, because I Timothy 5:8 states: 'If anyone does not provide for their relatives, and especially for his immediate family, he has denied the faith and is worse than an unbeliever.'

"Ephesians 4:28 adds: 'He who has been stealing must steal no longer, but must work, doing something useful with his own hands, that he may have something to share with those in need.'

"Have you ever heard that old saying, 'Don't let your possessions own you'? That's exactly what Jesus is talking about. In the parable of the rich young ruler that leads us into the verse about the rich man and the eye of the needle, this man was good, followed the law, and wanted to love God, but if it meant losing or giving away his possessions, he had to walk away. Giving away all you own is not a requirement for salvation, but casting out any idol that stops you from loving and obeying God is. If you let other things come first, they WILL own you, and make you miserable.

"If you, as Matthew 6:33 says, 'Seek ye first the kingdom of God, all other things will be added unto you'. Some Christians will be rich, others will be poor, and most of us will fall somewhere in between, but we will all be winners if we elevate God and Jesus to the place they deserve – First Place! Then what is added to us will truly be blessings, and not hindrances. In other words, with Jesus, we win!!"

The crowd stood, yelling and clapping as one.

"Philippians 4:13 boldly proclaims, 'I can do everything through Him who gives me strength.' And Romans 8:37 leaves absolutely no room for doubt; 'No, in all these things, we are more than conquerors through Him who loved us'. So, if we wind up being martyrs for Christ, our lives are not taken, they are given, just as His was for us. If we, like former Cardinal Albert Pujols, become multimillionaires for Christ, you should, as he has, become a Kingdom Builder. Use the talent and position He gives you to give Him glory and to accomplish great things! In conclusion, it is a win-win situation – pun intended! So, who wants to join the winning team, and be a star for the Morning Star?"

The harvest for this excuse was the greatest to date. And to think Tim had been afraid to confront it. But in the end, God raised up Tim's ministry partners and reaffirmed that victory would yet emerge from his own setback. As Tim watched the response, he felt like the MVP of the World Series, Super Bowl, Stanley Cup, and NBA finals all at once. He prompted Jamie and Meghan to sing *Victory in Jesus* as the harvest was reaped.

~

Jamie and Meghan had never felt so truly a part of TIME Ministries as they did now. People were actually coming up to them to express their decision of salvation. Several musicians, including a Hollywood, but not finalist level, *American Idol* contestant, now saw that their newfound faith and talent could work hand in hand rather than in conflict. One couple who had been in and out of church without ever accepting Jesus, were going through the very scenario Brother Tim had spelled out about having a college age daughter being drawn into full-time overseas missions. They now pledged to support her, rather than obsess over her safety, and the fact that she would be far away from them. The result? Their love for each other and their daughter grew rather than diminished as they put God in his proper place – number one!

Jamie and Meghan fell down on their knees in thanks and praise for being allowed to be a part of his work.

Winners, now and forever.

~

The second night, Tim got fired up about Heaven, the ultimate result of Christianity being for winners. The response the first night had been so spontaneous his sermon had been cut short. The concept of a life everlasting in the presence of God reunited with family and loved ones and all believers in a bond so deep earth had nothing to match it, serving Him forever, never growing tired, and only getting better as eternity goes on and on and on...

God knew what He was doing, as always, because it was on this second night that people responded more to this concept of the victory yet to come. In this way, victory now, and greater victory later, were both highlighted in their own right, only increasing the harvest.

Again, Tim met many wonderful people, including Cilia Tompkins, an *American Idol* semi-finalist just back from Hollywood. She couldn't wait to apply her faith to this experience, no matter how far it may yet take her. Also, Dave and Nancy Brisco, whose daughter, Elaine, felt called to India to be a missionary. Tim had to smile as he thought of those faith healers who would call out a person with a certain situation supposedly without knowing about it. Whether these events were always true or not didn't matter – this one was! Tim saw a younger version of himself in Derek Templeton, an MBA candidate with a brilliant business mind who found himself empty after pursuing success for its own sake only. Now he had purpose to put with his potential.

And then up walked Frank Delarosa.

"Brother Tim McDonald! I am indeed honored." He grabbed Tim's hand in both of his. His grip was both strong and warm.

"I'm already a believer my friend! I have been for over thirty years. The name's Frank Delarosa – President of Firm Foundation Network."

"Ah, I'm familiar with that. I watch it sometimes, in fact. The programs seem authentic."

"That's the whole point, friend. I'm not after what sells, I'm after what's true. And you know what? We're doing just fine! God provides! In fact, we've decided to relocate and enlarge our operations. We hope to have this completed in August."

"Praise the Lord!"

"I already know the first program I'm adding. I want an evangelist! I'm not talking about a faith healer or an end times prophet or a health/wealth preacher – I'm talking about a soul-winner!"

"Amen!"

"I have found the man I want. He gets results by wielding the sword of the spirit and speaking in love, not in flowery eloquent words."

"Has he agreed to come on board?"

"You tell me!"

Tim was dumbfounded.

"You're the man, I have no doubt! And I also have some great ideas for your singing duo!"

Tim felt a peace that passes all understanding wash over him. This was real!

"I'll pray about it brother, but I believe God is already weighing in! I feel such an affirmation right now."

"Will it help close the deal if I tell you our new headquarters will be in Charleston?"

Tears sprang into Tim's eyes, and without thinking about what he was doing, he grabbed Frank in a bear hug!

Christianity is for winners.

Game, set, match!

~

Tim had gone through quite a time of uncertainty in college as his faith weakened and the influences of other religions, cultures, and belief systems crept in. Although he rediscovered the Truth, many of the questions raised during this time had never truly been resolved. Even in Bible School. This had required a crash course, because now he had to face these issues head on.

There are so many religions out there – so many ways to Heaven. How can we know Christianity is true – and how can it not accept any other way to God?

Excuse number seven had to be confronted. Tim dealt with his own demons even as he dug in to once again expose the facts.

This one just might prove to be the toughest one yet.

Without God, Timothy Isaac McDonald stood no chance.
But with Him...

Excuse #7: So Many Religions

Ella Evans was feeling lonely.

As usual.

No, Ella was no hermit. She was entering her seventeenth year of teaching at Washington Elementary – this year it was first grade. She liked moving around from grade to grade. This helped her fight that age old enemy of educators, teacher burnout. She was well respected by her peers, and always helped with the planning of social events. She had pleasant, casual friendships with virtually all her colleagues.

And yet, she had very few close confidants.

And no boyfriend.

The problem wasn't Ella's attractiveness. She was quite beautiful. She just didn't know it. Part of the problem was her height. She stood a towering 6'2". Often people asked if she'd ever played basketball. Surprisingly, she hadn't. She wasn't really into sports. Her hair was a very deep brown and quite curly, and her horn rimmed glasses matched it perfectly. Her lenses could not contain her sharp intelligent eyes, as green as a thriving lush meadow in the middle of May. She bore the look often described as sexy librarian. The problem was, she had no clue.

Another paradox was this – Ella loved to talk, often laughed, and had a smile for everyone, and yet, she was quite shy indeed.

Ella longed to meet the man of her dreams, but she was scared to get out and try to meet him. Bars just weren't her scene, but neither were church socials.

Ah, church. That was another problem. Maybe her biggest. A couple of years ago, Ella had attended a conference on dealing with diversity of culture and beliefs. She had always considered herself a Christian, if anything. Now, however, after all of the different viewpoints and worldviews, she literally didn't know what to believe. Was there a God? Who is God? Is humanity good or evil by nature? Are we evolving into gods? Is there a Heaven? A Hell? Is there only one way to Heaven, or God, or are there many? Who is right? Or, is everyone right to a degree? The whole thing made Ella's head spin. One good thing, no one's opinion offended her – and as a result, she prided herself on totally equal treatment of all her students. Yet, deep inside, she felt confused. Her only relief came from exploring these different belief systems. There had to be an answer somewhere...

And then she discovered the New Age Movement. She was presently immersed in studying it more. Here, it seemed, you could have a little bit of everything. Eastern Mysticism, the Occult, Humanism, and even a little Jesus thrown in just to be safe.

So now her time outside of school consisted of researching this school of thought, along with others, and one other thing she had wanted to try for years, finally biting the bullet and joining about a month ago.

An online dating service.

Her pattern of a lot of talking but no serious action was holding sway so far. She had chatted up several prospects, yet had agreed to meet none of them.

But now, finally, maybe that was about to change. His name was Steven. It was hard to pinpoint what made him different than the others. Maybe it was the kind tone in his messages. Maybe it was the lack of obsession with sexual innuendoes. Maybe it was because he just sounded so nice...

Anyway, Ella felt a warmth toward him. She also noticed her heart accelerating as she logged on and searched for his handle – Firefighter Guy.

She was not disappointed.

To Learning Lady, From Firefighter Guy 18 Aug 14.
How was your first day? First grade, eh? You are one brave lady. It takes more courage to do what you do than it takes for me dousing the flames. When you get things settled I would love to meet you. No pressure. We could have coffee or something to start. Have you made any new enlightening discoveries in your search for truth? Your intelligence inspires me.
Waiting to be blessed,
F.G.

Ella smiled and carefully thought out just the right reply.

F.G.
My search for truth continues, but one thing I do know for a fact, you are the inspiring one. While it's true I risk my sanity daily, you risk your life, quite literally. Oh, and speaking of risking life and sanity, how does next Tuesday sound, say around 6:30 pm? I have parent/teacher conferences till six. I'll need a diversion after that. How does Starbucks on 3rd and Main sound?
L.L.

L.L.
I'm there. But listen, don't overrate my value. You know what I did last night? I got two cats rescued out of a tree and put out a small gas fire on a little old lady's stove.
F.G.

F.G.
Now I'm even more inspired. A hero to the elderly and to defenseless animals, a rescuer.
L.L.

L.L.
Do you like cats?
F.G.

F.G.

Yes, I have a white Persian named Fluffy. Is that corny or what?

L.L.

L.L.

That's adorable, but I've got you beat. I have a Dalmatian named Spot!

F.G.

F.G.

Okay, you win. I wonder if the two of them would get along.

L.L.

L.L.

I think it will be an adventure to find out!

F.G.

F.G.

About that truth you asked me about earlier – people come in all shapes and sizes, with different mindsets and perspectives. Don't you think, therefore, that God can come in more than one form? What if all the religions are right to a degree? God may just be too big for one belief system. Now, imagine if we all just worshipped together, however it was comfortable for each of us? We would all come together and unite toward making this a better world. Could that be Heaven?

L.L.

L.L.

You have an amazing mind and heart. I have some thoughts about that, actually. Perhaps I can share then when we meet, if I'm not too distracted by the beauty I will behold!

F.G.

F.G.

Just be warned, you may get more than you bargained for!

L.L.

L.L.

I'm not one of these guys hung up on Hollywood skinny. It's the inner you I'm intrigued by.

F.G.

F.G.

I hope you are serious about that! I know I'm excited to see you! I'm not hung up on physical appearance, either!

L.L.

L.L.
That's a good thing.
F.G.

F.G.
Well, I can't wait. But I've got to get off now – more paperwork of course! But later tonight, I just might return!
L.L.

L.L.
Promises, promises!
F.G

Ella spent the first part of Saturday catching up on errands and housework. Even when living alone, laundry still piled up, dust formed, and vacuuming and sweeping were still required.

Not to mention Fluffy's feeding, watering, and even her – aromatic kitty litter.

After this mundane morning, Ella rewarded herself with a trip to the mall. It was in Macy's that she found the perfect new outfit, a pale pink twin set with matching skirt. She purchased it impulsively. After all, she had to look sharp for her upcoming parent/teacher conversations, the new politically correct term for conferences.

Yeah, right!

Okay, so maybe there was a different reason for spending a little more than she had intended. She smiled as she headed to the food court and treated herself to some greasy, but still quite good, fast food Chinese.

Back at home, full and refreshed, Ella now turned her attention to her new roster of students and their first assignments – information about each one in their own writing. The seeds of intelligence in some of them utterly amazed her.

Stella, the pig-tailed, blue-eyed, blonde, heart stealer, was all about Hannah Montana – or, more accurately, about replacing Hannah Montana. Derek, already a star on his T-ball team, had his eye on Barry Bonds' single season and career homerun records, sans steroids. His shaved head and big-for-his age physique helped add to the picture. For many, it wasn't so much about what they wanted to be when they grew up (Spiderman, a Jedi, first president of the world, to name a few); it was the so too cute comments such as, "I want to trade my two sisters for just one puppy," and "I will be writing a journal on my first grade year – would you like to be in it?" Ella could not remember students being this bright in her day at such an early age. Thanks to the reading specialist, Mrs. Mayflower, some of these kids were already reading 60-80 words a minute.

It wasn't all bright and sunny, though. Some sad stories crept in as well. One girl, Tina, had lost her daddy to the jail for 'loving her wrong'. One very shy fellow named Wayne said his mommy had to leave because his daddy wanted him to have another daddy instead. More than one pupil also made comments about being hungry all the time, or being left alone. As Dickens proclaimed in *A Tale of Two Cities*, "It was the best of times, it was the worst of times." Amen.

On Sunday, Ella went to church her own unique way, by surfing the net. Today she pondered the Jehovah's Witnesses, who's New World Translation of the Bible gave them their own unique perspective. Their beliefs seemed to shift over time, yet no one seemed to work harder to win converts. Going door to door had to be brutal.

She learned that not all Muslims were terrorists. Some seemed like gentle souls who strove for peace, not war, as they tried to work their way to pleasing Allah. It was a shame this side of their faith never got any media attention.

Ella thrilled at the stories of Native Americans and their becoming one with nature and the Great Spirit. It was astounding what these people accomplished in their healing and survival techniques, only to be "Americanized" and forced onto reservations. Ella had a feeling these people would have their day, and it would be soon.

Eastern religion, especially reincarnation and Karma, next seized the Learning Lady's attention. Was it possible that we get to keep coming back until we get it right? That would line up well with God being a merciful Lord. It might even explain the controversial subjects of homosexuality and the transgender movement. Maybe a man felt like a woman trapped in a male body because he was a woman the last go-round, and vice-versa. Ella made a note to bring that up to Firefighter Guy during their next discussion. If only people of all creeds could just open their hearts and minds. Ella felt goose bumps overspread her as she ended things there for the day – quite a stirring church service indeed!

~

The parent/teacher conversations went pretty well as expected. The bright, happy kids' parents showed up, eager to get involved and help in any way, while the at-risk kids were for the most part unrepresented. Ella vowed to let her tolerant and open-hearted outlook lead the way to reaching, without exception, all her students and parents, equally.

She would make sure to send notes home with those whose parents didn't show to come up with an agreeable time to meet, even if it meant midnight on a Saturday.

Feeling resolved, Ella now turned to her next task, freshening herself up for her own conference. She applied some extra lipstick, a light fuchsia; some blush – a pink a shade more pale than her outfit; and some eyeliner – a deep green to complement her brighter green eyes. She smoothed out the wrinkles in her skirt, blouse, and jacket, then briskly made her way to Starbucks.

She arrived at 6:28 pm, exactly two minutes early.

She left at exactly 7:58 pm, her tall figure slumping despite the caffeine racing through her after three large espressos.

Steven had stood her up.

Why?

She found out as soon as her computer booted up the depressing but quite fair explanation.

L.L.

Sorry isn't good enough. Not for you. But my reason is true. Tonight was not about rescuing cats. It was about a house trailer that caught on fire out on the west side. The mother and one of her daughters are in critical condition.
The other daughter didn't make it. We did all we could. It wasn't enough. I'll be able to talk tomorrow a lot better. Will you meet me at your modem then? If you can forgive me and give me another chance, I would love to meet you Friday night. How about a real meal? You pick the place.
Gotta go. I am spent.
Talk to you tomorrow.
F.G.

How terrible! Of course she would forgive him. She had a feeling now more than ever deep in her gut that this guy was indeed a keeper.

She began a mental scroll of her favorite restaurants.

~

This time, Ella went all out – she actually donned a dress! On only the rarest of rare occasions – job interviews, weddings, and funerals – did she ever dare to do it. She felt as though it made her height even more of a deterrence. She had, however, bought wisely; choosing a navy blue and white striped number. Most women would choose vertical stripes to slim down their figure. Ella, though, had chosen horizontal instead, for obvious reasons.

She had chosen, and Steven eagerly agreed, on a cozy, locally owned Italian restaurant that featured soothing live music perfect for ambiance but not too loud for conversation, provided by a very gifted pianist. Ella hummed happily as she grabbed her purse and headed for the door.

Her phone rang.

"No, sorry!" She continued toward the door.

The phone continued, unabated, and like a siren song, it called Ella over to it.

"Hello?"

"Ms. Evans?"

"Yes?"

"This is Sophia Bonham, Tina's mother. Did I catch you at a bad time?"

"No, it's okay." Ella sighed inwardly.

"You said anytime we could meet with you. You could do it, even the weekend. This is urgent, or I wouldn't have called. Tina is screaming for her daddy to come home. I know you know the story. You'd think she would be sickened by him, but instead, he's all she wants."

"That is very common in abuse situations. A love/hate relationship almost always develops. On one hand, I'm sure Tina knows that what is happening to her is wrong, but on the other side of the coin, she craves that feeling of being special."

"Exactly! I was afraid we were even more messed up than we thought. Listen, could we meet? Tina adores you, even after just these few days."

"Sure. I'll meet you at the school in my room in twenty minutes."

"Thank you! Thank you! Thank you!"

As Ella rearranged her plans, in the back of her mind, she still pictured maybe making it to Vierda's in time afterwards.

In reality, the meeting lasted two hours, and although a lot of positives were accomplished, Ella knew this would be far from their last encounter.

She also knew she had just done to Steven exactly what he had done to her just three nights before.

She hoped he would be forgiving.

He was.

They agreed to try again – same time, same place, next Friday. Ella sensed that Steven was dead serious about following through with a face-to-face meeting this time. Not only was it all over his kind words, it was also the fact that he mentioned a couple of things she would need to know before next week.

Nothing bad, L.L., but I do need to be honest. I don't want you to be let down, that's all.
F.G.

Okay, F.G., as long as that works both ways!
L.L.

~

It no longer mattered one iota to Steven what Ella, a.k.a, the Learning Lady, looked like. In fact, Steven had already formed an image of her – a rather robust figured plain woman with short, sandy hair with no style or texture, old school granny glasses with virtually no makeup to enhance her nondescript appearance.

From her eyes, although drab, intelligence would nonetheless shine like a beacon.

Not to mention an incredible, unconditional kindness.

Steven, without casting a single glance at this woman, had fallen head over heels for her, as lovesick as a dog, perhaps even his own Spot, can become over its owner. Steven had been in a couple of close relationships over the years, but at thirty-seven, had never even considered marriage.

Until now.

With a woman he's never even laid eyes on, no less.

Was he crazy? Probably.

He did realize, though, that it was time to get real. First, the physical issue – no, Steven wasn't the ugliest man ever to grace the planet, nor was he anything like Ryan, that much more famous firefighter who had won the heart of Trista on *The Bachelorette*.

Appearance wasn't really the issue.

It was something else.

He hoped Ella was a sports fan. They had never discussed the subject, actually – because, if so, he had come up with a good way of explaining his situation.

If not, when they finally did meet, Ella might be in for more than a bit of a shock.

Or just a slight one, depending on her perspective, so to speak.

But that wasn't the main issue. Not by a long shot. It was the matter of Ella's search for the truth.

Because, unknown to her, Steven had already found it. And unless Ella came to the same conclusions in her search, there could be no future for them.

The thought of that quite simply broke Steven's heart. How, at this point in their relationship, that could be mystified him, yet it was spot on true.

How he would breech this wall was still yet to be determined. Yet he knew it simply must be done.

First, the so-called simple matter.

L.L.
Are you a Cardinals fan?
F.G.

F.G.
Not really, but I think they won something important a couple of years ago – am I right?
L.L.

L.L.
Yes! The World Series, in 2011. But I'm talking about 2006. There was a guy on that team. He's been traded since, but he always seemed to know what to do to win. His name is David Eckstein. He is my favorite player - even now. I followed him until he retired. The same reason I admired Muggsy Bogues, Earl Boykins, and Spud Webb in basketball. Have you heard of any of these guys?
F.G.

F.G.

I can't say that I have. But I would love for you to tell me about them.
L.L.

L.L.

For now, let's just say they made a lot of a little, kind of like me. You know what? Let's just meet. There's something you need to know about me - two things in fact, that might change your whole opinion of me. What I'm getting at with the sports figures is one - the other will have to be explained in person. Let's just do it all in person. Is that fair enough?
F.G.

F.G.

Fair enough. I will reveal my secrets as well. If this is going to continue, we need to face everything head on. I'm ready. Are you?
L.L.

L.L.
Absolutely!
F.G.

This time, as Friday night rolled in and the delectable smell and charming music of Vierda's flowed out into the street, no parent conversation or tragic blaze was on God's schedule. This time Steven and Ella's meeting was inevitable.

Ella arrived first, and ordered a large glass of sweet tea as the tuxedoed pianist rendered a lovely version of *The Rose*. Would this finally be the night? Ella's heart raced at thoroughbred speed.

Indeed it would be. As *The Rose* gave way to *Evergreen*, in walked Steven. Ella heard him announce his arrival to the hostess up front. It was hard to make him out in the dim, intimate lighting, but he certainly seemed decent. Rather well built, even. Something was out of place, though.

Then it hit her.

Amy, the hostess, who had first seated Ella, and was now leading Steven over to join, was a good eight inches shorter than her.

Yet now... Amy appeared to have an inch or two on the man beside her. So that was what Steven had been trying to say – a lot out of a little.

She hoped the lighting hid her blush. What would happen when they stood to leave and her own physical condition was exposed?

For now, she decided to say nothing. She was far too excited, even at this iconic turn of events, to spoil this first meeting with whom she was totally convinced was a most special man.

"Ella!" Steven's face ignited in a light of its own, "You are absolutely beautiful!" His blush, like Ella's, was mercifully masked.

"Hi!"

"Hello!"

They shook hands. Ella squeezed Steven's hand, briefly tracing the calluses on his fingers before releasing it.

Then – silence.

Neither knew what to say, these two who had been burning up the cyberspace chat line for over two months now. Liz, their waitress, broke the tension as she arrived to take their orders – spaghetti with meat sauce for the lady; fettuccini alfredo with Italian sausage for the gentleman. Both were already nervously sipping on their sweet teas.

Suddenly, Steven was struck by inspiration.

"Okay, David Eckstein, Muggsy Bogues, Spud Webb, and Earl Boykins – they all played their sport well – but all were thought too small, in some cases, way too small, to play on any level. But all these guys not only beat the odds, they became outstanding at the highest level – the pros."

Steven abruptly stood, drawing a few stares.

"I'm 5'4" or 5'5" – depending on my hairstyle and choice of shoes – yet I have chosen protector's profession. I honestly hope I can match these men's athletic contributions in my chosen field of firefighting."

Ella smiled warmly. "It sounds like you're well on your way."

Steven wiped his brow. He sighed in relief, and why not? She had not rushed out in horror.

Then Ella abruptly stood. This time, the stares were about double in number. Even a gasp or two and a giggle could be heard.

"I'm not hung up on physical appearance. Are you?"

Steven could not conceal his shocked expression. So he did all he knew how to – he laughed heartily, then held out his arms. She met his embrace. This drew a healthy round of applause. The pianist got into the act, breaking out into a rendition of Sinatra's *Strangers in the Night*.

The ice was officially broken.

"Okay, that secret's out of the way!"

They both fell into gales of laughter. By the time they got themselves back under control, their meals had arrived.

"Well, I guess I kind of gave you an idea how I got into firefighting. How about you? How did you choose a dangerous life-threatening occupation like teaching?"

"I'm crazy, and I'm totally fearless!"

Their laughter returned.

"Actually, my height had a say in my choice, too. You see, I was almost six feet already by the time I hit seventh grade, and I had reached my crest of 6'2" by high school. I was made fun of unmercifully. If I would have chosen to play basketball or some other sport, things would probably have been completely different – but it just wasn't me."

"Hey, you gotta be you."

"That's right. Well, anyway, none of my teachers really seemed to care that much. Oh, they reprimanded the rude comments, but still, nothing they did really changed anything. So I decided I would be different – a teacher who cared – truly cared, and I've done my best to fulfill that."

"From what I've heard, it sounds like you're doing just that."

"Oh, you've heard about me?"

"Just from a couple of parents. But I did not research your appearance or anything else about you. I wanted to be surprised."

"And boy, were you!"

"Yes, that's true. But it's all good, and I mean that." His smile spoke volumes to her still shy heart.

"Which leads me to my other big confession. Professionally, I am totally confident and secure. Socially? Not so much. I have very rarely even dated, and I'm thirty-nine, for crying out loud. So go ahead, call me the Thirty-Nine Year Old Virgin." She blushed profusely with her admission.

"Only if you'll call me the Thirty-Seven Year Old Virgin!" His blush matched hers, as relief flooded over and through them both.

They joined hands, and Ella resumed more in detail her tracing of his rough palms and fingers. Her hands were larger than his, but Steven seemed totally oblivious to this fact. They remained this way several moments, then both finished their meals with increased appetites.

For dessert, they chose a piece of seven layer chocolate cake made for two, with large gourmet coffees to accompany it.

Steven steeled himself, especially now that he was really becoming enthralled totally with this most beautiful woman.

It was time to come clean with his biggest secret.

His perception of the truth.

How would Ella react?

Steven's silent prayer rivaled that of the martyred New Testament saint who was his namesake despite the difference in spelling.

"Ella, I'm really liking you. I mean, a lot! So it's for that reason I have to level with you about something."

Ella grinned, "Let me guess, you're shrinking, and in ten years you'll be a dwarf!"

Steven returned her grin and laughed nervously. "Nope! This is pretty well it! Love me or leave me!"

Ella took his hand and rubbed her thumb across the back of it.

"I believe I'm really liking you a lot, too!"

Steven cleared his throat. "Okay, remember that as I tell you this. In your search for the truth, your open, probing mind always astonishes me. There is, however, one religion, one belief, one world view, you just have trouble handling. You say it's because they are so narrow-minded and outdated."

"That would be the Fundamental Christians. The ones that say either Jesus or Hell, that homosexuality carries a death sentence, that women have no right to choose abortion..."

"Well, I is one." Steven's childish misuse of grammar was intended to take out the sting of the statement.

It didn't.

Ella's face heated and fell.

"But you seem so different than that."

"I am, not in my beliefs, but in my attitude. Most of us are more loving than we are given credit. Unfortunately, there are some holier-than-thous that bring us down."

"Jesus I can handle. Many religions agree He was a great teacher and healer. How can you not admire someone who helps the blind to see and the lame to walk, not to mention his love for children?"

"He is all of that, but He's so much more! He's my Savior, my Lord, and my Best friend. I am not a Bible scholar, but I know He's real."

"How can you know He's the only way? The Koran professes Allah, Confucius has many wise sayings, Buddha was a great thinker..."

"I know that I know that I know.. It's hard to explain, but I do."

"But is He the only way to Heaven? I've read about Native Americans, New Agers, Hindus, Hare Krishnas, and yes, even Muslims, who are so sincere about their religions – Why can't they all be right to a degree? How can you put God in a box? Wouldn't He want to relate to all races and creeds?"

Steven knew Jesus did just that, but he could not intellectually argue the way Ella could.

"And who's to say reincarnation isn't real? It allows you to pay for your sin and have another chance. It could explain homosexuality. How could you fault a man attracted to other men because he was a woman last go around, or vice versa? And doesn't the Bible suggest it? I know there's something in there about John the Baptist being the second coming of Elijah? I believe Jesus even says that Elijah came back but no one recognized him."

Steven wasn't up on his scriptures as he should be. He made a silent vow to change that ASAP.

"Ella, my feelings for you are unchanged. I feel my heart surrendering even now. But, we will have to come together on this somehow for us to work. I'm going to pray. I do not have all the answers, but I believe He does."

"My feelings for you are unchanged as well. You seem so different than others I've heard or read about who believe the way you do. I am open to listening."

"That's totally fair, and that is exactly what I expected from you."

The conversation became light after this as dessert was completed (only a few crumbs remained), and the evening drew to a comfortable close.

And yes, the date ended with a kiss. This date would no doubt be the first of many. Was God in it? Steven had never hoped for anything as much.

~

Over the next few months, several things happened. Steven dove into his Bible, and he read some books by Lee Strobel and Josh McDowell defending the faith intellectually. He was amazed to learn that in tracing back time, there was a period of twenty four hours and ten minutes that could not be accounted for. This could very well explain the day the earth stood still for Joshua and the request that King Hezekiah made for the sun to go back a bit in its light on his floor as a sign God would heal his disease.

Steven was also enraptured by the fact of how well the Bible has stayed preserved, and how far back its manuscripts could be traced; way further back than any other writings. In fact, it wasn't even close!

Ella loved all this information, and seemed to take it to heart. Still, she resisted accepting Jesus as the only way. She did let Steven know that she was more fascinated with Jesus now, and that her studies of Him would be increasing. Unfortunately, she became enamored with the so-called hidden gospels, such as Thomas, Phillip, Judas, and Mary Magdalene. Those all seemed to confirm her belief in multiple religions intertwining, and Jesus being in the middle of it all.

Through all this, Ella and Steven continued to chat and to date. They grew close in so many ways. Ella began to secretly browse through bridal magazines, dreaming of the perfect wedding even though Steven was yet to pop the question.

As for Ella's teaching, this class was proving to be a special one. She had managed to have conversations with every single child's parents (or parent). She had sparked the intellect of the smart pupils while providing for the ones in desperate need. She had especially grown close to Tina Bonham and her mother, Sophia. Tina was still having separation anxiety about her dad, but Sophia was resigning herself more and more to divorce. Dennis was getting out of jail by year's end, and it was time to decide what to do. Ella told Sophia that for Tina's sake, there really wasn't a choice. End it! Now!

~

Steven almost did it at Christmas, but he still couldn't. Not yet. He wanted to present Ella with an engagement ring on that most sacred of days, but the sacred issues weren't yet resolved. He opted instead for a journey pendant, showing a love growing over time, along with earrings to match. For now, it would have to do. Steven prayed for something to help him finish breaking through to this woman, whom he now thought of as the love of his life.

~

Ella just knew he would do it at Christmas, so it was all she could do not to show her major disappointment at what was actually a most loving and beautiful gift. She knew the reason he was holding the last part of himself back. She wanted to simply believe, but to her, the truth still seemed far too big to be contained in a single point of view. Maybe 2015 would bring some sort of resolution to all this. She did not want to lose this man, whom she now thought of as the love of her life.

~

Ella received the phone call that would impact the rest of her life on Friday night, January 2, 2015, right at the beginning of the last weekend of Christmas break.

"Ms. Evans, th – this is Sophia."

The distraught sound of her voice pulled Ella awake instantly.

"Hey, hon – what's wrong?"

"Everything! I'm in the hospital. Can you please come?"

Ella's internal alarm was blaring as she quickly took down the information and her room number without bothering to ask for details. She got ready much faster than on a school day, and was by her friend's side in under half an hour.

"Oh, Ms. Evans – I blew it! I totally ruined everything! Oh, God, I'm so stupid!"

"Please, call me Ella." Ella took Sophia's hand, noting that it, her arm, and virtually everything else that was visible was covered in ugly squall-cloud purple and black bruises.

"He sounded so sincere. Dennis got out right before Christmas. He came home to us full of sweet words and apologies. He treated us like his queen and princess. He said all he wanted for Christmas was a second chance. Dennis is a macho guy, a man's man, yet he was crying like a baby."

"You took him back."

"Yes! I'm so gullible!" Sophia slapped herself in the face as Ella watched in horror.

"At first, it was like a second honeymoon, but then, on New Year's Eve, he advanced on Tina right at midnight. I wasn't feeling well – a horrible cold – and I'd turned in early. I figured the New Year would wait till morning for me." She broke down again into gut-wrenching sobs.

"Tina told him NO! She said her favorite teacher had told her it was wrong what he was doing, and that mommy should leave him! He slapped our daughter, then forced himself on her."

"You're mine! No one loves you like me!" he had screamed, which is what woke me. He screamed that you were a lesbo Amazon feminist Nazi, and that you and I were probably having an affair. I pulled Tina away, and hit him with all I had. He grabbed me by the hair, threw me across the room, grabbed Tina, locked her in our car, then came back and beat me unconscious. He sped off with our baby – MY BABY! She's still with him! NOOOOOOO!!!"

Sophia, as if realizing this fact for the first time, almost jerked off her IV in an attempt to get free. The nurse came running, and Sophia was quickly given a sedative.

Ella remained with her friend most of the weekend. Then, on Monday morning, she prayed to whomever that Tina would be back to school.

She wasn't.

It wasn't until Friday that Tina was finally back in Ella's classroom. Dennis had been found and was back in jail. Tina's grandmother was providing her a home until Sophia was released, which appeared to be that weekend or early Monday.

Yes, Tina was back, but only a shell of her former self. Ella would basically be starting from scratch. How could an evil person seem so sweet and so sincere? Who could you really count on? Lies could sound just like truth. She needed to talk to Steven in the worst way. She was glad it was Friday, their standing date night since their first meeting.

"Deep down, we're all liars. Deep down, we are all tempted. We are evil by nature. But we have a choice. A way out!"

These words no longer sounded to Ella quite as narrow and trite as they once did.

"I am beginning to see that somewhere there has to be some absolute right and absolute wrong. Be patient with me, dear, I'm trying!"

The two joined hands, as they so often did. Steven prayed, and this time Ella joined him, as the shell around her heart began to slowly crack.

In February, Ella visited Steven's church for the first time, and did not run out screaming. She even was intrigued by the revival tearing up the South and heading their way. Brother Tim, like Steven, appeared to have a sweet spirit, not a condemning one. When the crusade hit St. Louis, Ella agreed to go.

Ella attended one "Do's and Don'ts" session, and one "Christianity Is for Losers" service. Her mind marveled at the logic that was somehow more than logic. Still, however, she couldn't bring herself to surrender fully. Steven kept praying – so close! So close! What was God waiting for?

Then, like the balm in Gilead, came the seventh excuse – Too Many Religions. If Steven had to tie his love up, and drag her there, he would.

It was not necessary. Ella was bursting to go. Finally, someone had honed in on her exact questions and doubts.

Steven, thanking God in advance, drew his woman close. Hand in hand, they prepared for this service, pre-ordained perfectly by the Master Teacher and Fighter of Hellfire.

~

"Listen, young people, the idea of an absolute right and wrong is archaic! Obsolete! Over and done! Times are changing. Divorce is not scandalous – it's simply convenient for many – a way to prevent even worse problems! Homosexuality is not an illness. It is not even a choice! Remember when 'living in sin' was so disgraceful? Please! If we will just let each other be; the biblical new earth and heaven might actually occur then! Hey, I'm not knocking Jesus – He's cool! A great teacher, no doubt – but many religions agree on that..."

Timothy Isaac McDonald was quite shaken by this lecture from a Sociology professor his freshman year. He found several others concurring, both students and faculty. He began to see this might just be the key to real freedom and truth. He began to drink, something he had never dreamed of doing in high school. He studied Eastern religions; New Age practices, and even dabbled in the Occult. He found a mix of marijuana and Tarot cards to be quite mind-expanding on future predictions and everyday problems. He fell into the hippie views of "yo, whatever, dude!" and "if it feels good, do it." By the time he met Sarah at that fateful frat party, his virgin days were far in the past.

Tim almost became a true apostate. But it was not this that caused it. The real reason for that he could not yet process back through.

That would come soon enough.

But he had come through, by that grace that can only be referred to as amazing, and he was ready to face this first set of demons. Excuse number seven was now in the spotlight.

"Has anybody here ever checked your horoscope? Come on now, be honest."

Over three-fourths of the masses in attendance raised their hand, including Tim.

"How about Tarot cards, or a psychic reading?"

Again, very many responded affirmatively. Again, Tim included himself.

"Listen, people. There are a lot of beliefs and intriguing possibilities out there. Choices abound everywhere. Choices and changes, and new ways to look at things. So, are all religions at least a little bit right? Can you be a New Age Christian, or a Christian Buddhist? Is there anything to psychics, reincarnation, and higher consciousness? Is Jesus just a great teacher that can fit into all this? No! No! No!

"There is one person behind all these other religions. Not God – but SATAN! He thrives on confusion. There are two choices, folks – as Bob Dylan once sang, 'it might be the Devil, or it might be the Lord, but you gotta serve somebody!'

"Now, let me show you Deuteronomy 18:10-12 proclaiming, 'Let no one be found among you who sacrifices his son or daughter in the fire, who practices divination or sorcery, interprets omens, practices witchcraft, or casts spells, or who is a medium or spiritist or who consults the dead. Anyone who does these things is detestable to the Lord and because of these detestable practices the Lord your God will drive out those nations before you.'

"How about reincarnation? A lot of people try to say it's mentioned in the Bible when John the Baptist was Elijah returned – but Jesus clearly says John came 'in the spirit of Elijah' that is, in God's spirit and will. The true word on reincarnation is found in Hebrews 9:27-28, 'just as man is destined to die once and after that to face judgment so Christ was sacrificed once to take away the sins of many people, and He will appear a second time, not to bear sin, but to bring salvation to those who are waiting for him.' So forget good and bad karma, folks, we do only go around once, and then the choice is simple: Jesus leads to Heaven; anything else leads to Hell.

"I know! I know! Harsh, old-fashioned, and narrow-minded, right? Maybe, but it's the TRUTH! Deuteronomy 6:4 tells us the Lord God is one. Balaam the prophet tried to mix religions to compromise after his curse on Israel turned to blessing, and it did indeed foul things up. King Solomon dabbled in the New Age movement by multi-god worship compromise, and his son's kingdom became divided! That's right, the New Age movement is not new. In fact, it began in the Garden of Eden when the serpent told Eve if she ate the forbidden fruit, she could 'become like God'. Today, we are told that humans may well be evolving into gods. I choose to call it the Old Lie Movement. Jamie and Meghan will say in song now. Prepare to be rocked by *The Latest Lie!*"

Jamie and Meghan shifted styles as this old-fashioned Hell-and-Brimstone message got a shot of contemporary rocket power. The crowd plugged into it.

> *That's not love, they're playing with your heart*
> *Their methods tear your mind apart*
> *They weave a web around your life*
> *They laugh, as they gently take control*
> *But very soon, they will be exposed*
> *As just the latest lie!*

After the explosive reaction, Tim came right back out firing himself. "Straight is the gate and narrow the way! It's true! Jesus tells us that many take the broad and crowded path but few find the narrow but true road. And yet, that road is the ONLY way to Heaven. Jesus, that 'great teacher' that supposedly can fit into any religion says in John 14:6, 'I am the way, the truth, and the life. No one comes to the Father except through Me.' Acts 4:12 confirms this, 'salvation is found through no one else, for there is no other name under Heaven given to men by which we must be saved.' Jesus is either telling the truth, or He is a total lunatic – you cannot have it both ways! Yes, I'm an old-timey, screamin' preacher tonight, and that's not like me, but I'm like this because I almost fell for all this myself. For a while I lived only to gratify myself, and I tried all kinds of religions along the way to make it all mesh – but it's all LIES! Colossians 2:8 pulls no punches, "see to it that no one takes you captive through hollow and deceptive philosophy, which depends on human tradition and the basic principles of this world, rather than on Christ.'

"There are all kinds of cults, too, from Satanism to pseudo-Christianity, and everything in between. There are religions and non-religions and combinations of all these things. As far as Satan is concerned, the more the merrier. Did you know that people who study how to recognize counterfeit money do not spend their time studying fake currency? Instead they learn to recognize the real thing, so they can always know the difference. Yes, I do encourage you to learn about the cults and religions so you can help the people caught in these various untruths. But, it is much more important to know Jesus, the author of truth, and the Holy Word of God! I almost fell for Satan's trickery, but God wouldn't let me! He wouldn't – let – me!" Here, Tim cried openly, for more reasons than anyone except Sarah knew.

"So how about it? Who wants to join me on the King's Highway?"

The road to Heaven is indeed narrow but on this night, it was quite jammed indeed. The biggest one-night harvest yet – over seven hundred – walked it on this evening. Over the next three nights, the grand total ran to over two thousand – large even by the standards of TIME Ministries.

~

Ella Evans' mind, heart, and soul exploded with joy as she was one of the first to reach the altar. Steven, despite his strength, felt himself being dragged by Ella's overwhelming desire to be the first in line.

And he loved every minute of it!

~

Tim, as always, marveled at the diversity and uniqueness of those who found Jesus through his challenge of this excuse. Alec Gage, a hard-core Satanist, all in black laid all his soul's darkness at the cross. A psychic who was quite successful in her craft walked away from it all without a glance back. She ripped up her Tarot cards, shattered her crystal ball, and forever buried her title – Madame Theresa Joan. From Buddhists, to New Agers, to cultists of all shapes and sizes and flavors, and even Native American Spiritualists and Koran-toting Muslims – all were accounted for. And in the true nature of tolerance and diversity, all were wanted in the Family of Christ.

Tim smiled as he remembered the first couple to come, the tall drink of water named Ella Evans and her vertically challenged (at least next to Ella) significant other who had helped lead her to the Lord. He would later perform their wedding – 'the Learning Lady and the Firefighter Guy'! What a creative, imaginative, never boring, loving God he served!

~

Brother Tim had no time to bask in the afterglow this time, even though it was the brightest one yet. Because now, Tim's toughest test stared him straight in the eye. Nothing else remained. The demons that had almost prevented any of these other events that transpired, and that, despite everything, had never fully been defeated, now emerged in all their black anti-glory, ready to demolish TIME Ministries utterly and completely.

Even so, Tim mounted his spiritual steed, put on his full Armor of God, and prepared for the battle where absolutely everything would be at stake.

Excuse #8: Why Does God Allow Suffering?

No, her name wasn't Lois. But it might as well have been, because if ever there was a godly grandmother, it would have been Martha Morris. From Bible stories to home baked chocolate chip cookies, from homespun humor to a shoulder to cry on, Martha had all the bases covered.

Her husband David was a quiet man, but a strong support. That was fine, because Martha talked enough for both of them. Together, they formed a dream team of grandparents, and all seven of their grandchildren were frequent visitors in their warm, welcoming home. All were doted on equally.

Yet, there were two of them who were luckier than the others. The reason? They just happened to live next door.

Janet, the oldest, was lavished with Barbie dolls, pretty clothes, a dollhouse, and countless trips to McDonald's. Much more than this, however, she was shown and given a very clear model of unconditional love. The toys she received were often rewards for voluntarily memorizing scripture and having perfect Sunday School attendance. These things were never forced on Janet, however. It was all about love, laughter, and an always open sanctuary, even when things at home were less than perfect.

Janet's mother, and Martha's daughter, Tabitha, was no Eunice. She was at best a nominal, passive Christian whose religion centered on making sure her children were in church. As for herself, she figured she'd more than served her time growing up. Sundays now belonged to her. Bryan, her former jock husband, was all for a kid-free, work-free day at home.

As Janet grew up, there were some bumps along the way. She and her mother were just alike – outspoken and strong-willed. As a result, they clashed. On more than a few occasions, Grandma played peacemaker. Usually, Janet thanked God for having such a devoted advocate.

There were, however, a few exceptions. When Janet had done something that involved intentional disobedience to God, that's when Martha's other side emerged. Katie bar the door when that happened.

And so it was on that fateful evening of Janet's fifteenth year, when she found herself totally petrified to enter the house where almost always only pleasant memories dwelled.

This time, Janet had sinned, even by her lax parent's standards. The temptation, as is and was so common in the years of puberty, adolescence, and raging hormones, was a quite attractive member of the opposite sex who happened to be in Janet's youth group at church, and in most of her classes in high school.

Anthony Adams was on the basketball team – or more accurately, he was the star that anchored that year's varsity squad. At 6'3", he could score and rebound, and was averaging a double-double (double digits in both of these categories) for the season. A high GPA would no doubt seal the deal and ice the cake for a sky's the limit future.

And wonder of wonders, he had chosen to bestow his attention upon Janet. At first, it was just a strong platonic friendship, but as time passed and they grew closer, kissing and hand holding began in earnest. Stolen moments both at school and church became more frequent as the days passed.

Then came Valentine's Day.

He gave her bright red roses, and she favored him with dark rich chocolate. So involved were they in thank you kissing, then thank you petting, that they missed their 11:30 pm curfew.

By four hours!

No, their sin was not sex, although they did push the envelope about as far as they could have without performing intercourse. The problem was they fell asleep in Anthony's bedroom, and a red-faced Arnold Adams, a Sunday School teacher at their church, happened to catch them as he had gotten up for a snack and made a routine check of all his children's rooms.

No, they didn't have sex, but they might as well have, for all the fallout that resulted. Both were grounded from all but church activities for two months, and even there, the two were not allowed alone.

But for Janet, this was not the worst of it. She was turned over to Grandma for what would no doubt be the worst lecture of all time. Even worse, she was sure Grandma would cry because her precious granddaughter had let her down.

That was the worst of all.

Janet entered Martha's living room, where Martha was perched cross armed on her mauve and tan sofa. Janet tried to hide her trembling hands. Martha remained silent. David had chosen to run to Walmart to pick up a few groceries, leaving the two alone. Finally, Janet could take it no more.

"G-Grandma, I promise we didn't have sex. We just fell asleep. Anthony is a good Christian. Yes, we got carried away, but we both knew when to stop..." Janet's body shuddered with sobs.

Martha rose from her seat, took Janet by the hand, and led her to the couch, where she took the not-so-young child in her arms, rubbing her back and rocking her gently.

"I believe you. I really do."

The comforting continued for several minutes.

"Now, darling, you know, appearance as well as actions, are important. Even if something isn't so bad, it can still be a stumbling block for others. What if one of the youth group who wasn't saved, or who was considering pre-marital sex, had seen you at your boyfriend's, in his bedroom, at 3:30 am?"

"I know – I'm so, so sorry..."

"I know you are. Now sit up here and wipe those tears. You know, it just so happens I made a batch of heart-shaped cookies, and it so happens there are some left..."

"Could I have milk to dip them in?"

"Child, that's always been your favorite snack. The milk was automatically included." She kissed Janet, who returned it with her first smile since her rude awakening.

Grandma's biggest surprise, even sweeter than the cookies, came next.

"Listen, dumplin', I've been praying a lot about you. And you know what? I think you should take your punishment with dignity. But when it's over, I think you and Anthony should keep seeing each other. Take it slow, but I believe he's a special young man. Then, I want you to keep me posted, okay?"

Janet could not believe what she was hearing. She cried all over again, this time because she was so touched by her grandma honestly understanding just what she needed.

~

Soon enough, Janet graduated and headed away to college. She wound up dating a few other guys, but in the end, Anthony, who received a call into youth ministry, and she got back together and married. The wedding was glorious, but there was something important missing.

Martha.

~

Martha had one more grandson to spoil who lived next door. Elvis, Janet's younger brother, worshipped her even more devoutly than Janet, if that were possible. Martha never missed any of Elvis' baseball games – from Tee Ball through Little League, even when she suffered a broken arm and battled with chronic bronchitis and allergies.

Every Friday morning, Elvis had breakfast with Grandma and Grandpa as his mom went to the beauty salon and his dad went to work at the Coca Cola plant. Scrambled eggs, crispy bacon, and towering homemade biscuits with honey were five-star dining in Elvis' eyes. But even more delicious was the love that always surrounded him there.

Then came Elvis' tenth birthday, one he would never forget. By this time, he was no longer having his Friday breakfast, because Bryan, Elvis' dad, had been laid off from the plant, thusly Tabitha's weekly pampering had to be greatly curtailed. All of this did not stop Elvis from dreaming, both day and night, of the present he would have given anything to receive that year.

A bright green ten-speed shiny new bicycle; a Schwinn model, to be precise.

He had tried to save his allowance for it, but of course that had been cut back, as well. He tried offering to do special chores, but the money just wasn't there. Grandma and Grandpa talked lovingly but firmly about love and togetherness over material possessions, so even they would be of no help on this one. Still, in the heart and mind of an almost ten year old, hope burned bright. He just knew there would be a way.

The big day arrived, but the bike did not. Elvis tried to be excited about the baseball cards, new jeans, and super-powered flashlight he received.

He also smiled through his requested birthday meal of a Big Mac and large fries from Mickey-D's, and his D.Q. hot fudge sundae, in lieu of a cake, for dessert. He hugged his parents warmly and told them how much he loved and appreciated them. He meant it, too, but still…

Later that night, Grandma and Grandpa had him over for some special time. Grandpa, as usual, slaughtered him at checkers, but Elvis did get in a couple of good moves for a change. Grandma watched a couple of Scooby-Doo episodes and part of the Braves/Cubs game with him. Elvis began to realize this was a pretty good birthday after all, all things considered.

At about 10:00 pm, it was time to head home. Late for a school night, but for today it was just fine.

"Hey, boy," Grandpa called as Elvis was leaving, "your Grandma needs some help out in the garage. There are a couple of boxes she needs brought in. Actually, they're not heavy. I think she just needs a little more of your company."

Elvis beamed with pride. He did feel a little older.

"No problem, Grandpa!" Elvis grinned as he headed out to join her. He certainly didn't mind the extra time and attention either.

"Oh, hi, sweetie! I've got two of the boxes down, but this third one's a little bigger. Could you lend me a hand?"

"Sure, I'll be glad…"

But Elvis lost his ability to speak as he saw the 'bigger' item to which Martha was referring.

A bright green, ten-speed, shiny, new bicycle; a Schwinn model, to be precise.

~

Sometimes, she hit the situation head on; sometimes, she handled the matter in a much more subtle fashion. Either way, Martha Morris was a problem solver. One night in the fall semester of Elvis's sophomore year, she exemplified both approaches as only she could.

"Grandma, I don't get this. It says to reduce ($\frac{36a^5b^7c^4d}{24a^3b^2c^3e}$) to its simplest form. This might as well be Greek. I don't even like regular fractions, much less this algebra gibberish."

"Mom or Dad can't help, either, eh?"

"No, they're… never mind." Martha winced inwardly at this. There was big trouble here, but no one had bothered to confide in her, not even her own daughter.

"Ah, algebra. I bet you think I'm too old for that new-fangled math, don't you?"

"Grandma, nothing would surprise me about you."

"God has blessed me, dear heart. Now, let's start with 36 and 24. Could those be part of a times table?"

126

"Well, they're even – and, well, they both are; well, I think three would work and maybe four, too. Yeah!"

"How about six?"

"Hmm. 6 x 4 = 24, and 6 x 6 = 36. Yes!"

"But there's something even bigger."

Elvis thought deeply, his mind straining. He was no genius, but he was no slouch, either. Then it hit him.

"Twelve!"

"You got it!"

"12 x 3 and 12 x 2. So it's $\dfrac{(3a^5b^7c^4d)}{2a^3b^2c^3e}$. Now what?"

"a^5. That's like a x a x a x a x a, right?"

"Yes. I actually get that!"

"Good. So A^3 fits, right?"

"Yes. So it's A^2 over nothing?"

"Not nothing. $A^5 \div A^3$ is A^2, as you already figured out. Just subtract the exponents. So what's $a^3 \div a^3$?"

"a^0."

"Which is?"

"Oh! One!"

"Right. So there are no a's on the bottom, which means one, which does not need to be written, but why?"

"Because anything times one is itself! I see what you're saying! Wow! I actually get it!"

So on it went, until the final answer $\dfrac{(3a^2b^5cd)}{e}$ was achieved.

"I think I can do these, now. You are a genius, Grandma!" He embraced and kissed his beloved, maternal grandmother, something he was doing a little less these days because of his age.

Martha blushed with delight.

But then Elvis grew quiet, his face becoming sad.

"So why do I sense there are bigger problems here than polynomial fractions?"

"Grandma, if I needed to live with you, could I?"

Martha didn't miss a beat. "Of course, precious! But wouldn't your parents miss you a little?"

"I'm not sure." Elvis hung his head.

Martha waited patiently for him to be ready to expose at last what she knew had been building for a while.

"Well, Dad's decided Mom's too old for him. He's flipped for some hot-shot twenty something supervisor at his new sales job."

"Oh, honey..."

"He's leaving Mom for her."

Martha could not hold back this time. She took him into her arms. Elvis showed zero resistance.

"But it's not just him. Mom is cheating on him, too. With a used car salesman! Gimme a break! I don't want to be with either one of them. Please let me stay here, Grandma! Please!"

For a while, no words were spoken. Grandmother and grandson just held each other, both needing comfort from the other. Martha was ready to yank a major knot in both her daughter's and son-in-law's tail. Elvis felt doubly betrayed, and longed only for a house once more filled with love.

"Honey, if it comes down to it, you can most certainly live with your Granddad and me."

~

As it turned out, both his parents shook off the temporary insanity that often accompanies a mid-life crisis, and got back together. Elvis was relieved but he still spent over half of his home time next door, where he had always felt the most loved and the most happy.

~

Martha and David beamed with the pride only grandparents are privy to as Elvis graduated from high school two years later. Although his grades, especially in math, had improved, he was still not a top flight student. Although his guidance counselor had told him his dream of attending the University of South Carolina was not out of reach, she had also explained that he would have to work doubly hard, and he would probably not be receiving a scholarship.

She was right.

Elvis was in a bad spot. His parents (his mom now worked as an assistant office manager and dad had secured a promotion to sales trainer in the same company) made too much money to qualify for financial aid, but not enough to actually send Elvis to college. Elvis wanted so badly to have a chance to achieve something and become someone who had a career, not a job. But now, it seemed life was not in the mood to deal him a winning hand. He took a job at Sonic, deciding he'd become a manager there, if nothing else.

~

"Well, honey, I've been running some figures, and we finally have enough!"

"Oh, David! Are you sure?" Martha suddenly appeared twenty years younger.

"Absolutely, sugarplum. These two old fogies are headed to Europe for the dream vacation we've waited all our lives for!"

They both began laughing, hugging, kissing, then dancing around their house. They had given up so many items and trips over the years in place of this one big adventure both had agreed to one day share together.

That day had come!

They kissed some more, then David swept up the love of his life in his arms and they plopped down on the couch together in fits of laughter. Finally, they quieted as the reality of it all set in. This was so much better than instant gratification, which seemed more and more the norm for the younger generations. They joined hands and gazed with loving joy at the family photos featuring all their children and grandchildren whom God had so richly bestowed upon them to fill their lives. As they both turned to Elvis' graduation picture, framed in an ornate gold border, they both smiled and tightened their hold on each other's hand.

Both knew, without a word being spoken, that their vacation would simply have to wait, and neither had a single regret. They decided not to tell Elvis till later.

It was the hot season, right after the Fourth of July, and Elvis strolled into his home away from home fresh off a shift that saw hundreds of drinks in hundreds of combinations, and at least as many ice cream blasts and sundae treats whipped up.

"Hey, guess what, guys? I've been promoted to assistant manager! Can you believe it? I was told I handled tonight's rush with complete calmness, and best of all, they tell me they have big plans for me down the road..."

"That's great, sweetie, but what about college?"

"I can't afford it, you know that. Hey, it's okay. I'm still going to do well! So, when are you guys leaving on your big trip?"

"Oh, we decided to put it off!"

"But you've always wanted to go. Why?"

"We decided there was someplace we wanted to go even more!"

"What could be better than Europe?"

"Well, Columbia!"

"Columbia?"

"Yes. We're going on a trip there next month with your parents!"

"Grandma, you're a mess! Come on, what's really going on?"

"I'm dead serious. Oh, there is one more detail I didn't mention."

"Okay, I'm ready. Why do I feel like I'm being set up for a great punch line?"

"Okay, here it comes. You're coming, too."

"But my job..."

"Forget that! You're going to be a Gamecock!"

Elvis, who despite everything, had never stopped dreaming, felt a surge of hope and excitement laced with absolute confusion.

"What?"

"Hey, I didn't get you through algebra for nothing."

And then, like an eighteen wheeler pushing to make a delivery deadline it was way late for, it all hit him. His grandparents, the most unselfish people he had ever known, had given up their long-time, lifetime, hard-earned

129

dream so he could have his. He began to weep, all shame of doing so at his age forgotten.

"But you can't…"

"But we CAN, and we DID! David joined them then, and they all fell into a group hug that Elvis had no desire to end anytime soon! One day, he would become a business mogul, and give them back that vacation. In fact, it was this burning that gave him the courage to face his dream head on, and to earn better grades than he ever had at any other level.

At least at first.

~

Vanna sat cross-legged on the cold tile floor of her dorm room; head hung low, spirits hung even lower. No one could have ever pictured her in this state; after all, she was the hostess with the mostest, the Social Alpha lady, the true definition of a southern belle. Despite her freshman status, no one could deny she was a rising star on campus.

The reason for this darkest of depression, she had yet to share with anyone. The person she had always been able to confide in, her older sister Sheila, wasn't available to her at this time.

In fact, Sheila was the reason for her condition.

Sheila – the perfect big sis, had never looked down on Vanna. Instead, she had been an older best friend. She included Vanna in her slumber parties, and even the boy-centered talk as they both grew older. Sheila often took the blame when Vanna messed up, broke something, or otherwise fell short of the Billingsly family standard. That standard was quite high, as their mom had participated in more than a few beauty pageants and now was a pillar in Columbia's charitable and fine arts support community. Their dad was a leading workman's compensation attorney, and was respected by all. Sheila began to blaze her own trail – straight A's on her report card, dance lessons, piano lessons, then cheerleading starting in junior high. She cheered for the varsity all through high school, and was crowned Homecoming Queen her senior year. She received a full scholarship to South Carolina and graduated with honors. Through all this, she continued to pour out love, companionship, and sisterly advice to Vanna. Vanna, even before their parents, was first to learn of Everett, the dashing pre-med student who was Mr. Right in every way. Vanna was more than honored to be chosen maid of honor at their wedding at the tender age of fifteen. A year later, she became godmother – and favorite aunt – to Everett Garrison, Jr.

Vanna's path wasn't quite as smooth as her beloved big sissy's, but Sheila was there to hold her hand the whole way, even when her parents were too busy to appreciate what was going on. Sheila bore the tears of several bouts of unrequited puppy love. Sheila spent hours upon hours training Vanna for cheerleading tryouts. When Vanna fell just short, Sheila took her out for pizza, and bought her a new outfit out of her own allowance. That was Sheila.

For Sheila, kindness and compassion were no show. She was elected president of her church youth group, and excelled at memorizing scripture and witnessing to her lost friends without ever sounding preachy. She took God seriously from a young age, and never veered off that course despite countless temptations due to her beauty and popularity. Sheila could have chosen any career she wanted. She elected to become a teacher of the most severely disabled special needs children.

Vanna began to find her own niche as she entered high school. She was a great organizer and a people person who was a snob to no one. She, too, began to blossom with physical beauty, but like her sister's example, chose to nurture her spiritual side. She loved to visit nursing homes and cheer up the residents simply by paying attention to them and showing them kindness.

When little Everett came along, Vanna dove headfirst into her role of doting aunt. She wasn't afraid to change a diaper or feed her nephew his bottle. As he learned to talk and walk, Vanna began taking him out to the mall, even when her friends were along. She desired to be the same kind of aunt to Everett as Sheila was a sister to her.

"I want ice cream, Auntie-Poo!"

"I need a new toy, Auntie-Poo!"

"Let's watch a movie, Auntie-Poo!"

Auntie-Poo was glad to deliver on all these, and more.

Finally, it was Vanna's turn to leave home and head off to college – even though college was in her hometown. She, like Sheila, was allowed to live in the dorms and begin to get the feel of a more independent life. Sheila and Everett Jr. insisted on going with her to register, get her textbooks, and get settled in. Everett Sr. was now interning at one of the local hospitals and was way too busy to join them, although he would have loved to. Sheila still had acquaintances there, so before they left her on her own, Vanna had secured a bid to pledge Sheila's old sorority.

Vanna fit in well, and began to make friends faster than professors could whip out pop quizzes and term paper assignments. Her sorority pledging was demanding but worth it. Classes were challenging, but Vanna found she could handle them. It just meant burning the midnight oil and not being afraid to hang out in the library.

Only one thing wasn't going as planned – Vanna's own search for Mr. Right. She had been on a couple of dates, but nothing special. Then, at a sorority mixer, she had met Trent Kepshire, a second-string running back on the Gamecocks football squad. He smiled at her, but his attention stopped there. What to do? Only one option.

Call Sheila.

"Hey, sis! I need help – fast! It's an emergency!"

"What's his name?"

"Trent Kepshire – he's a football player!"

Both girls broke out into a fit of giggles.

"Okay, what's the problem?"

"He doesn't know I'm alive."

"Okay, here's the deal. This Saturday Everett is pulling a double – he usually is! Anyway, someone is dying for some Auntie-Poo time!"

"Oh, yes!" Vanna squealed.

"We'll eat somewhere, nowhere near the campus cafeteria, and we'll chart out a plan to turn this guy's head."

Saturday finally came. Everett Jr. and his two favorite women ate a high class meal at an upper crust establishment with the finest of ambiance – Chuck E. Cheese! Everett was loaded down with pizza and tokens, and Sheila served Vanna some first rate advice.

"Listen, sweetie. You have southern charm down to a science, even better than me. Find this guy, and lavish him with attention as a hostess would. Pour it on! He'll notice you then. It's natural, it's original, and it will work."

"Perfect! There's another party tonight! The Gamecocks won today, so he'll be in the right frame of mind!"

"Ah, perfect, indeed!"

The two shared a long embrace, then Everett Jr. joined in, finally all gamed out. No one wanted to say good-bye.

Vanna headed back to her room to get all spruced up. She could hardly wait to unleash her young womanhood.

~

"Did you enjoy seeing your Auntie-Poo?"

"Yes! Can we see her tomorrow?"

"Well, I don't know about that, but it will be soon!"

"I love her!"

"Me, too!"

"And you!"

"You, too!"

"And Daddy!"

"Me, too!"

Suddenly, a red sports car pulled out of nowhere. Sheila, caught completely off guard, slammed on her brakes as she tried to swerve out of the way. The driver, it would be discovered, was totally plastered after the big win by the Gamecocks. He too tried to avoid the inevitable collision, but he misjudged the distance.

"Honey, put your head down – we're going to crash..."

The impact was head on, and the force of the collision ignited both cars in flame. The sports car driver jumped out at the last moment and was hardly injured. As for Sheila and Everett Jr. they died instantly – which was merciful, because their bodies were burned beyond recognition.

~

Vanna wanted to quit school. She wanted to die. She tried to pray but was too mad at God to do so. She went into therapy briefly but again her anger was too great to accomplish anything. Finally, only one option remained. Vanna would throw herself into living for both of them. She got back into school, caught up on all her classes, got inducted into her sorority, and threw herself into hosting, planning, and partying.

She would lose herself in fun.

She learned how to keep up a front at all times, and, indeed no one knew the truth.

As for God, how could He be taken seriously if He could allow something like that to happen?

~

Elvis couldn't wait to show Grandma his first report card. Three A's and three B's! He had called her several times from school, but she hadn't talked a lot because her chronic bronchitis had gotten worse. Still, she choked back her tears of pride, and this made all the sweat and headaches worth it. Now, best of all, he had been told if he could keep up these grades for another semester, he might just earn at least a partial scholarship. This news burned inside his heart as he opened the door to his favorite place. Perhaps that dream vacation could occur soon after all...

He burst in, grinning from ear to ear, then fell silent as he saw his mom and dad, grandma and grandpa, and Janet all huddled together, and they were crying.

"Don't worry... dumpling. They're just being silly. The doctor says I have lung cancer, but I'm gonna beat it! You know me!"

Elvis joined in the huddle, his own tears burning hot tracks down his cheeks.

~

The next few months were horrible, even though Elvis experienced them from a distance. He had never experienced what it was like to truly hurt for someone else, as though their pain was his own.

Until now.

He felt her screams from the nightmare of chemotherapy. He felt the humiliation of Grandma losing about ninety percent of her hair. He felt her fever, her chills, and her nausea – and it all hurt – so much.

Elvis wasn't overly religious, but did believe in God. For Grandma's sake, he had memorized several scriptures and had attended church regularly. He figured Jesus was the way to go, and he had experienced salvation but Elvis figured he just didn't have it in him to get involved to the point of becoming a "Jesus Freak."

Still, he did believe, and although he had fallen out of church attendance when he entered college, he did still pray on occasion. Now, those occasions had definitely increased. One night, he stopped by the Baptist Student Union for a prayer and Bible study. For him, though, these guys and girls were just too fanatical for his taste. He had lost count of how many times he heard the phrase, "Isn't God awesome!" All anyone wanted to talk about was God – and Jesus – and praise and worship! These people had even shunned listening to radio stations that played popular music, for crying out loud. Only Christian tunes were Kosher! Please!

It was also around this time that Elvis began listening to his professors call for more broad-minded perceptions to life. Could other religions be real, too? Or was there a God at all? Elvis was not ready to go Agnostic or anything, but watching a true Christian like Grandma suffer like this --- Anyway, Elvis allowed his world view to expand a little. Maybe that wasn't such a bad thing.

A couple of his frat buddies had started dabbling in Tarot card reading, along with a little weed and alcohol to heighten the drama. Elvis refrained from the booze and drugs, but was fascinated by the cards. Could they really tell the future? Especially pumped was he one night when the cards clearly predicted a bright change in his life, and the very next day he received the word he would receive all A's, and a scholarship would be coming his way for next semester. Then, to top it off, Grandma's doctor told her she was in remission, and the chemo treatments were almost through! Grandma and Grandpa just might get that vacation yet.

~

"Auntie-Poo! It's dark! Please help me! Please come get me! I can't find Mommy!"

"I'm coming, sweetie! Don't worry!"

Vanna ran through the dark woods following the sound of her beloved nephew's cries. She entered a clearing, and found him at last – hung there, a dead burned skeleton – only the eyes were alive – bright blue, as Everett Jr.'s had been, and they were crying.

"I thought you went to heaven when you died, but it's so dark, and I can't find Mommy..."

"Everett! Honey! Is that you?"

Sheila's voice pierced the darkness, then her form returned it. She too, was a burned out shell.

"No! Where's God? It was all a lie! We're in Hell!"

Vanna awoke to sweated-through sheets. At least she had managed not to scream and wake her roommate. This was the third time she'd had this same dream, and that was just this week.

She wondered if her devastated soul would ever be the same, even as she began preparing for the party hosting and planning schedule that would fill her entire weekend. Thank God the semester was almost over. She needed a break. The problem was, that would mean going home, where the memories would assure that no peace would be found.

~

Right before school let out, Elvis officially received his scholarship notification, and it was even better than he thought! What a gift for his

134

grandparents this would be! Grandma could vacation, which should speed up her recovery even more. Her chemo was now complete, and she had been back to the doctor just this morning to confirm her continued progress. Elvis' feet were trying to dance as he practically skipped to their door. He waltzed in, letting out a victory whoop, and waving his scholarship letter!

"Hey, guys, I'm home! We've got lots to celebrate!"

Dead silence met his ears. That was strange, because their car was definitely in the driveway.

"Son, you'd better come in here. Now!"

Elvis's racing heart stopped in its tracks. Something was wrong. Please, not again. Elvis walked in to find everyone's head bowed. The dejection was palpable. But why?

"It's back, hon."

"What do you mean? I thought you'd beat it."

"My lungs did, but it had already spread into my lymph nodes. They had just concentrated on my lungs last visit. Now, they found that those nasty little boogers had gone into hiding. The problem is, they found my liver."

"So go after them there."

"We can't. Liver cancer can't be fought."

"No, Grandma!" Elvis sounded about half his age.

"Dumplin, those crazy doctors say I have only three months, but..."

"NO! NO! NO!" Elvis tore up his scholarship letter and stomped on the pieces. "I hate you, God! I hate you! If you're even there at all!"

Elvis stormed out, the hope of any kind of summer gone. As bad as he felt, he longed to take his Grandmother's place. Where was the comfort of all those scriptures now?

~

Vanna was all cried out. She accepted depression would simply be something she would always deal with. She strived not for good dreams, just no dreams. She knew she needed something to focus on that was positive. Maybe it was time to resume the search for Mr. Right. The first week of the new fall semester had her knee deep in social events once more. The Alpha Omega Pi and Sigma Chi mixer was the biggest of these. Maybe someone special would catch her eye.

~

"Sorrow, loss of a loved one. Sorry, bud, the cards just aren't with you."

"Been there, done that. Gimme another joint!" Elvis inhaled deeply. For at least a few moments he didn't have to think about watching Grandma's slow, painful death, watching the spry, sweet, saintly woman regress into dementia, then a comatose state as morphine became her only lifeline. Then, finally taking her last breath, and her funeral, full of admirers and tales of her good deeds no one had even been aware she had performed.

"Stupid cards! I'm sick of death! I'm ready to live it up!"

His dorm phone rang.

Elvis put on his sober air quickly as his mom's voice came over the line.

"Honey, I'm so sorry to tell you this. Your Grandfather had a heart attack."

"No! Please! How- How is he?"

"Sweetie, he's gone." Her sobs flooded forth. "He – died of a broken heart. I truly believe that!"

Elvis took the deck of Tarot cards and flung them everywhere. "I can't stand it anymore! I hate you, God! I HATE YOU!"

~

Vanna knocked herself out, as everyone agreed this was her coolest, classiest event ever! Almost all the members of both Sigma Chi and Alpha Omega Pi had pledged to attend. Also, many potential pledges were invited to mingle. Vanna had a personal agenda as well. No, it wasn't the football player from last year. He had since transferred. Instead, Vanna would choose a guy that caught her fancy, and give him the southern belle treatment suggested by her sister before everything had gone so bad and so wrong.

~

Elvis came back to school after another emotional, crowded funeral. He had totally had his fill of sadness, and there was no way he was missing the big bash. Maybe he would get laid tonight! Despite himself, Elvis flashed a boyish grin. Watch out, ladies!

~

"Hey, who's that cutie over there?"

"That's Elvis. He's an honor student now on scholarship. He's a rising star in the business department!"

"He looks a little lonely! I'd better go make him feel welcome." She poured him a rum and Coke and sauntered over to him.

"Hi, hon! Are you thirsty?"

Elvis looked up. "Hey, how did you know? Thanks!"

She took a seat beside him, draping her arm around his shoulder, her red, perfectly polished and manicured fingers beginning a massage that Elvis hadn't realized just how badly he needed.

"You look sad, sweetie, are you okay?"

"I've just lost my Grandparents – both of them in less than a month."

"Oh, baby, I'm so sorry!" She planted a kiss on his cheek, leaving red imprints of lipstick exactly matching her nails.

"I bet you could use some tender loving care, then."

"Ah! Yes. Thanks!" Elvis sighed, not believing his good fortune after so much tragedy lately.

"You just let Vanna take care of you!" She began stroking his hair as Elvis relaxed even more.

"Vanna, huh? Like Vanna White?"

"Exactly, baby. Everyone calls me that because I'm the Hostess with the Mostess!" Vanna giggled. Elvis joined her.

"I'm embarrassed to tell you my real name. It's kind of boring!"

"Honey, boring you are not!" Elvis's face flushed with the heat of his fully bloomed case of love sickness.

"Well, my real name – shh – don't tell anyone, okay?" She breathed it into his ear.

"Well, it is my utmost pleasure to meet you, Sarah Elizabeth Billingsly. Everyone calls me Elvis, but my true handle is Timothy Isaac McDonald, and the pleasure is all mine!

~

"You just relax, honey, and tell mommy all about it!"

It was a week later, and this time Tim and Sarah were alone. Sarah was once again working her magic fingers, first through his slicked back hair, then all around his back and shoulders.

"Oh, darling, you got me *All Shook Up*! *Let me be your Teddy Bear*!"

Tim's impersonation of his nick-namesake was, as always, spot on.

"So," Sarah cooed, "You never did tell me how come they call you Elvis. Now you don't have to."

"Thank you! Thank you very much!"

They both cracked up, then grew comfortably quiet. Sarah knew something was troubling this wonderful man, and was biding her time to find out. Tim was learning what it meant to feel like his heart was melting with love, even as his bitterness, hatred for God, and deep hurt lurked in his mind.

"Sarah, what do you think about God?"

"Whoa, baby! Where did that deep question come from?"

"I hate Him."

"What??!!"

"Right now, I do. How could He make my grandmother suffer like that? Then my grandfather, too. She was a saint! They both were! How could He give her cancer – a slow, painful death – then allow my grandfather's heart to break? Why?" Tim had unexpectedly begun crying freely. His face flushed. Sarah, without a word, gently wiped away his tears, kissed his cheeks and eyes, then resumed stroking his hair.

"It's okay, sugar. It really is." She gave him a more significant kiss.

"Oh, Sarah, I'm so sorry! I didn't mean to unload on you like that!"

"No apologies required, love! I told you I wanted to hear!"

"I just can't get past this. She used to memorize scripture with me, and he was such a rock. The old stereotype 'strong and silent type' actually fit him to a T. Together, they were the ideal role models. So what does God do? He PUNISHES them! I just don't get it – not at all!"

"Shh. It's okay, dear heart!" Sarah gave him another round of soothing kisses, even as she was wrestling with the very same questions herself. Tim would be the first person outside her family to hear the story of

Sheila and Everett Jr., but not tonight. Tonight was Tim's. Hers would come soon enough, of this she now had no doubt.

"When I was growing up, I used to eat breakfast at their house every Friday morning. Did I mention that they lived next door? Anyway, bacon, extra crunchy, scrambled eggs swimming in butter, seasoned to perfection..."

"Mmm! You're making me hungry, sweetie!"

"Me too. And the best part was the homemade biscuits, somehow – and they both helped prepare the meal – they made the biscuits like little mountains, all puffed up and delicious through and through..."

"That settles it! We're going to the IHOP, or Denny's, or somewhere!" Sarah pulled Tim up, and they headed out for a late night breakfast.

Over bacon, eggs, and biscuits, and a generous side of pancakes, Tim shared the tale of the magical Schwinn birthday bike, the Rescue 911 from algebra, and several times where unconditional love led to forgiveness when Tim did not exactly act his best. He also included Janet's story. As he talked, he found himself feeling better and lighter of heart than he had in ages. Sarah's beauty, so present across from him as he wolfed down everything on his plate, certainly didn't hurt.

Then a thought flashed through his mind. Could God have sent this Southern Angel into his life to help ease the pain, and give him a shot at the kind of love his grandparents had lived out for him? Oh, how they would have adored Sarah... And just like that, the anger returned. This process of healing would be quite a long one indeed, if it ever resolved at all.

~

The next weekend, a road trip to Myrtle Beach replaced hostessing and fratting around for the two. After an afternoon of surfing and an all-you-can-eat shrimp feast, Tim and Sarah took a moonlight stroll along the Carolina coast. The moon was a crescent, just like on the state flag, but it still cast a reflection on the gently lapping water occasionally fused with larger waves. The scene was breathtaking, as was the mood it cast.

After about an hour, the couple took a seat on the sand. This time, however, it was Tim who took Sarah's head into his lap, playing a symphony of his own upon her natural blonde, shoulder-length hair.

Sarah was finally ready to unload her own tale of sorrows.

"I had an inspiration growing up, too. For me, it was Sheila, my big sis, my heroine, my role model, my everything..."

A few sobs escaped.

"It's okay, darlin'. Tell Daddy all about it!"

"She was the perfect Christian, the perfect sister – and friend. She was so smart and popular. Yet I was never jealous of her, because she gave all she had to pave a similar path for me."

"She sounds wonderful. I would love to meet her."

"You – you can't..." Now Sarah's own floodgates burst open, unchecked.

"SHE'S DEAD! Killed by an idiot drunk driver!"

Tim's heart broke for her. He didn't say anything; he just rocked her, and continued his head and back massage.

"Oh, Tim! She was married to Everett, a doctor she met at school. She was preparing for a long career in special education. She could have been anything; an actress, a model, whatever – but her heart went out to the less fortunate. She was so natural. I was her maid of honor and both godmother and aunt to little Everett Jr. They were so happy."

Tim continued his comforting, even as his own sadness intensified.

"Then, last year, I was all depressed because this football player wouldn't notice me, so I talked Sheila and Everett Jr. into coming to see me and once again rescue me. We ate at Chuck E. Cheese, of all places. She gave me some great advice, but I never got to use it. On the way home, a totally wasted tailgater celebrating the latest USC victory hit them head on – and he lived! He was uninjured! And they..." Sarah lost all composure, burying herself into Tim.

With horror, Tim realized it wasn't just Sheila who had died that day. Tears of his own rushed out to join hers.

"Sheila had so much to give – and her whole life was in front of her – and little Everett – oh – they were both burned beyond recognition. I hate God too! Why? Why? Why? I've never shared this with anyone at school..."

They held each other, absorbing each other's pain for what seemed like hours, as the moon slowly carved its trajectory across the starlit sky.

"He called me Auntie-Poo! Oh, God, I miss him so! And Sheila, my best friend..."

Just as Tim had done, Sarah began to share pleasant memories, including the near miss at cheerleading followed by the new outfit anyway, many cases of Sheila taking the blame to keep Sarah out of trouble, the gorgeous wedding, the birth of Everett Jr., Auntie-Poo adventures, and the ensuing ache for children of her own, and how Sheila's connections had gotten Sarah into Alpha Omega Pi, which had led to her career path of hostessing and event and wedding planning.

Lastly, Sarah spoke of that advice given that day, to treat the guy like a prince, and to overwhelm him with her southern charm – the exact thing she had used to win Tim's heart.

"Hey, how about that? She's still loving and helping you!"

That thought, along with Tim's kindness, left Sarah more at peace than she had felt since the tragedy had occurred. Sheila would have loved Tim to death, and little Everett would have worshipped him...

And, just like Tim, she felt the hatred for God and the bitterness force their way back in. It would definitely take each other to get through all this.

If they ever could.

~

Sarah spoiled Tim for any other woman, and slowly the allure of partying faded, also. It was replaced by a drive to rise to the top of his class.

He increased his hours each semester and enrolled in summer school to boot. As a result, he was well into obtaining his MBA as his classmates were preparing for graduation and receipt of their Bachelor's degrees.

Sarah graduated that May herself, and right after she and Tim wed. Sarah and her mom planned the perfect wedding. All Tim had to do was show up, which he did with no regrets or hesitation. The music was provided by a concert pianist and an aspiring opera singer courtesy of the University of South Carolina music department. The reception was covered by one of the state's top traveling DJ outfits, and the food could have been featured in *Bon Appetit*.

The ceremony itself was performed by Brother Thaddeus Hudson, the Pastor of the Southern Baptist Church in which Sarah had been raised. Both had agreed on a Christian ceremony, but only recently.

Tim, still restless about faith issues, had spent the remainder of his college years researching other belief systems. For him, the Hindus had too many gods to keep straight; Buddhism, though not without wisdom, seemed to lead nowhere, and humanism was destined to fail, if all we had to count on was ourselves.

He also held dialogues with Jehovah's Witnesses, whose timetables for Jesus' return seemed to keep changing, and only 144,000 truly being saved seemed harsh. He did, however, have to admire their work ethic. Going door to door for them was not frightening at all. They took on the task with joy.

Next, he had given the Mormons a fair listen, but Joseph Smith seemed like a shady character, and personal revelations seemed to keep changing the rules on some issues. He did greatly admire their high moral code and loyalty, however.

So in the end, traditional Christianity had won out by default, but Tim was yet to find the answers he so desperately sought. Still, the God of his childhood seemed like the best shot – maybe one day...

~

Tim and Sarah settled into married life. Tim finished up his MBA and began working at the die-cast factory where he would eventually rise to management. Sarah began her event and wedding planning business, which was small and intermittent at first due to Gary and Brooke entering the scene. All in all life was good, as the city of Charleston wove its charms around them.

There was, however, something missing. What it was eluded them both. Tim found the bureaucracy of company politics to be cold and empty at times as he began his ascent. He loved the competition, but he hated the backstabbing and looking out for number one outlook which always seemed to prevail. This did not stop Tim from grinning ear to ear as he began to get promoted. Still, there had to be more, right?

Sarah felt the same. She loved her husband, her young children, and the people she worked with in her growing business. Yet, there had to be more – a purpose other than more money and more clients, right?

Not that those were bad things!

~

It was Nancy Whitten, a beautiful, dignified southern woman and a Charleston native, who would finally shed some light on the subject. Nancy and her husband Joe were preparing a vow renewal ceremony to be held on Church Street in honor of their twentieth anniversary. Sarah had handled this in her usual manner – both loving and meticulous – and Nancy could not have been more pleased.

"Oh, Sarah, this will be so perfect! You're such a doll!" Sarah then had found herself in the middle of a true southern hug, not an uncommon occurrence in these parts.

"So, how long have you been married, honey?"

"Just over five years!"

"And how many children?"

"Two. Gary's four, and Brooke is one!"

"Oh, how cute! We have three teenagers. Sweetie, don't be in a hurry for those years!"

"Oh, I've heard!"

"So, where do y'all go to church?"

"Well, we don't right now. We're both so busy. I mean, we're Christians and all, but well – we should – at least for the kids' sake as they get older..."

"Honey, you've got to come to our revival. It's under a tent! Is that cool, or what? We belong to Palmetto Baptist Church. We are a friendly, hugging congregation and we actually all get along fairly well. We aren't too little or too big, and we sing both contemporary and traditional songs! You and your family please come! You will love it, I promise!"

Sarah and Tim were both reluctant at first, but Nancy gently persisted. They finally attended on the fourth night. This would turn out to be a life-altering event in ways none of them expected.

The message that night was on surrendering to God. The evangelist had played football in college, and knew all about the thrill of competition and never giving up. He explained that there was one exception to the rule that giving up showed weakness; with God, giving up and giving in means victory! To surrender was to soar, and to admit weakness was the beginning of true strength. This hit both Tim and Sarah right in the gut. Both began to recall wonderful childhood memories of church, Bible stories, salvation, and baptism. Suddenly it all became real again; even more so than back then. As one, the two went forward to rededicate their lives back to their Lord. The next Sunday, they were in church. Then, several months later, they attended the marriage seminar where Tim would receive his initial calling.

Bible School challenged Tim deeply. Matters such as predestination and Calvinism, women's place in ministry, celebrating secular events such as Halloween, and popular current culture such as movies, television, music, and the arts were so confusing. Tim never got a good handle on every subject – does anyone, really? Still, his faith grew, and with it, his anointing.

~

Every preacher has stumbling blocks of his own. For some, it's tithing. For others, it's Hellfire sermons. For more than a few, it's self-sacrifice. For Tim, it was giving up his winner's mentality, dealing with cultural matters, and no truth in other religions, and all of them leading to Hell.

Still, he grew in Christ, and as a result, he bore more and more fruit, and he more or less found peace with all these hot topics.

Except one. The Big One.

Why did good people have to suffer for no apparent reason? His grandparents and Sarah's sister and nephew simply could not be reconciled in his heart and mind.

This unbelievable, unfathomable Excuses Crusade had been just as great a learning experience for him as it had been for his growing audiences. He was humbled by the harvest even as the farmer was barely understanding the seeds he was sowing. But God was so good, and Tim, in his weakness, was indeed growing stronger in the Master Sower, Planter, and Reaper.

But now, here Tim stood, face to face with his most fierce and personal demon.

Excuse #8 – Why Does God Allow Suffering?

There was no more procrastination or excuses of his own. The crowd was here, his largest yet. The sermon was prepared. Everything was in place.

It was show time on the Master's Stage of Life – both life now and life eternal.

~

"Yo! Slam it home, boys! Yeah, what's wrong, Lee-Bron? I do believe the Hawks done cooled off da Cavs! Yes! Steal that ball! Paul Mitsap with the J! Yes, a double digit lead! Hot 'lanta, baby!" exclaimed Gary.

"Um, excuse me, Garr-bear! I'm trying to work on a new recipe here!"

"Excuse me, babbling Brooke! What can be more important than NBA basketball? That's real ball, baby! My Hawks are soarin' – closing in on third in the East! Only Chicago and Cleveland to pass! Whoo-hoo!"

"Oh, please! It's just a game! At least you can eat my Teriyaki Chicken over rice and cashews!"

"Whoa! I might have to try some when you finish!"

"I'm making a small batch now, then a bigger one when Daddy gets home next week!"

Gary grinned. He was ready to shoot some hoop with his dad. He wasn't the best, but sometimes he schooled his son anyway. He had a way of getting lucky on those long three's.

"I have to admit, I miss the old guy!"

"Me too! I want to tell him about my new man in person."

"What is this, the third one this year?"

"Yeah, but by far the best. Wally actually enjoys cooking!"

"Hey, Mom? How about you? You missin' Dad?"

No answer.

"Mom?"

"Oh, sorry dear. I'm just doing some extra praying. Daddy's dealing with maybe the toughest excuse of all tonight."

"What's that?"

"Why does God allow suffering? And why do we have to suffer as Christians? You know, why can't life be easier? It makes a lot of people run from God and even get angry with Him. Daddy and I both have first-hand experience."

"Dad'll handle it! He always does."

"With God's help, but I'll tell you the truth – I could not give an answer for it, even now. I trust God, and I guess that'll have to do!" Sarah wiped away a tear and resumed praying.

"Yesssss!" Gary's war whoop broke the silence after a few minutes. "Hawks win! Hawks win! That ought to shake things up!" Right as he spoke these words, things did begin to shake.

"Whoa! See there?"

"Must be an eighteen wheeler or two going by."

The shaking intensified. Sarah's head shot up!

"I don't believe it! I think it's a real earthquake!"

Charleston is right on a fault line, and tremors were nothing new, but usually they couldn't even be felt.

Not this time.

Dishes began flying off the counter and Brooke's creation was spoiled. Then pictures began falling off the walls.

Suddenly, a filing cabinet leapt off the floor and fell into Gary.

"Oh, no, Gary!" Sarah rushed over to check her son, just as the TV cabinet fell over on her. Brooke, horrified, tried to call 911, but the phone was dead.

That's when a window shattered and the glass, along with a bookcase that had once sat against it, smashed into her. As her world went dark, so did the house, as electricity was cut off.

"What's wrong? Mommy? Bubbie? Sissie? It's dark! I can't..."

Chance, who had been asleep, must have thought he was having a nightmare. A chandelier chose that moment to fall, as Chance stumbled under it, making the nightmare one hundred percent real. He joined his family in total darkness unlike any before, as outside the ground moved in waves like the nearby Folly Beach and Isle of Palms, just as it last had 129 years ago.

~

Tim looked out at the crowd of at least ten thousand eager faces and cleared his throat to speak.

But no words came.

He began to pray for the spirit to take over, and as he did, a picture of his praise team filled his inner vision.

"Ladies and gentlemen, tonight's excuse just happens to be my toughest personal demon. Therefore, I'm going to call on two of the finest warriors I know to initiate this battle – Jamie Ray and Meghan Amhearst. From what I've been told, they have prepared a double punch, one upper cut and one slow knockout!"

With that, Jamie took the mic and spoke from his heart.

"You know, folks, we all have problems. We all face trials. In these economic times, this is all greatly multiplied. Our Lord never says we won't have them. In fact, suffering often goes along with standing on the truth without wavering and loving more deeply. But God never deserts us or forsakes us – that's a guarantee! The word proclaims it, and we believe it!"

The crowd responded with contagious zeal.

"God will lead us over, under, or around our troubles, even if it takes time and some stumbling along the way. And, even if we must face obstruction, pain, and trying times, the Lord still sticks right by us, leading us right through the middle of it all! And yes, friends, there is always an ending! We come out stronger and better on the other side! So put your hands together for a praise offering to the Great I Am!!"

A sizzling rendition of a brand new Jamie Ray composition *Lead Me Through* brought the house to its feet.

Lift me up! Pull me out!
Guide me under or around!
Help me keep the path of love
Ordained by you!
But when there's no other way
To face the trials of the day
Then take my hand, dear Lord
And lead me through!

The praise and worship continued long after the rollicking music concluded. Jamie and Meghan beamed.

"Now, I've got to tell you, music evangelism is tough. Both Meghan and myself have been through the mill both musically and personally. Tell 'em about it, Meg!"

Meghan shared her story of Troy Trenton, with all the personal and musical heartbreak included. She then told of Sandra and how she had orchestrated the meeting of Jamie. The magic that followed, and what they had been forced to give up to join TIME Ministries back when Tim was just starting. It was like a mosaic; making no sense at the start, but now unfolding more each day as a true work of art by the Master Painter. The crowd responded with genuine love and warmth.

"Now," Jamie resumed, "before Meghan and I met, I had what I considered a dream gig. I was playing piano and singing for a show band in a family musical theater, kind of like a Branson, Missouri show! It was perfect! I got to perform standards, both popular and gospel, as well as an occasional original – all in a family atmosphere! The pay wasn't the best, but I absolutely loved it! Then, one day, I was told my services were no longer needed because the owner's son was now ready to take over the keyboard duties. This song we're about to play for you was inspired by that event. Even in our saddest times, the Lord is working to bless us. Even when the river runs dry, He's always there, and if we'll just hold on, a brighter day will dawn!"

The twosome then proceeded to slay the crowd with *A Different Day*.

A different day, a second chance
Another change of circumstance
My river may run dry,
still His blessings are gonna flow my way!
He never said it would be easy
But He did say He'd never leave me
And when this evening's over
The morning dawns a different day!

The applause lasted a while, which allowed Tim to finally get himself together.

"I'm not going to lie, people. This one's personal." Tim then proceeded to recount the story of his grandparents, then Sarah's terrible tale of Sheila and Everett Jr. He had to stop several times as he teared up, but he made it through. The crowd loved him for it.

"I'll be honest, I still don't get it. But I do get this – God brought my wife and me together around our shared grief. Romans 8:28 proclaims: 'And we know in all things God works for the good of those who love Him, who have been called according to His purpose.'

"I wasn't a good Christian before all this, I became less of one because of all this, yet all the time God was working behind the scenes, making way for the perfect woman to enter my life, to make me examine God and religion more closely, and finally, to be called into His service. For that, I can say with no regrets – Praise God!"

The crowd erupted, screaming their own praises.

"There are so many people who have faced so much suffering. Children handicapped from birth, victims of senseless rape, violence, and abuse, untimely death, cancer or other diseases resulting in slow, painful death, mental illness – the list goes on and on. How can we explain it away? How can a loving God allow these things? For this, I do not have all the answers.

"Then there are major disasters such as 9/11, Hurricane Katrina, and our current economy. Why? Is it judgment or just nature taking its course? These events showed no respect of persons as both saints and sinners felt the wrath.

"Some things are the result of sin. Sin is real. We are all sinners, including the best of us, and sin has its price. Even Christians must still pay the consequences of their mistakes.

"Other things are part of nature. Sometimes God stops them; other times, for reasons unknown, He doesn't. Yet God never, ever loses control, even when it looks like He has – such as now, in these extremely difficult times.

"Sometimes, suffering and persecution is a direct result of our faith, because the world just doesn't get it. Jesus faced it, so why shouldn't we? Still, it seems so wrong for good to be repaid with evil.

"Listen to these two scriptures. The first in that wisdom book of Proverbs: 'Trust in the Lord with all your heart, and lean not on your own understanding. In all your ways acknowledge Him, and He will make your paths straight.' That's chapter three, verses five and six.

"And check this out: 'For my thoughts are not your thoughts, neither are your ways my ways, declares the Lord.' Isaiah 55:8 hammers this very helpful truth home for us.

"So, what can we do? How can we respond? Do we curse God? I did. Do we try to find answers somewhere else? I did. I can tell you that both of these responses are wrong!" Absolutely wrong!

"I think about what my grandparents meant to me, and the witness they gave with their lives. They helped me find salvation as a child, and it was that very same foundation that brought me back to God. I think of how Sarah's sister's advice to her on how to charm a guy worked after all – on me! I think of handicapped people who wind up inspiring us all despite of, and sometimes even BECAUSE of, their weaknesses. I think of how disasters can unite people and bring them back to God, and to each other. And yes, I know where my grandparents are now, as well as Sarah's sister Sheila and little Everett – and I REJOICE! Someday, we'll be reunited in a land of no death, no tears, and no goodbyes!"

The crowd, moved to total silence, now burst forth with rapturous response.

"Think about the scriptures I shared with you. They all say the same thing, really. God is in control! God loves us! He's working for our best interest, and he knows a whole lot more than we do! Therefore, I proclaim this to you – the key is trust! Trust the Lord, simple as that! No matter what happens, no matter what you've been through, are going through, or will go through, He is there for you! With Him in your heart and at the center of your life, eventually, the ending will be happy! So what are you waiting for? Come to Him now!"

And they did. Oh, how they did! Over two thousand in one night; by far the most successful night of harvest for the kingdom yet! The parents of both a blind and a deaf child; a husband playing caretaker to his young wife; a victim of both MS and a stroke; an entire family who had lost everything to Hurricane Katrina, and had fled north despite knowing no one in St. Louis; a teenager who had lost both parents in 9/11; and a piano player who had lost his livelihood due to the high guitar player who had accidently shot him in the hand. On and on the stories went, and Tim had never been happier. By the grace of God, he had stared down his worst demon and arose victorious. He could not wait to tell Sarah.

~

As soon as things settled down, which was well after midnight, he finally punched in her number.

There was no answer.

"Oh, well, it's almost 2:30 am at home. No doubt they gave up on me for the night."

Tim fell out on his motel bed, not bothering to undress. The next thing he knew, it was 9:14 am, and his cell phone was calling him back to the waking world.

"Brother Tim! It's Jamie! Meghan just called me! I was asleep, but not anymore! Turn on the news, quick! There's bad trouble at home! The big earthquake we've always feared has hit!"

Tim shot out of bed and punched on the remote. The news was not hard to find, as this was the lead story everywhere.

"The most devastating earthquake to hit the U.S. in over a hundred years has rocked the city of Charleston, South Carolina. Measuring 7.8 on the Richter Scale, its damage is both widespread and of Biblical proportions. It extends as far north as New England and as far south as Miami, where only minor effects were felt. But as far as Charleston, despite being well prepared, this is even worse than Hurricane Hugo twenty years ago. Many are missing, and already alarming amounts of serious injuries and even casualties have been reported..."

Tim punched in Sarah's number. No answer. He began to panic. He called the airport, but all flights there had been cancelled. "I'll get there if I have to walk!" he shouted to the empty room.

"Tim."

Tim stopped dead in his tracks.

"ONE MORE NIGHT."

Tim had never heard the audible voice of God like this. Could it be his nerves? Gasping for breath, he fell on his knees and buried his head in his pillow and blankets.

"Lord, please! I can't take this! Not this! If my family is gone – I can't..."

"YOU'RE RIGHT! YOU CAN'T. I CAN. ONE MORE NIGHT."

Tim called both Jamie and Meghan. Unbelievably, both said they felt compelled to continue one more night as well. So, in a way not even close to anything he'd ever known, Tim was forced to heed his own advice from the night before.

"TRUST GOD!"

~

"Last night, I thought I'd passed a major spiritual test. I felt better and more at peace than I ever had in my life! The harvest was beyond incredible! But today… today…" Tim broke down in loud sobs and fell onto the stage.

Jamie took over. "As many of you probably know, we are all from Charleston."

The crowd gasped as one.

"Tim cannot get in touch with his family. Tonight, it is HE who needs your prayers."

Choruses of "We love you, Brother Tim!" filled the building.

"God spoke to each of us – and we all received the same message: 'ONE MORE NIGHT!' So here we are! Praise Jesus!"

And they did, as Meghan and he unleashed several praise and worship tunes in a row. Tim then returned to his standing position, and did an unusual thing for a preacher.

"Trust in God. He's there for all, no matter what. If you've never been saved, do it! If you need to rededicate your life, do it! If He's calling you to serve Him, do it! That's my only message tonight!"

And they did. Not two thousand this time, but well over five hundred made their way to the altar. Many more stories were told that night, but it was one in particular which confirmed God's call to stay the extra night.

Dusty Jenkins, a middle-aged truck driver with a middle-age girth was crying like a baby despite his considerable size.

"I guess a lot of these excuses apply to me. I thought I was an all right guy, but then I got to drinking in college and – and I was involved in an accident where I killed two innocent people. I tried everything to make up for it, but church people treated me with contempt when I tried to say I was sorry. I couldn't understand why I got to live and that sweet mother and child had to die. I hated God so much, and that led me to hate myself. I had a failed marriage and two failed jobs. I couldn't quit drinking. I tried TV evangelists, but I never got hee-uhled. I tried AA, but it didn't help either. I felt everyone was always judging me. Then I decided on my own that I would make driving right a way of life. I solved my job issue, but nothing else. Finally, I heard about your crusade on excuses. I took time off work and followed you around. Something told me I was getting close to an answer, but I always stopped short of allowing Jesus into my heart. But tonight, I did it."

"What happened tonight, Dusty? I hardly even preached."

"Well, it actually happened last night. It was when you told the story of your wife's sister. I put two and two together, and realized – IT WAS ME! I'm the driver who killed Sheila and Everett! I had known their names once from the reports, but had repressed them because I could not stand to think about what I'd done. But now I'm ready to face it – I'm ready to repent – and I'm ready to beg – to plead – for you and Sarah's forgiveness!"

Tim thought he had seen and heard it all by now. Oh, how wrong he was! How out there was this? Tim did the only thing he could do in light of everything. He embraced Dusty in a tight bear hug.

"Welcome to the kingdom, brother! If Jesus can forgive you, surely I can."

"I want to make it up to you. I mean that I've been sober for five years now. I did, as I said, find a reason for making it stick. I wanted to drive for a living to become great at it – and I have. I've got my rig with me, and I'm offering you transportation going south. I've got some family in Charleston myself. Please, I know you can't get a flight there, and I know you need to go ASAP, and besides, I want more than anything on this earth to tell Sarah how sorry I am."

Tim studied this big lug of a man and saw a totally new creation before him. A feeling of rightness stole over him.

"You're on, brother!"

Another bear hug ensured, and this time Meghan and Jamie joined in, as they were brought up to speed. Everyone agreed as soon as they could get packed that the time to leave was now!

Sarah would not believe this in a million years.

If only she and the kids were still alive to hear about it. Tim tried calling again.

Still no answer.

~

Dusty Jenkins was a first class rig commander, and he proved it. An incredible thirteen hours of pedal to the medal, straight-through, power driving had them at Exit 199 to Summerville off I-26 East where Jamie and Meghan both resided. The damage was the worst any of them had ever encountered. That was saying something, since Dusty had once witnessed an F-3 tornado while driving through Kansas, and they all had seen what Hurricane Hugo had done twenty years ago. Meghan found her home in shambles, but Garth and Andy were unharmed. She and Jamie exchanged a tight, fierce hug as Meghan left for some well-deserved family time until the crusades resumed next month in Kansas City, then Chicago in May.

"Oh, honey, you should have seen it! The ground looked like the ocean. It was just like those history lessons on the carriage tours had come to life!" said Andy.

"Yeah, Mom! It was like, totally cool! Okay, so the house is damaged – it's okay, we're in good hands with Allstate!" exclaimed Garth.

Meghan's two favorite men picked her up and whirled her around.

"We're so glad you're home! We actually get you for a while!" said Andy.

"Yeah, and next month, I'm going!" beamed Garth.

"That's right. Kansas City, and this summer, you can go, too. We'll be recording before long, also – our serious album!"

"Yeah, and I get a part on it!" Garth warbled out a few notes of *Amazing Grace*.

"Hmm!" Meghan smiled. "We'll have to see what Peter Beck has to say about that."

"It's in the bag, babe! Don't sweat it!"

The family laughed, joining hands as they faced their destroyed home, knowing that home truly had not been destroyed at all.

Home was each other!

Meanwhile, Meghan's third most favorite man was anxious to see his top two favorite women. Oh, how he had missed them. They were okay, but was his house any better off than Meghan's?

No, his house was in shambles, as well, but his women were fine. In fact, both were sitting out on the porch, along with a third woman.

That most wonderful friend and Hairdresser Extraordinaire, Sandra Miller!

Hugs followed, fast and furious.

"Oh, it's so great to be home!"

"Honey, we don't really have a home."

"Yes we do! Each other!" Just as Meghan, Andy and Garth had realized, a house was a building, but a home was the people in it.

"It'll be okay. We've got us! The crusades are incredible. We even have a record deal! God has given us more than we could have ever hoped for!"

"Well, I would offer to cook, but…" said Andy.

Everyone laughed.

They all went out to eat at a nearby Chinese buffet which had withstood the quake. Jamie learned that Sandra's shop was damaged, but not down. Insurance would allow her to rebuild soon. It was only fitting that the beauty shop which marked the beginning of so many great things would once more regain its own beauty.

Finally, it was Tim's turn to face his worst fears. It seemed forever until he and Dusty finally pulled into his Charleston home.

It was still standing, but that was about all. Like Jamie and Meghan had already discovered, structures could be fixed or replaced.

The problem was that people could not, and unlike Jamie and Meghan, he could find no sign of his family. He and Dusty entered the house, and quickly observed the damage inside was just as bad. Bookcases, chandeliers, dishes, TV cabinets, filing cabinets, pictures…

And blood.

Way too much blood.

Tim lost his breath, falling to the floor, he began beating the floor and sobbing.

"God, please! Please not this! Anything but this!"

Dusty touched his back gently.

"Hey, brother, don't give up. They aren't here! Maybe someone…"

"Oh, thank God! Tim! You're back!"

The voice of Mildred Davis, their kind neighbor who also happened to be a nurse, came running as fast as her petite 5'3" frame could carry her.

"They're in the hospital. I found them! Come on! I'm scheduled to go in at three. They're hurt, pretty badly, but they're all alive!"

Tim and Dusty needed no further prompting. They headed for Charleston's largest medical facility. Mildred silently prayed that what she had just said was still true.

What she hadn't said was that one of them was barely hanging on by a thread.

~

Gary came out of a fitful dream of being schooled on the court by some 7 foot dude he had for some reason challenged to a round of one-on-one. This guy played basketball more like football, and his legs, ribs, and head were killing him.

Then he came to fully, and realized the pain was real. He had lost not to a future NBA prospect but to a massive earthquake. One broken leg, one sprained foot, one twisted knee, several broken ribs, and a mild concussion would keep his basketball action to viewing it on the tube only for quite a while.

That was fine by him. After all, his dad should be home soon. Just as he had this thought, in walked Tim.

"Oh, Gary! Thank God!"

"I'll hug you later, Dad, I promise! Right now I am in pain!" They both laughed with relief as they settled for grasping hands firmly.

"Dad I never in my life have seen anything like it! It was like the earth came alive, and it was mad!"

"I'm just glad you're okay, son. I actually have some time off, and I need it! We'll have some great times watching ball and taking tours! Well, touring may be tough, but we'll figure out something!"

"Yeah, it's crazy, but the historic stuff suffered the least damage. I hear St. Phillips' leans even a little further to the left now, which means the congregation will have to even become more right-winged to balance it out!"

Mildred and Dusty stepped in. Tim introduced Dusty and then Mildred checked Gary.

"All right, big guy. I believe the danger has diminished enough from your head injury that we can look at sending you home in a few days!"

"Cool! How about Mom, Brooke, and Chance?"

"We'll see. Just concentrate on you, okay, my man?" Mildred patted his hand, then rubbed it gently for a few moments. She then laid her hand on Tim's shoulder. "Let's go see Brooke."

They headed off to Brooke's room, and found her in almost the same exact shape as Gary. In her case, however, it was her arm that was broken.

Not her spirit, though, as her eyes caught sight of her daddy.

"You're home! Yesssss!" She grabbed him with her good arm and squeezed him as tightly as her soreness would allow. "They tell me I won't be able to try any new recipes for a while. We'll just see about that! I can cook with one hand! Oh, Dad, you've got to hear about Wally! He actually likes cooking! Nobody can talk to me like you can! Oh, Dad, I was so scared! That quake! Let me tell you about it…"

No wonder Gary had nicknamed her "Babbling Brooke"! He gave her a big kiss right in mid-sentence.

"I love you, sweetie!"

"You, too!"

Mildred checked her out as Tim again introduced Dusty. She gave Brooke the same promise as Gary. As long as the doctor agreed, she could probably finish recovering at home in just a few days.

Even if home meant a motel until they could either repair their home or find a new one.

As long as they were together, it did not matter – not one bit.

Mildred again took Tim's arm. "I believe there is someone else who needs to see you."

Sarah won the prize for broken limbs, as both an arm and leg were casted. Many cuts and bruises also covered her where she had tried to help their children.

To Tim, Sarah had never looked more beautiful. He could not stop kissing her.

"Hi, handsome!"

"Hey, baby, come on down to Memphis with me and I'll buy you a gold Cadillac – or maybe a cheeseburger."

The kissing resumed.

"I guess I'll be playing hostess to you for a while.

Sarah giggled through her pain. "So now you're the Hostess with the Mostess!"

Both Mildred and Dusty had grown quiet. Dusty would soon explain to Sarah how he and Tim met, and how revealing his true identity to Sarah would totally devastate her. Yet he had no choice but to tell her. Mildred was growing sick inside, for a different reason. It was time to tell them the truth.

The truth about Chance.

She walked over to them, taking Sarah's good hand and putting her other arm around Tim. She began to nervously rub her thumbs across each of the places her hands rested.

"Guys, I'm going to recommend to the doctor that Brooke and Gary will best recover at home in just a couple more days. Sarah, that goes for you, too."

"That's great, Mildred!"

Then, like an aftershock greater than the original quake, it hit them.

"What about Chance?"

"Yes, I need to see him, too."

"You can't. Not now."

"Why?"

"He's in the ICU!"

"What??!!" Tim and Sarah shouted in perfect unison.

"He suffered a much more serious concussion. We are praying there is no brain damage – but that's not the worst of it. A chandelier fell on him. He has several broken bones, and he has lost an incredible amount of blood."

Tim and Sarah were both crying softly.

"What can we do? We'll do anything!"

"He's got to have blood – and fast. If he doesn't get it by tonight, he may not make it. The problem is, he is AB negative, the rarest type, and we simply don't have enough. I already know none of you have that type. I'm so sorry. Gary and Brooke do not know. We wanted to make sure you guys recovered..."

"NO! NO! Why didn't you tell us?! NO!!"

"There was nothing any of you could do. We need to pray now! Now that I know the rest of you will be okay..."

"Okay? Okay?? We'll never be okay! NEVER! Not if anything happens to our baby! God, help us! Please! Pleeease!"

Dusty, who had been listening with horror, suddenly looked up at them. "Hey, could you check me?"

"Hey, man, this isn't your problem."

"It is if I'm AB negative! Besides, I'm your brother now. What would my salvation mean if I don't give it legs? Listen, years ago, I was in an accident, and I remember they took my blood to test me for alcohol. I failed." He hung his head. "But I also remember them saying something about my blood being unusual..."

Mildred paged the head nurse on Sarah's floor. "Test this man, NOW!"

This time, Dusty Jenkins passed. He gave all the blood he was allowed, and nearly passed out twice afterward.

Now, it was just a matter of waiting.

And praying like never before.

~

It was midnight when the word finally came. Chance was responding! In fact, he would be coming out of ICU with the doctor's okay, in two or three days.

Sarah clasped Dusty's hand.

"How can I ever thank you?"

"By forgiving me."

"Forgiving you?"

"Yes, ma'am. You see, that accident I was in – it was your sister and nephew – I killed them. I was young and stupid. It should have been me – not them." Dusty began weeping openly. "I felt drawn to your husband's crusade. Several of those excuses applied to me, but I finally saw the truth. God still loves me! I can't believe – He – has given me this chance – to – somehow – make it right. Please, Sarah. Please forgive me!"

Sarah took Dusty's hand, caressed it, and kissed it several times.

"You are forgiven! I can't believe how great God is! I may be laid up in this bed, but I've never been more healed than I am right now!"

She, Tim, Mildred, and Dusty all fell into a group hug, then burst into a chorus of *Victory in Jesus*.

Yes! Victory, indeed!

A Time of Recovery and Prosperity

"It was Boogan who saved you, not me." Boogan seemed to know he was being talked about as his big brown eyes blinked and he let out a doggie moan. Mildred was indulging him with an extra-long belly rub. He was large enough that Tim and Gary were able to participate as well. Sarah and Brooke stayed back – for now – as their hands had quite a way to go yet on the comeback trail.

"When the quake hit, Boogan must have run out the doggie door straight to my house, because I kept hearing a noise I assumed was just part of the shaking. Boogan knows I've helped you guys out with cuts and scrapes and various bug bites, so he came to get your nurse."

Everyone laughed, even Chance, who was still confined to his bed. It was still too early to tell if there would be any permanent physical damage, but his spirit and mind were just fine!

"Boogan's a heee-ro!" Chancie grinned, his dimples displaying themselves.

No one could disagree there.

~

Over the next six weeks came a time of recovery and prosperity, in so many ways for so many.

The city of Charleston was in a period of major restructure. The thousands of claims made to insurance companies did not help the economy, but in time it began to reshape the face of the Low Country. This process would take months, even years, but the Holy City had been through so much over time: fires – including one worse than the Great Chicago fire, in 1861; wars – both Revolutionary and Civil; and hurricanes, including Hugo in 1989. God works in mysterious ways, and this was once more demonstrated as Charleston actually began seeing a boom in growth and tourism – because of the earthquake. Historic carriage and walking tours now had brand new up-to-date disaster stories to add to the lore. The legend, mystique, and appeal of this classic town increased, which in turn helped to rebuild it!

In another twist, Jamie and Meghan wound up with only a two week vacation instead of a month.

Peter Beck called from Music City with great news. In light of the continued success and growth of the TIME Ministries Crusades, Peter's record company had decided to speed up the release of the *As High As It Can Go* CD. Due to the fact that the disc had yet to be recorded, the two singers had to make an emergency trip to Nash Vegas to do some serious laying down of tracks.

To this, there was absolutely no objection.

It was decided that in light of the magnitude of this event, both Garth and Isabelle should be present, along with both spouses. Hey, why not make a vacation out of it? This was a realization of a lifelong dream and the payback for so much blood, sweat, tears, and heartache over so many years.

Peter had laughed, saying "Just think, guys, you'll actually have all of the Excuse songs available, instead of half of them!"

Garth and Isabelle each got a part, as they joined in on the chorus of the title cut, with each voice getting just a touch of individual exposure. In this manner, the effect was charming, without being gimmicky. Jamie and Meghan could not believe how wonderfully the project turned out. This one was miles ahead of their first effort, which had basically been slapped together in the matter of a few hours. This time, Nashville's best took their time and produced a product worthy of radio airplay and national distribution.

After the final mix, which both families unanimously approved, Peter sat everyone down to discuss an outline for the immediate future as well as his long range strategy.

"Okay, so you guys are heading to Kansas City, then Chi-town. Use your current CD for those two, and push the soon-to-be-released one and take as many pre-orders for it as you can. In fact, I would offer the first at a discount when a pre-order for *As High As It Can Go* is taken. Then, when the Big Apple and DC hit in later May, we plan to do the same. We'll release the title cut while you're in Chi, and by the time you're in NYC, it should be starting its climb up the charts. Then we drop the CD. Does that sound like a plan?"

"Oh, yeah!" Everyone chorused as one.

"Now, if all goes as we hope, and Brother Tim's TV show kicks off late this summer, we'll set up some extra concerts for you. Meanwhile, be thinking of a ministry concept – something marriage and family related, we can build around your love songs CD. We'll then look at laying that down and getting it out there to an even wider audience."

Jamie and Meghan could not have been any happier.

"This is something that has been on my heart for years – why is it always – Christian songs versus secular love songs? It's God who made love, who is love, and who ordained marriage and family. Also, friendship, and even love for enemies should be addressed – not by them – but by us!"

"That's our vision, exactly!"

"Then let's do it! We'll pray and take it one day at a time – which reminds me – a CD of old time favorites with your trademark harmonies would be nice, too – and we'll let God lead on all of it. These are big dreams, but we serve an even bigger God – and as Jabez once prayed, 'Lord, increase my boundaries'!"

"AMEN!"

And with that, Jamie and Meghan headed back to Charleston, but only briefly, as Kansas City was now only a few days out on their increasingly busy itinerary.

~

Dusty Jenkins received a calling of his own. His heart began to be burdened by the fact that so many people out there had made horrible mistakes that caused harm to others. Although he did not consider himself a preacher or possess any musical ability, he still felt led to lead a ministry. It would be called *All Is Forgiven / All Are Forgiven*. He found he did have quite a way with just talking to people on their level, and could also crack a good joke or two. At first he began networking through his truck driving. The need was great, and soon he found this taking up a great deal of his time.

Which was more than okay with him, especially since he was blessed with a top flight assistant whose medical background and kind manner were perfect for the cause.

Mildred Davis, Tim and Sarah's favorite nurse and neighbor, had been single all her life. She had devoted herself to her career, and figured if God wanted her to have someone, He would send him along in His time.

Which, as it turned out, at age 42, had finally arrived.

Dusty had given up on love after his one attempt, but now he was a new creature. He and Mildred became friends and she was the first person other than Tim and Sarah to hear about his vision. Mildred caught the vision, as well as a love for this truly humble man.

God never ceased to amaze.

~

Tim devoted himself to the care of his loved ones. He watched NBA with his boy, even as the Hawks began to fade behind the Cavs, Pacers and the Bulls. He helped Brooke try out some new recipes, which despite his lack of culinary prowess, actually turned out quite okay. On one special occasion, Wally Jewell, Brooke's crush at the moment, got to come over and lend a hand. He made a good impression, and Brooke's recovery no doubt was sped up by his presence.

Sarah was treated like the queen she was. Tim massaged her good leg and foot, as well as her back. He brought her snacks and cans of soda or glasses of tea as needed.

"I taught you southern charm well, didn't I, darlin'?" She drawled.

"You sure did, baby!" Elvis breathed out as a round of hungry kisses ensued. He could already feel himself starting to miss her, as Kansas City and Chicago would still find her recovery concluding.

Boogan was showered with doggie treats, belly rubs, and table scraps. One of the local TV stations even got word of his quake time heroics, and he became the star of a feature on Lowcountry residents who had stepped up during this time of crisis.

For Chance, it was much harder than for the rest of his family. Being younger and having the worst injuries made this fact inevitable. Thanks to a great family doctor and to Mildred, it was bearable. As time approached for Tim to once more hit the Evangelism Trail, however, it was becoming apparent that Chance's right leg was not progressing. Physical therapists and other specialists were called in, and it was determined that some neurological damage had occurred, and as a result, Chance was probably going to be at least partially crippled. His left leg was fine, however, so a wheelchair would probably not be his destiny. Probably a walker to build his strength, then eventually a quad cane would most likely be his companion for life.

With prayer, however, who knew what would eventually happen? Chance's spirit again won the day, as he gave Mildred and his favorite physical therapist, Erin, a megawatt smile.

"I get free legs!" he blurted.

"Free legs?" questioned Erin.

It was Sarah who finally got it. "Three legs! That's what he means! How cute! His cane will be an extra leg. What a great way to look at the situation!"

Erin planted a kiss on Chance. "I think this young man can teach all of us a thing or two!"

No one could argue that one!

~

Tim, thanks to Dusty, added a new point to his sermon on Excuse #8 — the things we do suffer can make us more useful and genuine to others going through the same or similar circumstances. In that way, God truly does work all things for the good if we'll just allow it.

This was not the only change Tim made. He also felt led to include all eight excuses in each crusade. He did this by grouping 1 and 2 together, as they marked opposite ends of the spectrum. Some think they are too good to need Jesus, while others feel they are too bad for Jesus to accept. Likewise, 3 and 4 both allude to making people our standard rather than God. Five and 6 both deal with Christianity being defeated and imprisoned way of living rather than the abundant life it truly is. Seven and 8 would still require their own night, as each of these demands more time.

Jamie and Meghan loved it. It gave them extra music on the three two-excuse nights, and Tim gave them more time on the other two nights as well, to balance things out. As a result, the whole presentation flowed much better. This was much nicer and smoother than preparations in Atlanta and St. Louis had gone.

The results were the best yet, as each excuse won a large amount of converts. The harvest in the first five days was nearly 5,000, and their time was extended by a week, which meant no break in between Kansas City and Chicago.

Jamie and Meghan discovered their CD pre-orders were higher than they had ever deemed possible. Peter was impressed to the point that the single As High As It Can Go was released one week earlier than planned.

Tim was tired, so it was good that everything was set up so well. He spent way less time preparing. Even his time in prayer decreased. Still, the harvest poured in nightly.

Then came the call from Frank Delarosa.

"Listen, my friend. We won't have our new headquarters in your neck of the woods set up until late summer. However, the time for you is now! We will, if it's okay with you, film your Chicago, New York, and Washington, DC crusades, and interview you during each one several times, as well as your singers. This will actually be the beginning of *Now Is the Time*, your new show. What do you think, my brother?"

"I think I'm lovin' it! I believe you're right! Now is the TIME!"

~

Even as the two brothers were conversing, a different kind of meeting was being planned for the Windy City. The four participants in Atlanta, would join the quartet from St. Louis.

This time, Timothy Isaac McDonald would not be included.

This was war, and something had to be done, and fast. Fortunately, the Leader had come up with the answer. And now, with comfort and complacency settling in, and a big moment – a most crucial one indeed, had now been put in place by Frank Delarosa and Firm Foundation Network. The timing was impeccable.

TIME Ministries, right as it was racing to its highest pinnacle yet, would instead come crashing to its demise.

Part Three: The Third Meeting

"Ah, Wrigley Field! What an absolutely perfect choice for the site of this final Excuses Summit! One hundred and seven years of losing, and so many excuses explaining why!"

Boisterous laughter accompanied the opening remarks by Nick Chapman, who was in actuality, their leader.

But not The Leader.

"We've been hit, and hit hard. But fear not, brethren, the Big Boss has solved it all. In a mere matter of days, TIME Ministries will be done, completely discredited, annihilated!" said Nick.

"Preach it, brothuh!" yelled Brother Wesley L. Williams.

"Ayy-man!" exclaimed Terry Cantor.

"I'll give each of you a chance to speak what you have observed to this point. I'll go last. Then I will give us all reason to celebrate!" said Nick Chapman.

Brother Wesley cleared his throat. "I really thought that first excuse would work. After all, it's been one of the biggest stumbling blocks for millennia. Man wants to do it all himself. Adam and Eve couldn't wait to taste that fruit of knowledge. The Jews tried to perfect the law, and the Pharisees thought they had it going on. Now we have humanism and self-potential! I thought we had him right out of the box. But no, he has to pull out that dreaded Book and point out that only grace through faith can save. What a wimpy way to go. It's all so churchy!"

"Yeah, but Mr. Wonderful saw through all – but it's cool – a lot of those pathetic humans are still consumed with pride!" said Nick.

"And one of the voices pointing that out is about to be silenced!" said Terry.

"Let's get self-righteous up in here!" yelled Don Chambers.

"Praise Jayyy-zus – well, maybe not!" Terry raised his hands in mock worship.

"Lennard, whatcha got?" Nick got them back on track.

"This old world is in baaaad shape! The economy alone has everybody so scared and desperate! Multi-billion dollar financial fraud, people shooting others at random, people losing jobs and homes. Also, lust and perversion are sizzling. Anything goes – especially in these hard times! Anything to get relief, right? It's like people sit around trying to think up worse and worse things to do!" replied Lennard Garland.

"That's because they are!" grinned Nick.

"True. Soon, shock will be a thing of the past. Look what all is tolerated already!" Lennard concurred.

"Go, mankind, go!" Nick struck a cheerleader pose.

"So whose image are they REALLY made in, after all?" Don quipped.

"Good point. So now, even if they hear there's a way out of all that debauchery, they figure it's too late. Mr. Grace-and-Love-and-Mercy will never take them now. And yet, *Old McDonald Had a Farm* points out those 'whosoevers' and the pretenders in the Book who screw up and then get forgiven – please!" Lennard laughed.

"Well, our Preacher Boy's about to feel that way himself when the response suddenly just stops!" exclaimed Nick.

"Oh, do tell!" responded Lennard.

"In time, in time. Reverend Canter?" Nick turned to Terry.

Terry grinned. "Hey, wouldn't it just be the bomb if Timmyboy had a bad scandal of his own come out now? Is that the plan?"

"No, he's too open and honest – yuck! I hate those words – but he has gotten into a comfort zone after his so-called victories. He's not even praying as much. That's all the opening we need for our plan to work," Nick smiled.

"It is funny to watch the stars of God fall to earth – so pompous, and self-important – but in the end, only human. And now, our boy who defeated this line of thinking by saying 'Look to Gawd, not man – has himself let down his guard," Terry commented.

"Making him ripe for the pickin'!" piped up Brother Wesley.

"Can I get a halleluiah!" Nick shouted.

"Right up here you can!" Don took great pride in his excuse of church hypocrisy and conflicts amongst the church. "My reason is still working its magic. People can't agree on music styles, preaching styles, business matters, and the big one – money! As for using the church for selfish gain – that's as old as time. So all this talk about being one body and helping each other through problems instead of judging – you, Timmay – Get that plank out your eye! What, you don't have one? Well, as Gomer Pyle would say, "Su-prize! Su-prize! Su-prize!"

"Good one, Rev!" Brother Wesley proclaimed.

High fives and fist pounds were given all around.

Buddy Belcher took the floor, letting out a long, low sound in line with his namesake. "Our boy could not handle all those do's and don'ts. Are pumpkins with faces really evil? Will your feet be singed if you enter a dreaded movie theater? How dare you laugh at a sitcom! Throw away those playing cards and burn those vile Lotto tickets! And if that's not enough, I've heard him singing along with Tim McGraw country and Gavin Degraw pop. That is not Gos-pelll! And what about all those church services you missed! But best of all, now you've got your sermons so down pat, you're not studying The Worrrd as much – nor are we praying, are we, preachuh-mah-yun?"

"Brilliant performance, dude!" Nick slapped Buddy's back.

"Thank you! Thank you very much!" Buddy took a bow.

"How ironic of you to imitate the king!" Nick grinned.

More unbridled guffaws erupted.

"Yes, sir. Our boy played the faith and grace card... again, but that old legalistic trap is hard to break, right Brothuh Williams?" Buddy quipped.

"Ayy-mah-yun!"

"Let's see what he thinks of grace when he no longer has it!" Buddy declared in triumph.

"Precisely. Now, it's your turn, President Obama. Oh, I'm sorry – Tyrone! You know, I always have said you guys all look alike!" Nick applauded his own joke.

"Racist! You could go to Hell for that! (laughter). Yep, our boy was all about winning – getting that MBA, landing that cushy job, oh-too-cute kids – even if one might prove to be a stumbling block, so to speak!" replied Tyrone.

"Yes, I'll address that further momentarily. Now, please continue, homeslice!" Nick high-fived Tyrone.

"He gave up his wealth and success to follow Gawwwd, then he lost his show just as he was starting to get it back! Wake up, brother! You could go a lot farther if you'd just tell the people what they want to hear. Anyway, I digress – pardon me. So, won't he be shocked when his new and better show crumbles? This will hurt him, his family, his singers, the so-called Firm Foundation Network – what a loser!!"

"Loo-ser! Loo-ser!" Their eight-part "harmony" was, well, not so glorious.

"And all this 'more than conquerors' stuff? Puh-leeze! We'll see how he feels when we get the final word after all. Can he really do all things through Jay-zus? Maybe not so much!" Tyrone concluded his spiel.

"Here! Here!" everyone roared.

Samir Muhammed stood up, bowing to his cohorts in mock humility. "You know, I nearly had him in college. When all that pain had him in its clutches, he was searching. And even after that, he's always wondered why there can't be some truth in other beliefs. Then he woke up, I guess some would say, to the straight and oh-so narrow. "But he's right! There is only one god. That god just happens to be behind all those other ways of thinking. Do you know what the fastest growing religion in America is? Don't look at me and my Muslim aura, because if you said Islam – bzzzzt! Wrong answer!"

"Really, I'm actually a bit surprised. What is it? New Age? Mormonism?" Nick inquired.

"No, it's Wiccan!" Samir replied.

"Wiccan? You mean witchcraft?" Don looked shocked.

"Yep, people are eating it up. There are a million different variations, so it's very flexible which suits modern society. Well, women especially love it, because of the 'girl-power' goddess element, and it's also eco-friendly!" Samir commented.

"You know, it really doesn't matter which one is number one, as long as we keep people away from The Way, because all other ways lead to our way, the way to one Hell of a party!" Nick thundered.

At this point, they could no longer contain their excitement. They began rolling around, dancing, and singing. If, that is, it could even be called that.

Finally, things quietened enough for Nick to make his long awaited speech.

"I'm the one who had him. Those precious, saintly grandparents of his were his foundation. Oh, how he cursed at God, truly hating Him – ahh – now that felt – goooood!"

"You go, man! We're gonna have a revival in this land!" Tyrone danced and raised his hands.

Nick continued, "Indeed we are. Then, when he heard about what happened to his baby-doll-WHOA! You know, the noble gentleman that he is. We had them both. In fact, this was the one thing they truly had not gotten over. Really, can we even explain why the so-called Most High allows such tragedy to occur? Then, our fine holy roller thought he'd finally risen victorious when all those poor misguided souls got saaa-ved. Just because he showed them God is smarter than man and supposedly controls things for his own good, or is it Gawd's own good? Anyway, then came the two-pronged plan. That quake should have wiped out his precious family, but nooo! Who could have seen that stupid dog coming? A dog, for crying out loud! Give me a break!

"But even then, the driver that killed Sarah's loved ones shows up twenty years later. Man, the boss gave me a promotion for that one. But Sarah forgave him! That's absolutely insane! And he winds up saving that little brat's life! Ah – but when this total collapse occurs, they will then have plenty of time, or is that TIME, on their hands to reflect on the joy of raising a cripple, especially as they get older! So tell me, who's in control? Is it Gawd? I don't think so!"

"So, what's the plan exactly?" asked Brother Wesley.

"Yeah, it sounds great, but everything else has been slapped back in our face!" Don pointed out.

"Not this time, boys! What the Big Guy has provided for us is this: The Ninth Excuse," Nick proclaimed dramatically.

"What are we going to do, show up on Timmy's doorstep right at the last minute again?" questioned Terry.

"Nope. Not this time. This one is totally going to catch him by surprise. Remember, he's not studying and praying as hard as he was, and that will indeed be his undoing! His total undoing," Nick sighed with delight.

"Okay, so what is it?" Buddy was bursting to know.

"Anybody want to guess?" Nick asked.

"How about, 'If Jesus is so great, what's taking Him so long to come back'?" Tyronne offered.

"Ah, that's a goodie, but no! At least not for this." Nick replied smugly.

"I know, 'Why would a loving God send people to Hell just for not believing'?" Buddy belched as he spoke.

"Now there's a beauty! That one might give Ol' Preachy a run for his money, but not the one which will finish him off." Nick continued to glow with his knowledge.

"Okay, so you're killing us here. What is it?" Brother Wesley demanded.

"What it is, my friends, is the one excuse that can trump all the responses to all the others. It's the only one that can stop people dead in their tracks, even if they totally understand what they need to do. It is the one that will mark the true end of TIME! Like my pun? Anyway, it's all in place. Tomorrow night, Timothy Isaac McDonald, child of the Lah-umb, will no doubt don his best suit as he marches out on stage to address his largest audience in this very key city. The cameras will be rolling, and many homes across the country, for the very first time, will finally experience the miraculous revival everyone is talking about. What he will not know is that this excuse, the most powerful of all, will be whispered into the minds and hearts of all the lost. As a result – it's Apocalypse Now! The lights will go down, and TIME Ministries will be no more!"

Nick took a bow and turned on his heel with a flourish.

He then shared with them the excuse.

~

Twenty-four hours later, as Tim prepared to commence his most urgent crusade yet, the eight were still partying and acting totally crazy. Now, however, it was time to calm down, sit back, and watch their masterpiece unfold.

Excuse #9: What's Your Excuse?

As the Firm Foundation cameras were all set in place, and the crowd of close to fifteen thousand gathered in fevered anticipation, Tim was poised, ready, and relaxed. After all, it was time. Kansas City, especially the final week, had virtually run itself. Tim reflected on this as the minutes counted down to takeoff in the City of Broad Shoulders.

The first night of week one saw the two opposite ends of the spectrum exposed, compared, and contrasted. No amount of self-righteousness would ever save, yet no amount of vilest sin, if truly confessed and repented from, could prevent salvation. Over eleven hundred responded.

The second night brilliantly depicted the folly of putting any man or woman on a pedestal, as well as the futility of letting self-centeredness, personal agenda, and gossip tear down a church body. "We are the Body of Christ, not of a preacher or deacon – and working together is vital, just as it is with our own bodies!" The harvest was about the same as it was the first night.

Tim used his own story as well as Jamie and Meghan to demonstrate Christianity does not spell defeat. In addition, choosing what is right or wrong can differ from person to person on some issues, but never at the cost of the cause of Christ, or the stumbling of a weaker believer. Again, the altars were flooded with the fruits of God's labor.

Many different worldviews and religions were examined next, and it became clear only one way shone – The Way. So many, from so many belief systems, turned away from the old and toward the new – the Truth!"

Tim's favorite sermon was now the Eighth Excuse, and why not? His demon, along with Sarah's had been conquered. The authenticity of this only added to the new citizens God's kingdom gained upon the final evening's conclusion.

Tim was doing something else differently. Since so many major crusades were coming up, he was now more mindful of pacing himself. Between the breakthroughs down South, and in St. Louis, then the trauma of the quake and all the increased care he'd dished out at home, Tim found himself more exhausted than at any time in his life. He decided to delegate meeting the new converts to the many volunteers and counselors local churches had provided. Also, he allowed Jamie and Meghan to become more involved with this aspect of the ministry.

After all, they were totally pumped. Their song was now on the radio, and starting to catch on! Jamie and Meghan were driving to the crusade on night one of week two when it happened. The Christian station in Kansas City was providing a pleasant soundtrack of Chris Tomlin, the Booth Brothers, Michael W. Smith, Hillsong, then Jamie Ray and Meghan Amhearst! Hearing *As High As It Can Go* suddenly appearing beside these established artists, and fitting in nicely in fact, was both awe-inspiring and humbling.

"Wow, what a sound! That sounds like an anointed song by a brand new duo that bears serious watching. Praise God!" The announcer's comment was the sweet icing on this cake which seemed like it could only be Angel Food.

Now came television exposure, and their largest venue yet. Were the two up to it? Yes, as long as they remembered it was the three of them. With God, all things were both possible and doable.

As for Tim, he had breathed a quick thanks to the Lord before crashing last night. Today, he hadn't even had time to pray because so much had transpired. Getting here, getting everything set up and organized, meeting with Frank, and running sound checks. He and his praise team were not even able to have their usual meeting before the service commenced. Tim still felt okay. So much prayer and preparation was what had brought them here in the first place. Right? Anyway, the TIME had arrived. The currents were flowing; the air was cracking with them. Tim opened his mouth, and Chicago began.

As did *Now is the Time*.

~

They call her the Angel of Mercy. How ironic, since Dr. Kayla Cunningham had fled her parents' Pentecostal church at an early age. To Kayla, all it seemed they did there was lay hands on you, speak in weird languages, and say "Praise Jesus" to just about everything. Where were the good deeds? Where was the action?

Kayla's bright mind and kind personality made her quite an admired figure at school. Not only were her grades almost all A's, she tutored her struggling classmates so they would share this same success.

Yes, Kayla was all about caring for people. It was this, not the prospect of riches and respect, that drove her into the medical profession. She worked her own way through school, and still managed to balance it all and maintain a GPA that kept her near the top of her class. But did she stop there? No! She also, as she had in her junior and high school years, helped her classmates stay caught up rather than competing with them.

Upon graduation and completing a grueling internship at one of Chicago's most prestigious medical facilities, she had several offers to mull over. What did she choose to do? She went into the inner city and became part of a clinic that helps AIDS victims, poor single moms, and children who otherwise could not afford a doctor or medical treatment. She not only treated these less fortunate folks, she also found ways to give them food and clothing. She sacrificed her weekends as well, often working Saturdays and Sundays, and even holidays, when no one else wanted to help.

So why was the Angel of Mercy here at this incredible crowded TIME Ministries crusade? Honestly, she wasn't quite sure. No one had invited her. Maybe it was just curiosity, or maybe, it was a deep yearning for something she had never found, despite all her works.

As Brother McDonald explained how true strength came from not ourselves but from God, and all the self-righteousness in the world could not earn anyone a ticket to heaven, and especially that verse in Matthew 7 about not everyone who says "Lord, Lord" necessarily even knows Jesus; in fact, he turns them away. Her soul began to stir. Maybe there was something to all this.

She looked around at the huge crowd, the lights, and the television cameras. She had never liked the limelight. Maybe she could sneak up front in the crowd, and not make a big deal out of it. She did want to go, she knew that; and yet, maybe... maybe she needed to think about it more first...

~

Jason Shapiro had never liked women. It had started with the one who brought him into this sorry world, dear old mom. She smothered him with love – at least that's what she called it, and dominated him completely. She chose all his clothes, spoke for him, and only let him have friends if she approved. She wrote his name on his underwear and embarrassed him time after time. Everyone called him "Mama's Boy."

Then, when he tried to start dating, things really got bad. "Mommy Dearest" called Sherry, one of the nicest girls he'd ever met, a whore – simply because she was wearing nail polish at age sixteen. Also, she would tell humiliating stories about him as a child. Jason had been a bed-wetter up until fifteen or so, and even this was fair game for her tales. She was jealous of anyone else having his affection and attention.

He did not give up on Sherry, nor she on him. She confided that with her it was her father who abused her with words. Not only that, but physically as well. They became romantically involved, and on graduation night they decided to get married.

"Oh, no you're not!" snarled the Dominatrix. That whore will NOT ruin MY baby's college and future. Now, you come here to your Mom..."

He did, all right. He slapped her hard, then screamed he no longer loved her and never had. He knocked her on the floor when she tried to block his way out the door. He never returned. But oh, the power that surged through him. Never, never again, would anyone, especially a woman, control him.

Sadly, it was Sherry who soon found this out, when she harmlessly suggested a different shirt than the one he had picked out to wear to a job interview. He slapped her hard, saying it was his decision. Sherry cried, but did not run away. After all, this was exactly what she was used to.

So began a long tumultuous pattern of abuse, separating, forgiving, then more abuse. Finally Sherry just knew she had the answer – a baby! She produced for him a son whom they named Jason Jr. For a while, times were better.

Until Sherry forgot to change a diaper.

And Jason Jr. wouldn't stop crying.

Not only did he beat his wife senseless, he also hit the innocent child hard enough to cause head trauma and a trip to the E.R. Of course, Sherry, out of fear, said it was an accident, and they came home to try one more time.

Again, things quieted, this time for a few months. Until that is, the night Jason Jr. crawled out of his crib and knocked over Jason Sr.'s just poured glass of beer all over the brand new carpet they had just installed. Jason Jr. smiled, and slapped the rest of the bottle over. Jason Sr. exploded.

Sherry made the mistake of defending her son.

The result? Two black eyes and six cracked ribs for Sherry, and a badly broken arm for the little boy; because his dad would not stop twisting it in his anger.

This time, they both left him.

Rage was all Jason could feel, but soon the pain came. His family refused to forgive him no matter how many times he pleaded.

He felt totally unloved, and beyond any help or hope.

A co-worker had casually mentioned the TIME Ministries Crusade and how it seemed unanswerable questions were being addressed, and people in all kinds of situations were finally finding God.

But Jason never could. He was simply too bad a person for even Jesus to love.

Still, he went.

As the Biblical examples were given of the very worst still being saved, and the current stories were shared of the people who had come forward despite their many horrible deeds, Jason felt a small ray of hope. It was tiny, yet unlike anything he had ever experienced. For the first time, that religious term "grace" came alive for Jason. He felt himself being drawn to walk the aisle.

But what would people think of what he'd done?

Still, he felt the gentle tugging...

But he didn't deserve another chance. What if he went down there then turned around and let God down again?

He needed to think carefully, maybe learn more about this first...

~

The music was sharp. The sermon was bulls-eye and spot-on, and as the invitation began, Tim could not wait to see the flood gates of Heaven's harvest fill up the altars and the stage. He closed his eyes and let the words of *Just As I Am* work their magic.

Finally, after all six verses, he opened them to see how long this might go.

But it was his mouth that flew open wider.

Only about fifteen to twenty people had ventured down.

"I sense God is not done tonight! I know this word was received, and I know it was given by God. No amount of self-power will work, and yet the very worst of you can make it work through Jesus! He is the only way for the best of

168

us and the worst of us! Please, come to His throne! He longs for you to enter His Love!"

And yet, no one else did. The evening, which had seemed so slick and polished, now concluded awkwardly. Tim was able to meet all the converts this time, as it only took a few minutes.

So much had happened over the last few months. Maybe everyone just needed to go back to the motel early and crash. After a brief prayer of thanks for the few who did step forward, everyone did just that. Tomorrow would be a new and better day. Right?

~

Indeed, the next day did dawn beautifully and only went uphill from there. Tim felt refreshed and ready to get the harvest back to its high volume. Frank assured everyone that last night still looked good for TV, and the disappointing response could be edited over by some interviewing about past responses to these excuses.

Jamie and Meghan got an extra boost when *As High As It Can Go* was featured in a triple play, sandwiched by Casting Crowns and MercyMe. This was feeling more real all the time.

Even the weather seemed to agree. The temperature rose into the mid-seventies, and the wind was not nearly as noticeable as usual. Even the Cubs won their matinee at Wrigley. Could this finally be the end of the 107 year curse?

TIME Ministries started its service right on time, after a brief meeting and prayer. Everyone felt refreshed and well rested. It was time to deliver a home run for the Master.

~

Jeff Burgess had no outstanding physical qualities, yet a light seemed to shine around him. He wasn't the brightest student, yet people came to him for answers, and somehow he would know them. Although there was nothing extraordinary about him, he managed to woo, and eventually marry the Homecoming Queen, Laura Liles. How did he do it? He was a natural born salesman.

It started at a young age, when he sold his parents on the fact that he had been born again at church camp. In truth, he thought church was silly, but it won him lots of praise, a few gifts, and no more nagging. He also conned his way out of going to school more than a few times, conveniently on days where major tests were being given, or uncompleted assignments were due. Somehow, though, he always landed on his feet, and never failed a single class.

In Junior High, he began charming the ladies, and by high school he was dating regularly. No one got to him like Laura, however, when he discovered her his sophomore year. It took him two years to win her, but boy, was it worth it! He finally accomplished this by staying friends with her consistently, assuring her he'd be happy just to remain that way. The more she saw his interest was not fleeting like the jocks, or just another conquest for the best looking guys, and the less pressure he put on her, the more her own interest for him grew. They became engaged the summer after their senior year, and were wed after Jeff completed his associate degree at a nearby community college.

Jeff landed a sales position at a growing GMC and Chevrolet dealership. It was commissions only, but that was okay. Jeff had found his niche, and became determined to acquire for Laura all she needed. And wanted.

The first thing he did was charm Zales Jewelers into letting him have a credit card, and bought for his princess a solitaire diamond ring to replace the Walmart special that had been her engagement ring. Naturally, matching earrings and a necklace were soon to follow.

Next, Kohl's and Macy's cards were acquired, and Laura found her once modest wardrobe much more fitting as she began her quest for employment in medical records. It paid off, and she secured a front desk position with a group of ear, nose, and throat specialists that also included work with patient charts and billing. To celebrate, they responded to a couple of mail offers for one gold Visa and one platinum Mastercard. Ah, the American Dream!

And for a while, that dream only grew. Jeff kept up paying all the cards, and the credit limits kept increasing. This led to fancier jewelry, nicer clothes, and two wonderful vacations: one to Florida; the other, a weeklong Caribbean cruise.

Then Jeff hit a sales slump, and lost his job. Suddenly, the friendly credit card companies began sending late notices. This was closely followed by phone calls, which steadily became more constant. Jeff turned on his charm and made payment arrangements. The trouble was, he didn't get rehired as quickly as he thought.

But then he did. A Chrysler/Pontiac company gave him a shot, this time with a guaranteed salary plus commissions. Determined not to ever hurt Laura, he dug in, and immediately excelled.

While working one day, he heard one of the other salesmen talking about how he got credit cards off his back by getting a consolidation loan with a personal financing company. He jotted down their name, turned on his magic, and signed a $7,500 debt consolidation deal. No more plastic, and only one low monthly payment! To celebrate, he used one of the cleared out cards to buy them a new bedroom suit to replace their much over used old one. Surely that wouldn't hurt.

For the next several months, life was good. Jeff became a top five salesman, and Laura was awarded a much deserved raise. This time, a night out at the movies and dinner at a high scale restaurant found their way onto another of the now vacant cards. A weekend of shopping at Kohl's and Macy's gave them each several new dressier outfits to match their new level of success. Then, an impromptu visit to an Ashley Furniture Store led to a new living room couch and pair of matching chairs. Hey, why not? No payments for a year, right?

Then Jeff's dealership hit the skids, and downsizing became necessary. Jeff's numbers had fallen again, and he was the newest employee. Then another surprise hit – Laura became pregnant! None of the creditors sympathized, however.

Jeff found a new position at a buy here, pay here used car lot, but it was not as lucrative as before. The couple found themselves getting cash advances from one card to pay the minimum payment on several others. Soon, they were totally maxed out, and no one would give them any new cards or raise their spending limit.

The next step was credit counseling, but they found the one lump payment to be only slightly lower, so the reduced interest was not a benefit in the short run. After about three months, they missed a payment. The next month was no better, and they were dropped from the program.

Now what? There was no equity in their home, as it had been stretched to the limit with home improvements. Jeff even tried praying, but God's voice could not be heard.

Then an ad for a debt settlement company caught Jeff's ear. With this deal, you only paid a fraction of what you owe, which was now in excess of $35,000! But hey, this made sense! Over four years, they would only really be paying about $19,000. Jeff jumped on it.

What he didn't realize was that the money had to accumulate before any accounts could be settled. As threats of lawsuits and debtors refusing to participate increased, Jeff was at his wit's end.

Late one night, unable to sleep, he uttered a prayer. "God, please, I need a miracle."

He turned on the TV, and inadvertently landed on a prosperity preacher's program. His name was Earnest Rich, and his promise was simple. Give to God, through Earnest's ministry, and receive ten-fold, maybe even a hundred-fold, in return. Jeff saw this as the answer, especially as he heard testimony after testimony of how this had worked for Earnest's followers. Jeff sent the refund check for cancelling with the debt relief company (only about half of what he had paid them), straight to Earnest. Then he sat back and waited for God to deliver.

Absolutely nothing happened.

Now, with Laura threatening to move out, and the real threat of bankruptcy looming, Jeff did not know where to turn. So when one of the guys at work invited him to the TIME Ministries crusade, he figured he'd do about anything just to get his mind off of his problems.

~

No promises of instant wealth here, but Jeff discovered something better. Instead of a credit card, a loan company, a debt relief agency, or a health and wealth evangelist, the answer lay in God, Himself. This problem of

Jeff and Laura's seemed unfixable for man, but not for God. Jeff knew he had to start here – to make his faked salvation experience real. From there, God could help him with debt and with winning back Laura and their soon-to-be-born baby daughter. He could not wait for the invitation.

But wait! Who was to say Tim McDonald wasn't a fraud himself? And what would Laura think? Becoming a religious nut might just be the last straw. But yet this did make sense. Okay, fine. He just needed time to process all this...

~

In the eyes of Leslie Fredericks, God had never made a neater, cooler person than Jessica Talbert. Jessica taught the fifth grade Sunday School class at High Point Methodist Church, but to say she taught it was simply far too inadequate a description. She truly loved the children as her own. She kissed them, she tickled them, she hugged them, but she scolded them, too. When the need arose.

Jessica was beautiful, fun, sweet... Leslie simply ran out of adjectives to describe her. This twenty-something angel knew how to make the old stories and characters of the Bible come alive. Once they took "torches" which were actually candles, and re-enacted Joshua's march around the city of Jericho as they paraded around the church. Another time, Jessica brought in some wafers coated with honey, explaining that this was close to what it was like when the Israelites ate manna from heaven while in the wilderness.

Naturally, becoming a Christian was a topic of conversation. This class was at the right age to start understanding the concept of being saved. One by one, these children did just that, and justly, Jessica was seen as a true soul winner for Christ. Leslie was just about ready to make her choice.

Then came that late spring weekend when Leslie and her mom, Linda, went for an all-girls trip to a secluded resort on Lake Michigan which featured lots of shopping, fellowship, good food, and a women in ministry meeting whose speaker just happened to be Linda's sister, Joyce.

After a thoroughly enjoyable day, Leslie was resigned to sit through the meeting. She had just settled back to listen when Linda's cell rang. Linda had debated switching it off, but she was an E.R. nurse and it was her weekend to be on call. The news was not good. A bus of tourists had crashed into a tree when the vehicle's brakes went out. It was going to be a long night.

Linda rushed Leslie home, then sped to the hospital in a cloud of dust. She did not notice the Ford Focus, bright red in hue, parked behind the garage. Leslie, however, did. She wondered who could be at her house. It had to be one of her daddy's friends.

Leslie opened the door, and heard laughter coming from upstairs.

Familiar laughter.

It was Jessica. Leslie crept up the stairs to see what was going on. She was right. It was Jessica all right. Daddy and she were continuing to giggle, and it sounded like – kissing? That couldn't be. Then it sounded like they were moaning, but it was a happy sound.

The bedroom door was closed. Leslie carefully cracked it open.

And her childhood innocence came to a crashing end.

~

Jessica was relieved of her position. Linda demanded a divorce. It turned out these "visits" had been going on over a year. Leslie felt so betrayed. She lost her favorite teacher and hero, and on top of that, her parents would no longer be together. All intrigue and credibility that church and the Bible had once held in her heart were stripped away.

Getting saved was obviously nothing but a sham.

Years of being shuffled back and forth between mom and dad became emotionally grueling. She refused to go to church, and began rebelling in small ways, such as choosing the wrong friends, wearing too much makeup, and using strong language. It was getting to where she would use any excuse to just get out of the house.

So it was, that when a group of her new peers suggested a trip to the TIME Ministries crusade, she jumped at it. How could mom object to this? So what if they were actually going there to make a mockery of the message and try to stir up a little trouble.

But as Leslie was drawn into the cool music and the dynamic words of Brother Tim, she began to long for that old excitement she had known before her childhood world had ended. She was amazed to hear about stories similar to hers. This man had a point. It's not God's fault when churches or church people go astray. It's because they aren't following the Lord that brings on hypocrisy, gossip, and splits in the Body of Christ.

Okay, so maybe this could be for her, after all.

But as one of her friends started poking her to listen to a rude joke about a priest, a preacher, and a rabbi, Leslie knew she had to act the part of the heckler, even as her soul felt a longing. Maybe she would explore it further when the situation was different...

~

Same smooth flow of service, same perfectly delivered music and message.

Same low response.

In fact, if anything, it was even worse than the last night – only twelve, as it turned out.

What was wrong?

Everyone had an opinion. Sarah noted that Tim was maybe pushing a bit too hard, something she had noticed last night also as she, proudly despite the outcome, was watching her hubby on the tube.

Jamie and Meghan wondered if it might be that the excuses had simply run their course, or maybe it was their music holding it back.

Tim thought Sarah might have a point, but did not agree with his praise team.

"You guys are great, and you know it. I just keep sensing God is trying to work but for some reason people are resisting."

"You know, we're all crazy if we don't think spiritual warfare is going on here. Why wouldn't the devil come after something that is winning so many souls? I think we need to pray," Frank suggested.

They did. As they formed a circle and joined hands, Frank took the lead.

"In the name of Jesus, we reclaim this work of God! By His blood, no dark forces are welcome here!"

Tim's mind began to wonder. It had to be something about his sermon.

Then it hit him.

Maybe, in this market, the change he envisioned would be just the thing.

He went back to his room, did some hasty re-writing, then fell out flat in his bed. The fatigue was really getting him, but tomorrow would dawn a different day, as Jamie and Meghan's song declared.

He smiled then, because he knew his singers would love this new mode of attack.

~

For as far back as he could remember, Wendall Abrams felt as though he were drowning. The reason? One man, the Right Reverend Charlie Lippert. His church was called Holy Freedom Assembly, but there was no freedom to be found there.

None at all.

Men were required to wear suits, even boys four and older had to be in shirt and tie. Ladies had to wear dresses, and so did girls. Pants or blouses won you a suspension from the congregation.

Television? Not a chance, unless the Reverend preapproved the program – which scarcely occurred. Radio? Gospel music only. Computers, the internet, even cell phones were frowned upon. Anyone caught at the movie theater was automatically shamed in front of the church, and a second offense resulted in dismissal. It did not matter what the movie was rated or what its contents were. Only certain books were allowed, with a strong emphasis on primarily Bible reading. "What othuh book could you possibly need? Certainly not a trashy romance novel or horruh storeh! Lust and violence must be eliminated!"

If your children weren't saved by a certain time, ol' Chucky baby would do a personal home visit and examination of your child raising methods and family activities.

Wendall simply faked his own conversion at age eight. He knew by now just what to say. How could he not?

Both middle and high school were such a drag. No dating allowed until graduation, and of course, not prom – dancing was an abomination unto the Lawwwwd!

At eighteen, Wendall hopped a greyhound to Chicago with all the allowance money he had every gotten. He wanted to follow his beloved Cubbies without feeling any guilt for doing so.

His parents did nothing to stop him. In fact, they helped him along until he got his first job in construction.

Wendall watched TV, especially sports. Wendall saw every movie that come out, and loved them all. When he turned twenty one, he went out dancing at several different clubs.

And he dated.

Ah, yes, red heads, brunettes, blondes; Wendall tried them all.

Until Rhonda came along.

Rhonda was sweet. Rhonda was hilarious. Rhonda was beautiful. Rhonda was a Christian.

Ouch! Wendall knew he could never go back to that hell again. Yet Rhonda wouldn't give up. She heard about his church, and assured him hers was nothing like that. Wendall tried, but the horrible memories kept winning out, and he and Rhonda began to struggle in their relationship.

Finally, he knew it was all or nothing. He broke it off, and set out to go have wild times once more.

But he felt so empty.

One night, soon after, he was walking by Wrigley Field. He smiled, just for a moment forgetting his troubles, as he daydreamed about the Boys in Blue finally winning the Series this year. They had the team to pull it off! He had saved up enough money for season tickets...

That's when he saw the advertisement for TIME Ministries and all those excuses. His eyes went right to "Too Many Do's and Don'ts!" He was so there!

Now, indeed he was, as Tim's spell weaved itself over him. Reverend Charlie had never explained it like this. Christianity did lead to freedom. Even the rules led to better, fuller living. Wendall sensed he still had a chance at everything...

But what if it was all just a trap? Would Rhonda and her church be like this, or like his childhood prison? Well, it was certainly worth researching further. He would ponder this very carefully over the next few days...

~

Ashlyn Abernathy had one problem. She was simply too beautiful!

Her parents filled her schedule with beauty pageants, dance recitals, and talent shows from her elementary years right through high school. She could sing, she could dance. She could look beautiful.

But her passion was acting.

Of course her high school guidance counselor discouraged this; after all, even someone with everything going for them would face a very rocky road indeed, pursuing an acting career.

Also, there would be no guarantee that this road would not stop suddenly at a dead end.

Or head straight off a cliff.

Ashlyn headed off to the University of Illinois to begin her dream, with plans to go either west to California or east to New York upon graduation to seize her dream.

But there was another aspect to Ashlyn – a blooming inner beauty. She had a heart for the unfortunate, and a desire to do something important with her talent. She had not been raised in church and knew nothing about God except snippets here and there from friends, radio, and television.

Between getting her requirements out of the way and getting parts in as many productions as possible, Ashlyn was running at breakneck speed. Still, she found the time one evening to attend a Bible study. It was an interdenominational group, so Ashlyn felt at ease as a seeker.

But then came all the talk of giving up your ambitions, not seeking wealth, and losing yourself to find life. How could this ever mesh with a self-promotional, ambition driven career like acting?

And yet, she thought God said not to hide your talents, but to use them.

She left the meeting in total confusion.

Ashlyn made it through school somehow, compiling quite an impressive acting portfolio and résumé along the way. She decided New York was the way for her to go. Both Broadway and soap operas were beckoning. Broadway might just be the right fit for her various talents, and soap operas might be the key to steady work in the meantime.

Still, there was this God thing...

She returned home to Chicago to say her goodbyes and prepare for the big move. As she was driving around reflecting on her life and memories of the small Windy City suburb she had called home all her life, she saw a small billboard advertising TIME Ministries' Excuses crusade. She pulled over to take a closer look, and was most intrigued by Excuse #6 "Christianity Is For Losers." She immediately decided to postpone her move to attend.

Now here she was, listening to the beautiful, uplifting *As High As It Can Go*, a song which had found its way to Christian radio and may even cross over. Now this was getting interesting fast. Jamie and Meghan would no doubt be able to relate to her.

As Brother Tim told stories and quoted scripture debunking the loser label for followers of Jesus, Ashlyn began to squirm in her seat.

But, she was about to move, and start a new life. Maybe she should get settled and situated first before she makes any more life altering decisions...

~

Jamie and Meghan were loving this. They got to perform all their songs and share their testimony. Tim had decided to hit all the excuses tonight. He reviewed the first four, then faced down the harder four. He kept it short and simple, yet left out not one important point. Maybe this change in approach would wake up the Second City and reignite this revival.

~

Shayna Griggs had been a victim of the male species all her life, but no more. She had been the victim of a dominating dad, a mean-spirited brother, and a sex-starved boyfriend. She was sick and tired of a world ruled by men.

But then, one glorious night at her new best friend Chloe's house, she was shown the key that opened every door.

True girl power – or in this case – goddess power.

Shayna Griggs was shown the quite literal magic of Wiccan. After hearing her tale, she was inducted into Chloe's coven on Friday the Thirteenth in March of her senior year.

No, this wasn't devil worship or anything. In fact, it was white magic. Kind of like Glenda, the Good Witch of the North in the Wizard of Oz; or more recently, Hermione Granger in the Harry Potter series.

It was unbelievable! It supported earth and the environment. You could actually learn to cast spells – revenge (but not deadly) on the people who hurt you, and blessings for the people who were kind.

And, oh, the friendship! Shayna knew her coven sisters would lay their lives down for her, and she would do it right back for them.

Shayna felt truly born again – saved, if you will.

Her first spell was a secret one on Chloe. She was facing an F in pre-calculus, and needed a ninety or above on the next two tests to pull it out of the fire.

Chloe's grades? A 91% and a 93%.

Shayna flushed with excitement and power. This was real! She performed a spell on herself, so she would be irresistible to the cutest guy in her class.

Three days later, he asked her out.

Oh, yeah, this was awesome!

Would revenge work, too? Dear old dad tried to give her a 10:00 pm curfew on the night of her big date. That simply would not do.

So she uttered her first hex.

A week later, her dad suffered a mild stroke.

Wait a minute. This was too much. She figured it was revenge enough on her last boyfriend, who only wanted sex, then dumped her once he got it, that the guy who could have anyone had chosen her. So, how about big brother, Kerry? It was so unbelievable how mean spirited he was, yet now, he was a policeman, for crying out loud. She figured his favorite part of his job would be to hand out speeding tickets with no mercy.

177

She was correct.

He always bullied her, making himself appear angelic to their parents. She just had to try this new ability out on him.

That very next night, Kerry was shot in the foot while trying to run down a convenience store robber.

This was getting downright scary.

Okay, so daddy's stroke left no permanent damage, and Kerry's foot, while quite painful, would heal. Still...

Shayna began to do some research at the library and on the net about Wiccan. What she discovered was that there were at least a hundred different versions of "the craft," as it was often called. This, coupled with the results of her spell casting that was way too strong to be coincidences, made her start having second thoughts about her involvement.

But, oh, those wonderful, deep friendships, especially Chloe...

So when Chloe suggested they go check out the latest nut case Bible thumper to come through town, Shayna couldn't say no. Chloe figured they could hex the service so that no one would come forward.

And so it was that Shayna found herself listening to Christian music and listening to a Christian preacher for the very first time in her life.

Like fiery darts, the words were hitting her right in the heart. There were so many religions out there. What was really right? Jesus made it clear there was only one way, and He was it – but, He didn't just speak it, He backed it up.

Then Wiccan was mentioned by name – and Deuteronomy 18:10-12 very clearly forbid spell casting and witchcraft. Shayna was ready to go straight to the altar, but then she saw the gleam of hatred in Chloe's eye. How could she offend her very dearest friend? And yet, oh, this was so hard! She needed time to think what to do...

~

Barry and Gwen Bordeaux, along with their two kids, Dirk and Allison, had the American Dream by the tail. Barry had an on-line business earning him five figures a month, and Gwen was one of New Orleans' top realtors. Both kids were enrolled in private day schools, and had the best of everything. Only a natural disaster of Biblical proportions could ruin their ideal lifestyle.

And then, one did. Her name was Katrina.

Gone was their 3,900 square foot home. Gone was Gwen's clientele, as well as most of her product. Barry's empire was also based on commercial property and local tourism interests. He was quite literally wiped out overnight, just like the dot coms before him.

Worst of all, both their sets of parents were killed in the flooding and wind damage. This family grew irate whenever someone suggested that New Orleans was party town and a den of iniquity, therefore the punishment had to be from God.

Their parents were all Southern Baptist.

Two of their best friends, one Methodist, the other Catholic, both lay near death in understaffed hospitals.

So, where exactly was God, anyway?

Neither Barry nor Gwen had ever taken Him too seriously. They believed man's answer lay in himself. But who had the answer for this vicious category four hurricane?

For several months, the family stood firm in the Big Easy, but life was no longer easy. Not at all.

Barry had a sister in Chicago, so for lack of a better plan, the four of them left home behind for good and headed north. Soon, the Bordeaux breadwinners were back at work, but it was nothing like before. Public school, a much smaller house, and a tight budget were now the order of the day.

Susanne, Barry's sister, was a devout Christian so she did her best to convert her little bro as well as his lovely wife and kids, but they would have none of it. Otherwise, however, their relationship was a comforting one, and it grew steadily closer.

Susanne's son, Sammie, was devout as could be. He seemed to glow within with a love of life. The way he spoke seemed far beyond the wisdom someone only seven should possess.

This did not change, even when the little guy was diagnosed with a rare form of bone cancer that had already spread undetected over half his body. It was hard to tell who was in more pain, Sammie or Susanne, as the chemo treatments increased in intensity.

Again, Barry and Gwen could see no sign of God anywhere.

One day Susanne called, sounding hopeful for the first time since the cancer had cruelly intruded.

"Hey guys! There's a minister coming to town whose results haven't been seen since Billy Graham! I'm taking Sammie! He wants to go! Maybe we'll find an answer there! Please, come with us! Just this once, okay?"

With great reluctance, they did. Susanne appeared totally crestfallen that Brother Tim wasn't a faith healer. Still, the music and message were absolutely amazing. Sammie smiled and clapped along with the songs. Even all four Bordeaux family members found their attention captured.

"Sometimes suffering isn't from God at all. Sometimes it is, not as punishment but as a means to get us to draw closer to Him. Also, the more we go through, the more help we can be to others! They will take us more seriously if we can truly come along beside them in their need and empathize with them..."

Barry looked at Gwen. Gwen looked at Barry. Both had tears in their eyes. Then they both looked at Sammie, who was probably in the last few months of his precious, young life. What a waste. Tonight was just too soon to make such a huge decision. There were still too many unanswered questions. It certainly did merit strong consideration.

Just not tonight.

~

Tim had poured his heart out like never before. Jamie and Meghan had performed impeccably. God's spirit was moving.

Yet the people were not.

The response was the lowest yet. Tim's head was spinning, as was his stomach.

Suddenly, it hit him. There had to be a different excuse he was missing. He racked his brain, then he spoke in hurried, urgent tones.

"I know God is not through here tonight! I also know that there are other excuses I have not talked about – but none of them will stand up. How about this one – 'If Jesus is real, what is taking Him so long to come back?' or, 'How can a loving, merciful God send people to Hell simply for not believing in Him?' II Peter 3:8 addresses the first of these, and 3:9 takes down the second one: 'But do not forget this one thing, dear friends: with the Lord a day is like a thousand years, and a thousand years are like a day. The Lord is not slow in keeping His promise, as some understand slowness. He is patient with you, not wanting anyone to perish, but everyone to come to repentance'.

"God is above and beyond space and time. He is not bound to it as we are. Just as Jesus came right at the right time the first time, so will He come right at the right time the second time! So why is He taking so long? Verse nine spells it out – it is His will and desire that everyone would come to repentance – or be saved, if you will. But, He does not want robots for servants. He gives us free will to accept his free gift! Because God is just and fair, He gives us every chance to make the right choice. If we do not, then we have only ourselves to blame. God does not send anyone to Hell; we send ourselves! He wishes that no one would have to go! Or, maybe you are wondering what your friends or family, your school mates, or your co-workers will think if you make this radical decision. 'If anyone would come after me, he must deny himself and take up his cross and follow me. For whoever wants to save his life will lose it, but whoever loses his life for me will find it. What good will it be for a man if he gains the whole world but loses his soul?' Or what can a man give in exchange for his soul?

"Nothing is more important than Jesus, and yet, when you believe in Him and make Him Lord over your whole life, your life becomes whole! Remember what we talked about earlier? Christianity is for winners, not losers – but He must come first for it to work! Now, again, I open up the altar! I invite you to give up your excuse, whatever it may be, and come forward for Jesus!"

Just a handful responded. Something was still wrong.

"Lord God, I know there are so many more who need to come tonight! What have I done to hinder your work?"

Tim began to weep. He then fell prostrate, Jamie continued to play *Just As I AM* until the end of the verse, then things grew as quiet as it was possible for such an enormous gathering.

"TIM."

Tim looked up.

"IT'S NOT WHAT YOU'VE DONE. IT'S WHAT YOU HAVEN'T DONE."

Tim's heart broke. At last he knew. He had been cutting his prayers short, and just letting the crusade run itself. A spirit of repentance overflowed from this beloved child of God.

"Ladies and gentlemen, the Lord has laid on my heart the reason for the lack of response. It is me! I have not been praying like I should. I have become way too lax in doing my Master's work. I know now that He has forgiven me! Can you?"

The silence ended with a deafening roar. Even as it did, Tim still heard the still, small voice speak.

"PROVERBS 27:1."

Tim dutifully opened his Bible, and quieted the crowd, reading with fire in his voice.

"Do not boast about tomorrow, for you do not know what a day may bring forth."

Even as he read this, the voice spoke again.

"MATTHEW 24:44."

Tim flipped there as quickly as he could, and proclaimed: "So you must also be ready, because the Son of Man will come at an hour when you do not expect Him."

"ONE MORE... RELEVATION 20:15."

Tim turned to the back, then found it.

"If anyone's name was not written in the book of life, he was thrown into the lake of fire."

As Tim finished, he saw a vision of all eight "men" who had been sent to torment him. He saw the conclusion of their most recent meeting and heard the uttering of the Ninth Excuse. Instantly, everything fell into its proper place, and Tim began doing what he does best.

"When I was about nine, my grandparents took, or rather, dragged, me to an old-fashioned revival meetin'! I had never heard a preacher like this guy. Hellfire and Brimstone? Oh, yeah, and that's when he was having his lighter moments! Anyway, he told a story that seared into my brain. There was this teenage boy who had been in and out of trouble for years. He had just gotten his driver's license, and was starting to finally get his act together. He actually showed up at the church where this evangelist was in revival. He came under conviction, but failed to come forward. Afterward, the preacher caught him as he was getting into his car. 'Son, do you want to be saved?' 'I believe so, sir. But I want to be sure. I'm going to go home and think about it this afternoon. I will probably be back tonight, then I will come forward. I just need a little more time, that's all.' As he was pulling out of the lot, a truck jackknifed and hit the driver's side killing him instantly."

The crowd was deathly quiet.

"Folks, I found out the story was true. I got saved myself soon after. Of course, I went on to backslide in a major league way, but I know God never gave up on me. He never left my heart.

"People, all we have is today. We simply don't know what will happen tomorrow, or even later tonight, for that matter. I know now that is the Ninth Excuse. The Bible can refute any excuse we can come up with, with or without me. Satan knows this, so he lets us see this, only to say, 'okay, I'll do it, but not now. I need to think about it. I need to talk to someone first. I want to do this or that first before I get serious about this.'

"Wake up, brothers and sisters! Don't be defeated by hesitation!"

The crowd began to stir.

"No, I don't have a prophetic chart to show you the exact time of Jesus' return, but hear this: He is coming back, and every day that passes is one day closer! And even if it's 10,000 more years till this happens, or it it's later tonight, we still don't know when our time on earth will end! We learned that in Charleston, as the earthquake did come like a thief in the night. So do not delay!

"If you feel the call to salvation, do it now! God has pricked my pride in so many ways tonight. Even my new program is called *Now Is The Time*! The answer was right in front of me, but I became so content in my own strength, I totally missed it! Whatever you do, don't miss it! Hell is real, and if you leave this earth unsaved, that's where you're headed! It's all or nothing folks! And God is doing everything He can to keep you from going there! Heaven is the ultimate victory, but new, full, abundant life in Him starts now! It must start now!

"You cannot do it on your own goodness, no one is too bad to receive it. Look to God, not to man, for your role model. The church is intended to be the body of Christ, not the center of gossip and fighting and secret sin. God's rules free us, man's imprison us.

"Christ is The Way to highest, truest victory, and He's The Only Way, not the best way, to Heaven! And, no matter what you have gone through, or will go through, He will use it for your good, to draw you closer to Him, and ultimately bless you more! So now, I ask you, what are you waiting for? Now is the time for the decision of a lifetime!"

Dr. Kayla Cunningham almost didn't come back tonight because of work. But she did. Jason Shapiro almost headed to a bar to fight his self-loathing. Instead, he came back. Jeff Burgess was low on gas money, but felt compelled to scrape up enough to come back one more time. Leslie Fredericks felt uncomfortable when her friends thought it would be fun to come back for another round of heckling, but for some reason she joined them. As for Wendall Abrams, Ashlyn Abernathy, Shayna Griggs, and the Bordeaux family, they were still all here, and as it turned out, receptive. All of these searching souls abandoned their doubts and came forward. Chloe joined Shayna, as the rest of the coven sulked off. But those would-be witches were in the minority.

Over 7,500 others also heard and responded to God's call.

Hundreds of others were called to duty as counselors. Tim didn't honestly care if the night ever ended.

As for Nick Chapman and his band of merry men, they sulked off in exactly the same manner as the Wiccans had. They knew they were in deep water – make that fire – with the big boss. Oh, yes, there would be other ministries to bring down, but this stung. It stung bad. Why, oh why, did that man have to go and start praying and depending solely on the so-called Most High?

~

Sarah and the kids had never been more proud of their family head. Soon, they would be joining hem, and when the Firm Foundation Network relocated to Charleston, they would be truly together, as it should be.

For now truly was the TIME, is the TIME, and would always be the TIME, to serve the God of all Time.

Reality Television, indeed!

Epilogue

Excuse #1: Self-Righteousness

Madisyn Wilson, although a wonderful person before her conversion, had never been perfect, nor was she perfect now. Her kindness and thoughtfulness did, however, increase manifold. She let her witness flow naturally through her leadership skills, and as a result, many of her employees at SunnyBook were led to the Lord, including the Wiccan and the Atheist.

Paul Sanders kept right on doing what he was doing, and won more than a few converts himself, including Clinton. Paul won something else, too – the love of the woman of his dreams. He and Madisyn began dating, and in time they were married. They went into business together, starting a Christian Business Directory called the Son Pages. It started with greater Atlanta, and soon expanded to cover much of the southeast.

Yes indeed, life was abundant.

And Madisyn Wilson Sanders was, at last, truly strong.

<>

Excuse #2: Beyond Forgiveness

A few months later, Diamond in the Rough Ministries was founded and sponsored by Our Savior's House, the nondenominational church attended by Ilise Jackson. Sean Diamond was its leader, and Ilise acted as "missionary momma" as its mission to reach gangstas and street people flourished. Through it all, Ilise's softest spot remained for her "firstborn" spiritual son, but she loved the hundreds more to follow equally as much.

In time, Sean even got his "revenge" on Slick Rick and Krime Dawg, just not in the way he had first envisioned.

Both became converts as a result of their former comrade's work of God.

<>

Excuse #3: Evangelistic Scandals

Danny Driver became Rookie of the Year in 2015, with a .373 average, 35 home runs, 114 RBI's, 45 doubles, 17 triples, and 143 runs scored with 50 stolen bases. During the off season, he and Christy wed.

In 2016, Danny signed a to-die-for contract that would keep him in Atlanta for the next decade. He didn't disappoint, as all his stats improved.

In 2017, he hit .411, becoming the first player in seventy-six years – Ted Williams last accomplished it in 1941 – to hit over .400. Danny Jr. was born at a robust 8 lbs., 12 ounces – right in the middle of that historic season.

What Danny considered his best accomplishment, however, was finally seeing the light about the Light. He became TIME Ministries' greatest supporter, because this organization was totally centered around, and led by, a legitimate hero – not Tim McDonald, although he had won Danny's total respect, Jesus Christ. Besides the financial help, Danny became a frequent guest on Tim's television program and won to it many more viewers than Tim alone could have. He and Sarah became like second parents to Danny. Now, no matter how incredible Danny's career stats may turn out to be, he knew that what he wanted most to be remembered for was being a man whom God could be seen through.

And he was.

<>

Excuse #4: Hypocrisy and Not Getting Along

Jo Windsor went on to college, then to seminary, as a full-time calling into missions flowed over her like living water. Most unbelievable of all, the paths of her and Stanley Sturgiss, intersected once more – as each discovered their shared overseas destiny. They re-met, fell in love, and became an exemplary couple on the International Mission Board's roster. The two settled in Romania, where they spearheaded quite a revival in their own right.

And yes, Matt Sturgiss and Rob Windsor were reconciled, and they and their families became fast friends.

Yes, church can be beautiful after all, when Christ truly becomes the head of the body!

<>

Excuse #5: Too Many Do's and Don'ts

Just before their graduation, a double wedding ceremony was held in the college chapel uniting Brent and Stacy, and Randy and Tracy. All their friends and families attended, and not a dry eye was in the house. Brent and Randy indeed got their talk show, *The Cancelled Guilt Trip*, dealing with cutting edge issues and featuring Christian musical and comedy talent, including the host - finally free to use all his gifts. Stacy and Tracy secured an educational program on the same network, helping to revolutionize Christ in childhood education of all the traditional school subjects. True happiness and true freedom, were both alive and well. And to think, it all started with a divine appointment in a college campus cafeteria. The network that signed them, incidentally, was Firm Foundation Television!

<>

Excuse #6: Christianity is for Losers

Jamie and Meghan stayed with TIME but they also expanded. They got their own show on Firm Foundation on building strong Christian marriages and families.

As High as It Can Go received five Dove Awards and one Grammy.

Together We Are Beautiful, their first love song CD, received two Dove awards and three Grammies.

The title cut crossed over to mainstream radio as did *Too Lovely To Be Lonely*, and *Sweet, Southern Love*, a song inspired by Tim and Sarah.

Also, the two started a Christian family restaurant in downtown Charleston called Southern Harmony House.

It held its own quite well in this culinary paradise.

Never for a moment did the two ever regret turning their talents and lives over to the Lord, whose Name is faithful and true.

And victory eternal.

<>

Excuse #7: So Many Religions

Having Tim McDonald perform their ceremony definitely trumped the lavish reality TV wedding of Ryan and Trista. Like Ryan did, however, Steven remained a firefighter, and over the years rose to assistant chief, with a possible top position still to come when the current chief, himself a believer, retired.

Ella continued teaching, but she also became an apologist for the faith, and began to build quite a ministry in her own right. Upon retiring from education when her years of service were met, she pledged to go full time with it.

The two did manage to squeeze in two children before the biological clock ran out – a miracle in itself. Steven Jr. showed early signs of growing tall, while Tina Sophia would always look up to her mom, literally and figuratively.

<>

Excuse #8: Why Does God Allow Suffering?

Despite all of personal agony this eighth excuse had been for both Tim and Sarah, God wound up turning it to blessing. An incredible 2,500 souls were saved, and long awaited redemption occurred not only for Dusty Jenkins but also for Sarah, who could now at last put her past where it belonged – in the past.

<>

Excuse #9: What's Your Excuse?

Firm Foundation made its way to the Holy City, and TIME Ministries grew and flourished right along with it. Tim learned to listen with a discerning ear for any and all excuses that prevented people from knowing the Lord. He also remained open to God's will for his messages and for new ministry ventures.

New ventures did indeed come. Sarah and Brooke got a mother/daughter cooking, decorating, and event planning and hosting show from a Christian perspective. Gary became a tour guide for real, and in the process received his own calling into the ministry and to follow in his dad's footsteps.

Now Is The Time did features on different people who had become believers as a result of the crusades. In addition, an evangelistic program for churches based on the excuses was started. As a result, Tim became an extremely busy, but even more, extremely happy, man.

One of the nicest surprises was the newest praise team member who came on board. Supported by a cool, brass colored, quad cane, Chance

McDonald touched a chord in millions of hearts with his pure, sweet voice. Once more, God used tragedy to weave his blessings.

~

Dr. Kayla Cunningham became a missionary without moving an inch! Her inner city clinic became a light for the soul and heart, as well as the mind and the body.

Jason Shapiro won back his family, and founded a desperately needed ministry for men who struggle with anger, violence, and abuse issues.

Jeff Burgess and his family were blessed with a surprise inheritance, and started an on-line financial planning business based on Biblical principles. What set this one apart from others was this one helped people already in debt and financial ruin, along with tips for avoiding this situation.

Leslie Fredericks found a new church, new friends, and her own call into youth and children's ministry. She wanted to create what Jessica once had, but this time make it last, and not be a letdown for anyone.

Wendall Abrams did not win Rhonda back, but he did find love with her best friend, Deborah. He became a church builder, both literally and figuratively, as he both constructed the sanctuaries, then taught Christian ethics as a roving public speaker and Sunday School teacher.

Ashlyn Abernathy headed to the Big Apple, where she became a shining talent for the Lord in the much under-represented arts, acting, theater, and entertainment world.

Shayna Griggs, along with her best friend, Chloe, started True Magic, a ministry for kids struggling with Wiccan and the Occult.

The Bordeaux clan discovered Dusty and Mildred Jenkins, and war was declared on repressed and depressed victims of disasters and crises.

Thank God! Praise the Lord these people either came back, or stayed around for the exposing and downfall of the Ninth Excuse!

So, whatever reason Satan may put in your heart or head not to believe in Jesus and follow Him, the Bible can overcome it.

Whether you are self-righteous, self-loathing, let down by a hero, hurt by a church, trapped in legalism, feel like doing right always leads to losing, confused by all the choices of what or who to believe, or going through unimaginable pain and suffering no one but you could possibly understand, Jesus is waiting, and longing to love you! Do not wait another day, not even another moment. Have you done it yet? If not, only one question remains.

What is YOUR excuse?

THE SONGS

Strong
Words and music by Christopher May

1st verse
My worries overtook me
So I withstood them all
Because I can't stand weakness
My pride won't let me fall!
I'll fight the pain inside me
I'll win, it won't take long
For you see, I need no one! I am strong!
1st chorus
No, you'll never see me fall down on my knees
Or hang my head in hopeless defeat
There's no need to help me along
I depend on myself, I am strong!
Interlude
2nd verse
But the bitter hurt just wore my heart
Right down to the bone
That's when I finally cried out
"I can't take this alone!"
I wept in true repentance
"Dear Lord, I was so wrong"
That's when he took me in and made me strong!
2nd chorus
Can you believe I'm finally falling on my knees
Begging for my soul to be free?
Now each day he helps my love along
*For the first time in my life, I am strong!
Repeat 2nd chorus * twice

Even us saved folks can have trouble with this. My wife will tell you that! When we are weak, He is strong through us, making us truly stronger! What a Lord!

Sinner's Prayer
Words and music by Christopher May

(Intro) 1st verse

I've never talked to you before
I've never dared come to your door
Every chance I've had, I've blown
I know it's no one's fault but my own!

Chorus

You see, my life's a mess
And you're my only hope
To ever walk away and start again
*Now I know I need you
Yes, I know I love you!
Here's my heart! Sweet Jesus, Please come in!

(Repeat Intro) 2nd verse

Yes I know I've got to change
My old friends will think I'm strange
It's scary, but I've learned it well
Without you, I'd be headed straight to Hell!
Straight to Hell!

Repeat chorus - # Twice end with a hint of *Just As I Am* music

I was an interim youth minister once (once!), and that particular group of kids inspired this contemporization of the sinner's prayer. Anyone can pray this, no matter what they've done. My prayer is that they will.

You Are Lord, You Are God, You Are King
Words and music by Christopher May

1st verse
Matchless is your majesty
All creation's yours to claim
Yet you look inside your children's hearts
Then gently call each of us by name!
2nd verse
You defy all space and time
Yet you're there for us each day
Through you, all is possible
You alone are worthy to be praised!
Chorus
Let us stand, and let us sing
Through your son, salvation reigns!
You are Lord, you are God, and you are King!
3rd verse
Mighty are your miracles
You are light, and you are love
Through grace to us your mercy flows
Sweet spirit descending like a dove!
4th verse
Your word is real and wonderful
All your promises prove true!
Our future is forever
Through Jesus, our only way to you!
Repeat chorus twice

In college, I took a Christian Doctrines class. As we pondered the greatness of God, I knew I had to write a praise song with a dramatic build and feel. This is the result.

Sittin' On My Blessed Assurance
Words and music by Christopher May

1st verse
Serve the Lord Sunday mornin' right on time
I gotta make sure that back row seat is mine
If the music's good – the sermon short and right
I might even show back up tonight!
2nd verse
But the organ's getting old,
it doesn't sound so great
As I drop my quarter in the offering plate
Now the preacher's droning on how we're
All called to serve, and frankly,
He's getting on my last nerve!
Chorus
Seems the budget's gettin' tight this year
We need more program volunteers
Well, God bless ya, brothuh! I promise I'll
Pray – at least every other – other day!
Call me a pew potato, a benchwarmer, too
But I'm doin' all that I can do
I'm all signed up on heavenly insurance
So I'm sittin' on my Blessed Assurance!
Interlude
3rd verse
I can't teach Sunday School –
I just don't know enough
And visitation – whoa! That sounds way too rough!
I'd join the praise team, but I just can't sing
So praying someone else will
Just might be my thing!
4th verse
Hey, try to see things from my point of view
I even helped decide the carpet should be blue
I always bring my Bible for all to see
And I try to read one verse – a week!
Repeat chorus twice
Coda
Are you a pew potato
A benchwarmer, too
Are you really doing all now
That you can do
Just because you're signed up
On heavenly insurance
*Don't go sitting on your Blessed Assurance
Repeat * twice

I once served as music minister under a pastor who loved to use the title of this song in his sermons. I always warned him I was going to write a song about it, and I did! This is meant as Christian comedy with a message. Hopefully, it will make you laugh even as it makes you think.

Ordinary Man
Words and music by Christopher May

1ˢᵗ verse
I'm not a well-known minister
Or a great leader of men
But through your love, sweet Jesus
My soul is saved from sin
2ⁿᵈ verse
I know that I'm not perfect
But I'll do all I can
Have mercy on me, Lord, sweet Lord,
I'm just an ordinary man!
Chorus
I sing about all kinds of love
I write just what I feel
And though my songs are not the best
At least I know they're real!
Yes, I know there is no doubt
Of one thing that is true
*All of these emotions are a gift from YOU!
Interlude
3ʳᵈ verse
If salvation were based on works
I know I'd be ignored
But I am spared because I know
You are the one true Lord!
Repeat 2ⁿᵈ verse
Repeat chorus - * twice
Repeat 2ⁿᵈ verse

I have always believed that Christianity is a lifestyle, not a religion. I have written about all things, but from a Christian perspective. Once someone challenged me, saying I wasn't religious enough if I wrote or sang anything except gospel music. Ordinary Man was my response, made in love.

Too Lovely To Be Lonely
Words and music by Christopher May

1st verse
She has put her life on hold
For her family's sake
Running a household solo
Is often tough to take
2nd verse
But God sees her soul's symphony
A song that should be shared
There's no doubt He's listening
No question that He cares!
Chorus
She's too lovely to be lonely
Too strong to be held down
An undiscovered treasure
Just waiting to be found!
*In our Lord's perfect timing
Someone shall surely see
She's just too lovely to be lonely!
3rd verse
She builds the dreams of others
While putting off her own
She listens to people's problems
While facing hers alone
4th verse
But she'll get where she's going
All she is, will set her free
At last the lyrics in her heart
Will find their melody!
Repeat chorus twice
Repeat *

Most of this book flowed from my imagination, but the story of this song is true.
And yes, it worked!

Together We Are Beautiful
Words and music by Christopher May

1st verse

So much locked inside of me
But no one tried to turn the key
They were scared to accept me as myself
So I stood all alone, without a love
To call my own

2nd verse

My heart was aching from the cold of
Not receiving the warmth of love
There we were, two lonely people lost
Till God led us to meet
Our sadness fell down to defeat because

Chorus

Together we are beautiful
Forever we are love
The right words for the right song
Perfect combination
*Once empty, our hearts are now full
Together we are beautiful!

3rd verse

Soft and gentle is your touch
Just knowing you're here means so much
Neither of us knew things could be like this
Happiness has won! And our love's only
Just begun because

Repeat chorus

Bridge

Prettiest harmony! The blending of you and me!
All my life I've waited
Finally you've arrived
You touched my dreams and wishes
And made them come alive!

Key change – Repeat chorus

* twice

I sang this to my wife during our wedding, and have sung it for many weddings since, including my niece's. We Christians really should be the ones writing and singing the love songs!

As High As It Can Go
Words and music by Christopher May

(Intro) 1ˢᵗ verse
I want to go where no one has ever gone
I want to do what no one has ever done
Chorus
He'll break the barriers down
And turn this world around
He'll take my strength as high as it can go
The more of him I know
The more I want to grow
He'll take my strength as high as it can go!
(Intro-key change) 2ⁿᵈ verse
I want to love whom no one has ever cared for
I want to cry for whom no tears are shed for
Repeat chorus with "Heart" instead of "Strength"
(Intro – key change) 3ʳᵈ verse
I want to mend what they say can't be changed
To create what's never been arranged
**Repeat chorus with "Mind" instead of "Heart" then "Praise," "Serve,"
"Worship," "Adore," "Soul" and last with "Life"**

This is my desire in Christ. I hope this book and these songs can truly be the beginning of this!

<u>Rewrite of *As High As It Can Go*</u>
Words and music by Christopher May

1st verse
I want to go where no one has ever gone
I want to do what they say can't be done
Chorus
He'll break the barriers down, and
Turn this world around
He'll take my strength as high as it can go
2nd verse
I want to love whom no one's ever cared for
I want to cry for who no tears are shed for
(Repeat chorus – "Heart" instead of "Strength")
3rd verse
I want to mend what they say can't be changed
To create what's never been arranged!
Repeat chorus – "Mind" instead of "Heart"
Bridge
Praise Him, praise Him, praise Him!
Serve Him, serve Him, serve Him!
I want to worship and adore Him!
Repeat Bridge
Repeat chorus "Soul" instead of "Mind"
Repeat Bridge twice
Repeat chorus "Life" instead of "Soul"

This rewrite, my last touch to this book, gives this song a little extra kick. The key changes are natural, moving the song to an appropriate "High" climax.

The Latest Lie
Words and music by Christopher May

1st verse
Their smiles are sweet and caring
As rapture fills their eyes
It's easy to be fooled by their disguise
Itching ears so desperate for
The lessons that they teach
Don't hear the double meanings in their speech!
Bridge to chorus
They slowly reel you in, erasing any doubt
Before you know it, there is no way out!
Chorus
That's not love, they're playing with your heart
Their methods tear your mind apart
They weave a web around your life
They laugh, as they gently take control
But very soon, they will be exposed
As just the latest lie!
2nd verse
Blinded by their visions
The only truth they know
But it's what the people want, so they grow!
They mock the true believers
They say that we're so lost
But the compromise is never worth the cost!
No, never worth the cost!
Repeat bridge to chorus and chorus
Interlude
2nd bridge
It's not too late for the victory!
The war's already won!
Come back to the light of the son – God's son!
Repeat chorus

I once played in a band made up entirely of members of a pseudo-Christian cult, The Way International. I once knew a friend who was a fortune teller. I have seen what Satanism is about, and what it can do, and I am certified to give seminars on the New Age movement. All of these people make me feel the same thing – love! They are being deceived by cult leaders, and need our prayers – as do the cult leaders, for that matter. There is nothing new or exciting here, only the same old lie movement that Satan started in the Garden of Eden.

Lead Me Through
Words and music by Christopher May

(Intro) 1st verse
Life here on this earth
Is sometimes filled with hurt
Yes, storms will come
And they'll rain upon us all!
2nd verse
But I've finally found the key
You're always here by me
Even when my chosen road
Runs right into a wall!
Chorus
Lift me up! Pull me out!
Guide me under or around!
Help me keep the path of love
Ordained by you!
But when there's no other way
To face the trials of the day
Then take my hand, dear Lord
And lead me through!
(Repeat Intro) 3rd verse
In my coldest, darkest night
I can still see your light
Worries may drown my mind
Yet I find rest!
4th verse
When I'm utterly confused
I still stand on your good news
That this, too, shall pass
And eventually, I'll be blessed!
Repeat chorus twice
Lead me through 4x

*This is my newest song. This economic crisis is certainly hitting us head on, as it
is with virtually everyone we know. Even when the only way around a problem
is straight through it, God never fails. Just to prove it, God brought me to my
current church during this time, and at the same time revealed the church I
thought was the right one didn't work out, but instead helped me find this one.*

A Different Day
Words and music by Christopher May

1st verse
I may be sad now,
but the Lord's still in my heart
For in Him, hope never fades away!
Though all others may forsake me
His words from me won't part
And when this evening's over
The morning dawns a different day!
Chorus
A different day, a second chance
Another change of circumstance
My river may run dry,
still His blessings are gonna flow my way!
He never said it would be easy
But He did say He'd never leave me
And when this evening's over
The morning dawns a different day!
2nd verse
My friend, let me tell you –
our Lord is for real!
Put Him first,
and in all your life He'll stay!
Yes, the whole world may forsake you
But He knows just how you feel
And when this evening's over
The morning dawns a different day!
Repeat chorus – replace "Me" with "You" and "Your" for "My"
Also, after "Easy", add "This is true"
Coda
He never said it would be easy
But He did say He'd never leave you and me
And when this evening's over
The morning dawns a different day

In the story, Jamie Ray speaks of losing a job at a family theater that was such a perfect outlet for his music. This happened to me in real life, inspiring this song. When you have unusual, hard to achieve dreams, things can get lonely. When you are trying to serve the Lord, this is even more true. In this case, a different day did dawn a few months later, when I met, became friends with, and sang with the lady who inspired the character Meghan Amhearst.

I Did It All For You
Words and music by Christopher May

1st verse

I came into this world
Far from my home above
And through this life I walked
To pave a path of love!

2nd verse

And though the cross I knew
It had to be my fate
I went through it all
To conquer sin and hate!

Chorus

I did it all for you
So why won't you believe?
I come in peace and love
Why practice to deceive?
I'll always be with you
If in my word you'll stay
I did it all for you – please don't turn away!

Bridge

And I will come again
To take you all with me
To that Holy Place
Where life and love run free!

3rd verse

I want to see you all
And leave no one behind
So please try to give sight
To those who are blind!

Repeat chorus twice

No, you did not overlook this song in the story. It is not there. No song occurred for the Ninth Excuse, because it happened so spontaneously, but this one no doubt would be in the future. When I read about Jesus – fully God and fully man – weeping over Jerusalem, I had to write this. It stands as an answer for all excuses!

Sweet, Southern Love
Words and music by Christopher May

1ST verse

Alone, I was so alone
There was laughter, there were friends, but it was all pretend
Home, so far away from home
Let down and deceived by all I had believed

1st Bridge

Then through the black of night
Came your warming light
Comforting and kind
To soothe my soul and medicate my mind!

Chorus

Now I'm melting in your arms
Intoxicated by your charms
An angel with a word
From Him above!
Surrounded by your soft embrace
All my tears evaporate
*As I'm enveloped by your sweet, southern love!

2nd verse

My heart, completely shattered and bare
Unrelenting pain – feeling like I'll go insane!
I smiled, appearing not to care
No one ever knew, nor even had a clue!

2nd Bridge

Across the room, I saw your face
So strong, yet somehow out of place
It was God's plan I concede
To complete our hearts, and meet
Each other's need!

Repeat chorus twice
Repeat *

As it turns out, this one is even newer than Lead Me Through. As I read back through the story, I felt Tim and Sarah were worthy of a love song of their own. Also, while I was writing this, we made our own move to Charleston, which also helped set the stage as our own love seemed to grow sweeter.

Tim McDonald thought that it was more than enough challenge when he was called as a bi-vocational pastor. God then upped the ante for the full-time calling to evangelism. But suddenly, Tim finds himself leading the biggest revival crusade since the hayday of Billy Graham. It centers on people's excuses for not accepting Christ. As the excuses become more challenging, Tim experiences spiritual warfare firsthand, especially when he must face the one excuse he himself has never found peace with...

~~~

ABOUT THE AUTHOR

Christopher May, despite being legally blind since birth, began his writing career in 1995 while working with his wife as her special education assistant by day, playing music by night and raising three children. He has now written over six Christian thrillers and has written over 400 songs. He received a B.S. degree in Broadcast Performance (Murray State University, 1982), a B.S. degree in Ministries (Mid Continent University, 1999) and became an ordained Baptist minister in 1994.

Chris resides in Summerville, SC with his wife, children and their three rescue dogs. He is an associate pastor, worship leader (with his praise team, Chris May and the Blind Side Band), Sunday School teacher and continues to volunteer in his wife's special education classroom. Chris is also a member of the Christian rock band ABIDE.

You can contact Chris at chrisnmary45@gmail.com

Books by Christopher May:
The Difference
Therapist
Labor of Redemption
Raising Hell
Excuses
Eyes on the Prize (co-authored with Rick McComsey)

Made in the USA
Charleston, SC
01 February 2015